## PRAISE FOR DON'T START ME TALKIN

"Tom Williams' *Don't Start Me Talking* reminds me of why I started reading in the first place—to be enchanted, to be carried away from my world and dropped into a world more vivid and incandescent. Here is a heartfelt and irresistible novel about the Last True Delta Bluesman, Brother Ben, and his steadfast harp player, Silent Sam. Williams handles this ironic tale of the Blues, race, pretense, and life on the road, with intelligence, grace, and abiding tenderness. Read this remarkable and exhilarating novel, friend, and I promise you'll start reading it slowly so it won't ever end."

—John Dufresne, author of *No Regrets, Coyote*

"A master storyteller, Tom Williams enters the living history of Delta Blues and emerges with his own thrilling tall tale, alive with American music, American legend, American heart."

—Matt Bell, author of *In the House upon the Dirt between the Lake and the Woods*

"Tom Williams writes like Paul Auster might if he were funnier or like Stanley Elkin might have if he'd ever been able to stop laughing. Darkly charming."

—Steve Yarbrough, author of *The Realm of Last Chances*

"Tom Williams' *Don't Start Me Talkin'* takes the wheel of a coffee-brown '76 Fleetwood Brougham, settles you into its supple leather seats, and tours a world of fried meat and plush polyester through smoky juke joints—a must read for fans of low down sounds everywhere."

—Preston Lauterbach, author of *The Chitlin' Circuit and The Road to Rock 'n' Roll*

# DON'T START ME TALKIN'

## A Novel by Tom Williams

CS

CURBSIDE SPLENDOR

RECORD CORP

1. Good Evening Everybody  2. Take Your Hand Out of My
Pocket  3. Going in Your Direction  4. Keep It to Yourself
5. Don't Start Me Talkin'  6. Bring It on Home  7. I Can't Be
Alone  8. Your Funeral & My Trial  9. Sad to Be Alone
10. Fattening Frogs for Snakes  11. Eyesight to
the Blind  12. One Way Out

# DON'T START ME TALKIN'

A Novel by Tom Williams

CS

CURBSIDE SPLENDOR
RECORD CORP.

1. Good Evening Everybody 2. Take Your Hand Out of My Pocket 3. Going in Your Direction 4. Keep It to Yourself 5. Don't Start Me Talkin' 6. Bring It on Home 7. I Can't Be Alone 8. Your Funeral & My Trial 9. Sad to Be Alone 10. Fattening Frogs for Snakes 11. Eyesight to the Blind 12. One Way Out

DISCARD

CURBSIDE SPLENDOR PUBLISHING

Published by Curbside Splendor Publishing, Inc., Chicago, Illinois in 2014.

First Edition
Copyright © 2014 by Tom Williams
Library of Congress Control Number: 2013957480

ISBN 978-0-9884804-4-5
Edited by Leah Tallon
Designed by Alban Fischer
Cover photos by Jacob S. Knabb

Manufactured in the United States of America.

www.curbsidesplendor.com

## 1

## "LET'S CALL THIS A TEST," BROTHER BEN SAYS.

"See if there isn't a lesson worth learning."

"A lesson?" I say, closing my magazine. "Lesson in what?"

"Humility." Brother Ben smiles as he strides down the sidewalk, showing me the way.

It's said that when Robert Johnson arrived in a new town, the first thing he looked for was an ugly woman who owned her own house. That way, Bob could

# Good Evening Everybody

depend upon a place to sleep, food on the table—he'd supply the liquor—and a bed partner likely as starved for affection as he was. Having just checked into the L.A. Convention Center Holiday Inn, Brother Ben and I hover near the intersection of Wilshire and Lucas. More than good loving and a full bottle, Brother Ben, the Last of the True Delta Bluesmen, wants clean sheets and room service.

It's two days before the start of my fifth tour. Ben doesn't keep track any more, as he says the number of shows he's done would only depress him. Instead of rehearsing or working out the fine points of our itinerary, we're headed to Silver Screen Motors to buy a new car. That is, we would be headed there had I not showed Ben the issue of *Blues Today* I still presently clutch. In it, the special Readers and Critics' Issue, we're ranked number one by critics and readers have us at number two behind Blind Deacon Roland and the Professor as traditional blues acts. A likely reason for our jump of two places is the deaths of Ott Sikes, the fife and drum player from Senatobia, and the Texas ragtime pianist, Henry Lou

Bascombe. Along with those rankings, for the first time my name's on the list of top ten harp players, an idea so incredible I open *Blues Today* again. Ben catches me turning pages and says, "Put that away. We're conducting a test."

I obey, stick the magazine in my back pocket as Ben steps off the sidewalk. He raises his hand and waves. Two o'clock in the afternoon, early February, and he's trying to hail a cab. Here we are, two black men, too far from the hotel for a doorman to reel one in for us. Oh, he's sharp, that Brother Ben. Knows what I'm thinking before I figure it out for myself. In this instance he knew why I was waving those polls at him. Now his test is simple. Will we get a cab? Neither of us resembles a Laker, Dodger or action film hero with a new blockbuster advertised on every other billboard. And if I believe my ranking beneath Sugar Blue as the tenth best blues harp player in the world will get someone to stop or take a second glance, I'll be on this street corner a long, long time.

Three cabs pass, fast as ambulances. "Ok," I say. "I get it."

Ben's smile straightens as he shakes his head. "I don't think you do," he says and waves frantically while cabs four and five don't slow down. I chew on the notion that L.A.'s a difficult town for anyone to get a taxi in, while six, seven and eight speed by, the last one's "ON DUTY" lights shutting off as it passes. It's driven by a dude darker than me. An African, likely, told by his dispatcher he'll get shot by fellows matching my description. I flip the cab off as it passes, then consider directing my middle finger to Ben. I pocket my hand instead.

So we stand here, Ben now smiling as every wave fails to get us inside a cab. I tug his jacket sleeve—I want to smack him with the magazine—and say, "You're right."

Still waving, he says, "Right about what, Pete?"

With no one around on the sidewalk, we're secure enough to use birth names, though I never call him anything but Ben. "Something you got to say?" he says.

I curl my lower lip between my teeth. I don't want to say it. I don't want to see him turn with that look confirming his wisdom and my naiveté. But if I don't, he might keep us here past dark. And there's still the matter of a car. As if preparing for one of the occasional harp solos he allows me on stage, I take a breath. Then I say, "No one knows who we are. We're just two brothers fool enough to think a cabdriver might pick us up."

Ben's arm relaxes. He stops waving but still faces the street. "And?" he says.

I take out the magazine and tap it against my palm. I'm not mad at him. I'm more amazed at how this time I thought I might have more say in how we spend the next four months together. What was I thinking? I need this lesson. I say, "And I still have a lot to learn."

Ben's hand falls to his side. His other arm lands on my shoulders. "Number one with the critics?" he says. "Not bad, huh?"

• • •

McKinley Morganfield. Chester Burnett. Lizzie Douglas. Henry Roeland Byrd. Hang those names on a marquee and see who comes running. Change them to Muddy Waters, Howlin' Wolf, Memphis Minnie and Professor Longhair, shoot, you've got the best of the blues. B.B. King, whom we call the "other B.B.," is really Riley. And Sonny Boy Williamson II, the man whose music led me where I am today, came into this world as Aleck Ford. He then took up Rice Miller, was known for a while as Little Boy Blue, but his most famous appellation he snatched from another harp player named John Lee, who supposedly went looking for the other Sonny Boy and got his ass whupped or a lesson in harp-playing or both, depending upon your source. Ben and I are in pretty good company, what with the names on our drivers licenses: Wilton Mabry and Peter Andrew Owens.

But it's Brother Ben and Sam Stamps, AKA Silent Sam, who ride in the back of a Yellow Cab driven by a tense and quiet white man. We're not in character for his benefit. Though we're not playing a gig in L.A., we'll be performing as soon as we arrive at Silver Screen Motors, the vintage car lot where Ben buys all his touring vehicles. After the cab pulls into the tiny space of driveway that's not cut off by the huge concertina wire fence, we pay the driver, watch him speedily depart down Figueroa. Then Ben presses the intercom button to gain Louis Habib's attention. A graying, slender man with impeccable taste in shoes, Mr. Habib is quick to call himself Persian and praise the U.S. of A. I've heard his story of escaping from the Ayatollah four times but have always suspected he's from Detroit, not too far from my own hometown of Troy. What we need from Habib is a machine that inspires dropped jaws when we pull up to the various concert halls where we'll perform. Part of his myth is that he's deathly afraid of flight, so Ben's MO has always been to drive himself to venues. And for the same reason he plays pawn shop acoustics and dresses us both in the most garish rags of man made material, the only cars he believes his loyal fans—the blues faithful, he calls them—want to see him behind the wheel of are Cadillacs and Lincolns, maybe a Pontiac if it's long, with chrome that blinds and fins so sharp they'll wound a careless finger. Back home in Biloxi, where none of his condo-association neighbors knows him as anything but Wilton Mabry, a retiree who's always up for eighteen, a Volvo quietly resides in his garage. "The safety record, Pete," he claims. "Plus those new seat warmers are a dream."

Now the gates open via remote control and we tip on in wearing pointy-toed, calfskin shoes—perfect in the club, not so on hot asphalt. It's warmer here than it was when I left New Orleans, my home of the past three years, and I'm glad for my sunglasses, too. The long, buffed hoods and roofs collect the sun's rays, shooting them off like laser beams in all directions. I do believe I'm sweating in my black Orlon shirt, a remnant from the last tour. It sticks too close and I flap my arms to loosen it.

Engaged with two customers who stand near a Model-T, Mr. Habib doesn't see us approaching. His voice rising, both hands fly above his head. If I didn't know better, I'd think he was Fresh Off the Boat, like my friends at the Michigan State University International Center used to say. Yet the man has owned this lot fifteen years, I've learned, renting vehicles to movie studios and marking them up later to sell to those who'll brag Denzel drove their Jag in his latest. Meantime, Ben has started shopping. I step beneath an overhang, watching him mime a shuffling, arthritic gait while running his palms over the mirror-sheen surfaces of Fleetwoods, Continentals, DeVilles. All are classics, lovingly restored by the detailers and mechanics here, only Ben won't keep our newest once the tour ends. Claims it's more financially prudent to donate them to charity and take the tax deduction. Thinking of the day care centers, Boys & Girls Clubs, and literacy councils in Jackson and Greenwood with castoff Caddies can be a pleasant image, you ask me. And Ben's never wrong about taxes. The last two years he's been nagging me I need to quit 1040-EZ's and apartment living to take advantage of that homeowner's deduction.

"No, no, no," Mr. Habib suddenly says, so loud I can hear him over the traffic noise. "You try to steal from me."

Ben joins me in the shade. "Found it," he says, pointing to a long brown ride between a sparkling red Corvette and a silver VW Beetle with a Rolls Royce grille. I shade my eyes with my hand and nod, while Mr. Habib shouts, "Final offer. Final offer." He raises both hands, tangles them in his fringe of graying hair, then turns and says, "Brother Ben! My favorite customer!"

That's not the voice I'm used to. He nears us, looks over his shoulder at the two conferring men then turns around. In a voice so American he could sell funeral plots in Topeka, he whispers, "Studio types. Always trying to cut a deal." His blousy short-sleeved shirt shows no sweat marks while he pumps Brother Ben's hand and mine simultaneously. "The last one still running?" he says. "The '72?"

"'74," Ben corrects. He's managed to shrink, as if generating a Mississippi accent has taken off pounds and inches, and perhaps a vertebra. "And she pow'ful, Mr. Habib. A luxururus machine."

"Good, good. Now you're back for another?"

The studio execs break their huddle. One calls, "Mr. Habib?"

He ignores them, nods slyly at Ben and me. "See anything you like today?" Together, we three form a rich brown spectrum, with Habib lighter than cream-heavy tea, Ben the color of a pecan shell, and me in the Hershey Bar range. I remove my hat, swipe at my forehead with my black sleeve.

"I likes them all," Ben says. "Ever' time I comes to the land of Californee I wants every car I sees." Habib just blinks at the echoes of Mud's "My Eyes Keep Me in Trouble" and Johnson's "Sweet Home Chicago." I put my hat back on and wipe away a smile on my shoulder. I'm quietly humming the harp line of "My Eyes" when both execs holler, "Mr. Habib?"

"Let them call twice more?" he whispers to us. "What do you think, Sam?"

Behind my sunglasses, I blink. My contacts shift and settle, and my lips are dry and stuck together. I've been staring, a little jealously, at Habib's smart, black and white spectator shoes. Takes me a second to loosen my lips, but before I say a word the execs have neared, their loafers creaking. "Mr. Sam Stamps," Habib says in Ali Baba mode. "Man of few words."

Ben chuckles and wheezes while his surreptitious elbow catches my ribs, a subtle clue for me to join in. The studio execs now are near enough for me to see their tanned faces, smell their subtle colognes. Smacking the back of one hand against his palm, Mr. Habib shrieks, "What you give me, huh?" Ben keeps slumping as if the hazy Southern California sun is melting his bones. There's a lot of funny stuff going on right now, and I'm still laughing when the execs and Habib look my way, until Ben's shoe slips over mine and he puts all his weight down on it.

● ● ●

"Now then," Mr. Habib says, leaning back in his chair. "What can I do for my favorite customer?"

We're inside his office, the AC chilly enough to raise gooseflesh on my neck. Habib's office is large enough to occupy all three of us and his massive desk. Framed photos of Iranian landscapes hang crookedly on the cinderblock wall behind him. A U.S. flag as big as a king-sized sheet stretches across the glass wall near the showroom. Ben leans an elbow on the desk, takes off his hat to mop his brow. The handkerchief comes back dry, I'm sure, but he pockets it swiftly, his hands appearing nimble one moment, bent and aching the next. None of Habib's rug merchant act is on display now—though ten minutes ago it secured for the Model T a rental fee twice what the execs wanted to pay. Shoes up on the desk, his soles look smooth, like they've never touched a surface that might wear them down. He says, "I got a whole new fleet of Caddies two months ago. Did you see them?" He looks at Ben, then me. I nod, while Ben pours it on, thick as cane syrup. "Which the coffee-colored one?" Ben says. "Caught my eye, sho' nuff."

"The '76 Fleetwood Brougham," Habib says, his voice softening like a teacher asking questions to the dumbest kid in class.

"Bro-am," Ben says, sounding out his phonics. He turns to me. "You the educated one, Sam. Tell me how that spelled."

He's not talking about my marketing degree from State. He's referring to the high school diploma Silent Sam's peoples are so proud of. I shake my head and shrug.

"B-r-o-u-g-h-a-m," Habib says.

"Sound like some expensive letters," Ben says, cackling. Habib says something about price, just as Ben's dry laugh turns to a racking cough that doubles him over. Habib stands, asking if Ben's all right.

"Fine, fine," Ben says through a voice close to the grave. His neck jerks twice as he coughs again. "You right," he croaks. "Let's get down to bidniss."

"That cough sounds terrible," Habib says, looking at me.

Ben's foot touches mine, a signal the negotiation's started with him on top. He's warned me to pay attention to how he haggles in a way that doesn't seem like haggling. He says I'll need to do this when I'm performing on my own someday, though neither of us is ever specific on when that day might come. Right now, I don't even own a car. As poor a light as that shines on a native Michigander, it's true. One of the reasons I picked the Garden District of New Orleans to live in was its streetcars and buses. I can get most places by my own two feet (and Pelican cabs aren't too difficult to get when you call the dispatcher). Only time I'm ever behind the wheel is when we're touring, and usually then on the interstate where I can do the least harm.

Absently, my hand touches the copy of *Blues Today*. I wonder what Habib would say if I showed him the polls. Among his celebrity photos on the wall, Ben's is prominent, above Harvey Korman and just below the good son on *Dallas*. That favorite customer business sure can seem real. The man cuts at least a couple hundred off every purchase I've seen Ben make. Because he loves Ben's music? Or because Ben's driven so many cars off this lot, always paid Habib in cash? ("Mississippi John Hurt carry Diner's Club?" Ben once asked me.) I can't be certain of anyone's motives anymore. When you spend so much time being someone you're not, you suspect everyone's got a con. And you lie waiting for the tipoff that tells what the hustle is.

"Deal then," Ben says abruptly, his trembling left hand extended—he never shakes with his "picking fingers." Habib stands, forces Ben's hand into a soul shake. "My man," he says. Then he turns to me for a high five. I wipe my palm on my sleeve to oblige him. "Be back with the keys."

Ben starts counting bills on the desk. Fourteen hundreds form a pile he taps together like cards. "And you're quiet, why?" he says, his voice without clear emotion. For a few seconds I don't reply, staring at the enormous American flag and shaking my head. I already know his retort to my belief that the polls indicate our music matters most to fans, not the act we put on. I know he'd tell me something like, "But we got to look the part of bluesmen just to make them hear." No point in even bringing it up. Besides, I hear Habib shaking the keys. He hands them to Ben as he spots the bills on his desk. "Don't you want to take it for a test drive?"

"Oh, I trusts you," Ben says, unfolding himself from the chair but not quite reaching his full height—six one on his Mississippi driver's license, though most would swear he's no taller than five ten. One reviewer called him, "the venerable and diminutive heir to such luminaries as Son House and Charley Patton." Now he nurses a phantom ailment near his spine with his hand. "But I'm gon get behind that wheel in a hurry." He smiles at Habib first, then me, sharpening his eyebrows in a way that says, "You're on your own."

"What about the title and such?" Habib says.

"Sam can handle the paper," Ben says, shuffling away. At the rate he's moving, he'll arrive at the car about nightfall.

"So," Mr. Habib says, putting the papers in an envelope. "Where are you headed on the tour?"

The AC cuts out. Habib's just chit-chatting, still my heart thuds and catches in my chest, as it always does when Ben's not dominating the room. I'm sure he designed this particular moment into as much a test as the earlier experiment with the cabs, only now he's determining how well I can handle myself alone. I lay my tongue on the floor of my mouth, move my lips only slightly. "Las Vegas foist," I say. "Then purty reg'lar."

"That's strange," Habib says. "Don't you usually start in Portland?"

I nod and tug at my collar, which chafes the back of my neck. It is strange, us playing Vegas, but most of the time, on tour, I just follow Ben's lead. He's been on the road so long, I've got to trust the direction he's taking us.

"Still, Las Vegas," Habib says. "That should be a splendid time." He shakes a slim finger at me. "But keep an eye on your money, Sam. Country folk like yourself often wind up in tears at the roulette table"

"Will do, Mr. Ha-bib," I say, knowing good and well how to pronounce his surname, having attended high school with Mickey and David Habib. He hands me an envelope containing the papers and we walk out of the office to the lot, where Ben's at the wheel of the Brougham, coffee-colored like the one Chuck Berry sings of in "Nadine." It lacks fins but is longer than a city block, with a vinyl top and a hood ornament bigger than an awards plaque. Ben beams like an aged Sambo, honks the horn two notes. When I show Ben the paperwork, he feigns a lot of blinking as he pulls his chin with his hand. In "Where I'll Die," he sings, "I never stayed long in no schoolroom, never learned no ABC's," a lyric which assures people like Habib of Ben's illiteracy. "Look all right?" he says. "We let Mr. Mabry take care the rest."

"As a manager should," Habib says. "Give him my best, will you?"

Ben and I nod. Habib walks around to the driver's side, gives Ben another soul shake. "You'll outlive us all, my friend," he says. "Don't run off with a showgirl." Then he turns to me, his face darkening. "Brother Ben doesn't seem so well this time. He needs you."

I nod again, amused at his concern for Ben, and his well wishing of Wilton Mabry, a man he believes he's never met. I also feel talked out after my ten or twelve words.

Habib tosses his arm over my shoulder. "This is some great nation, is it not?" he shouts. "Men like us, we've made for ourselves a new day."

Oh well. I slump, prepare to hear again the midnight escape from Teheran. The whole story sounds suspiciously like the plot of a movie I once saw, and Habib's role gets more heroic with each telling. Always he has to leave someone behind, a cousin, a  favorite uncle, last time his wife's deaf grandmother. Ben and I could share some equally harrowing sagas: of Ben's wife, Martha, dying suddenly and mysteriously after fifteen years of marriage or of my dad's fatal heart attack when I was three. Only those aren't Brother Ben and Silent Sam's stories. They belong to Wilton Mabry and Peter Owens. Now, though, as Habib's eyes close for the journey back to his departed homeland, a wrecker with a convertible Thunderbird honks its horn. "Next year," Habib  says, thumping my back, then following the wrecker to the garage, waving. I glance at the price of the Caddy on the window. 2400 dollars. I shake my head as I get in the car, whose wood grain control panel dazzles. I sink into the plush bucket seats and brush my fingers against the pile carpeting. After shutting the door, I say, "How?"

Ben interrupts. "He made a killing on those Hollywood boys. Plus, he always takes care of his favorite customer. Especially when he feels sorry for me." He fakes a cough, as dry as the desert Habib claims he left behind.

I keep shaking my head as he eases the car onto the street. It's as if he knew what I was about to say, which isn't that strange a phenomenon, I must confess. For the Last True Delta Bluesman not only has the ability to outduel the slickest used-car dealer in the West, he's able to read minds and foretell the future. What else do you expect from a man who in "Call Me Your Lovin' Man" claims he's the seventh son of a seventh son?

• • •

Wardrobe next. And though the kind of swap meet rags we want are available in every neighborhood with an African American population above ten percent, Ben always depends on the stores along Crenshaw to provide the tackiest and ugliest. Today's expedition to the two-for-a-dollar bin yields an armful of shirts quite popular circa 1975. Ben singles out for me a long-sleeved, iridescent number. "Looks like the color of motor oil," he says, laughing his everyday laugh, not the stylized one he employs on stage: "Gon get up in the morning, huh-*huh*." I meander toward the jackets and suits, wondering on what occasions did the former owner wear this leisure suit the color of mustard. It's in my size, though: 42 Regular. Meanwhile, Ben's more efficient. Along with a dozen shirts, he selects for us six pairs of polyester flares, guaranteed to rise up and show off the opaque, ribbed socks we favor. He drapes some suits over his arm and grabs a pair of black, ankle high boots with roach-killing toes and zippers on the side that'll fit both of us—I wear an eleven, Ben a ten-and-a-half.

Spot a brother my age—twenty-seven—dressed in any and all of these outfits and you'd either ask him where the costume party is or give him directions to the soup kitchen. Yet when Ben and his first harp-player, Reggie "Bucketmouth" Carter—and yes he could fit a whole harp in that mammoth mouth of his—veered into the seventies, after playing all the sixties coffee houses and festivals in dusty brogans and faded Big Smith overalls, a lot of people wore these synthetic monstrosities. Only for bluesmen did they stay in vogue long past their expiration date. Everyone from John Lee Hooker to Junior Wells to the other B.B. looked like an extra from *Superfly* until about five, ten years ago. Nowadays, you've got blues men dressed like rappers, others like cowboys or rock and rollers. The ladies, like Koko and Etta, prefer gowns, the more sequins the better. And the other B.B. seems only to appear in a tux, which no fan expecting a demonstration of an authentic Delta past will allow. Ben thinks we may as well not monkey with a good thing. Just accept these uncomfortable threads as the necessary password that allows us to enter the venues where we get paid to play. After each gig, we're both out of them faster than any crawling king snake can shed its skin. For now, we hand over forty dollars and earn from the cashier a lopsided grin, then head to the latest pimp wagon to haul our slick asses back to the hotel.

• • •

"You want some advice?" Ben says, a question he's asked me so many times he rarely waits for my answer anymore. "You best lay off that red meat." We've just ordered room service—Heart Healthy special for him; cheeseburger platter for me—and lounge in his room. Ordinarily, we share quarters, but Ben's sprung for two tonight.

"I'll be all right," I say. Out of our stage clothes, we're comfy in slippers and bathrobes. Seated at a small table, Ben fills the compartments of his weekly pillbox. Nothing going in is prescribed. There's no medical conditions I have to know, no emergency numbers to contact in case he starts clutching his chest like Fred Sanford. He counts on homeophathic remedies and supplements to keep him in a physical condition that steadily reminds me of the ten or fifteen pounds I need to shed. "We got enough strikes against us, Pete," he says now. "Hypertension, diabetes. You best get some greens and grain in your diet. Cruciferous vegetables, too."

"Charley Patton keep an eye on his fat grams?" I say.

"And how old was he when he died?"

A bad choice. I search the pantheon for a long-lived bluesman. "Lightnin' Hopkins drank gin and fried eggs for breakfast."

Ben shuts the seven compartments of his plastic tray. "Well then let's get you chopping cane like Lightnin'."

"Chopping cane?" I say. "When's the last time you were out in the fields?"

He grins, drums his hands against his taut stomach. I pull mine in. "Don't let's get started on that," he says. "What grows in Michigan?"

"Cherries," I say, recalling seventh-grade Michigan History. "And boy when massuh found out you was eatin his crop. . ."

A knock at the door stops me cold. Most likely, it's room service, but you never know. Ben's always willing to let fans visit wherever he's staying—in fact, he encourages them—and the two of us sharing a room displays the country-negro frugality that balances our garish clothes and fancy cars and creates the overall image Ben believes we must cultivate. I doubt we'll get such a visitor now, but I creep to the door, tighten my robe and say, "Who dat?"

A moment passes, long enough to make me suspicious. I say again, "Who dat?"

This time, I hear "Room Service," in a pleasant young woman's voice, so I open the door to retrieve my food along with the steamed vegetables and brown rice for a man who on stage purports to smoke dynamite and drink TNT.

• • •

At nine, Ben racks out—the Last True Delta Bluesman needs his eight hours—and I tip to my room to listen to Sonny Boy and examine the dates and locations of the tour. A few radio and TV interviews along the way, with most of the gigs at places we've played before. A lot of colleges, though it's rare we see students. Their professors are always present, as are the record- and health-food store owners and all others who graduated but never found reason to leave Missoula, Ithaca or Athens, GA. This time around we're the featured performers at a conference at Indiana Northern University, my first gig of that kind. We play Eau Claire in addition to Madison but will get to Detroit about half way through. Not to play, though. I need to see my mother and her husband, Grover, who are soon headed to Ghana, the motherland. She's been planning such a trip since Alex Haley published *Roots*, only I bought the tickets because two years ago I couldn't make it to their wedding. And once again, we'll bypass Ben's hometown of Clarksdale and the Beale Street Blues Awards, though we're nominated for Best Traditional Act, as we are every year.

In all, of these next four months, much of my time will be spent in rooms like this one. I'll play harp, practice to speak like a Mississippian with a high school education so I sound true to people who probably count me and Ben as the only black people they've conversed with. The brothers and sisters I'll see, other than my mother and her husband, will be waiting tables or sweeping up. They won't be in line holding tickets for the Brother Ben Show. I always assume a few are in the crowd, just outside my peripheral vision—half the time, on stage, my eyes are closed, anyway.

From my case, I take out the Military Band Hohner in G I bought for the tour and haven't broken in yet. Its weight in my hands is a comfort as I play some Sonny Boy, "Good Evenin' Everybody," which was a modification of his King Biscuit Time intros. The point then for Sonny Boy was as much to sell flour as to make sounds like no one else had ever heard before. For me now, nothing feels more right than the smooth metal running cool across my lips, my tongue slapping holes to chord, my hands cupped or flapping like wings, yet I stop when my eyes open and I see my black shirt hanging on the doorknob. That's part of the other show, the one we'll be putting on, before and after the music. After four years, I don't know how much longer I can keep it up. But I get to play harp. I get to play harp.

• • •

First time I heard a harp was on a radio show called "Who Covered Whom." The station was Detroit's Cool Q 102, and I listened every Sunday so I could appear in school on Monday, dressed like everyone else in a rugby shirt and jeans and Weejuns, and talk about what records were played on "Who Covered Whom," as if knowing Little Eva did "The Loco-Motion" before Grand Funk might obscure that I was the only twelve-year-old in Troy who was black *and* fatherless. One Sunday, the DJ played Slowhand Clapton's "Eyesight to the Blind"—from the soundtrack of *Tommy*, a popular midnight movie among the stoner set—then Sonny Boy's original. The sheer sound, so rough and raw and real, reached inside and shook me. I didn't know how anyone could have made the sounds Sonny Boy did. I almost believed those trills and slides emanated from within, like song from a bird. Plus, I knew instantly, unlike with Jimi Hendrix on the same station, that Sonny Boy was black. And I wanted to learn how to kick up such a racket myself.

Once I bought my own harp and instructional books to go with it, I was soon stumbling through "The Star Spangled Banner" and "God Bless America," meantime listening to Sonny Boy and Little Walter and wondering if I'd ever sound like them. Later, at Troy High and at Michigan State, I joined several bands—the Mr. T's, Sheik and the Trojans, Motown Mojo, Jack and the Dull Boyz—but we sounded like George Thorogood or J. Geils. Having grown up on Apple Blossom Court instead of Dockrey's Plantation, I feared I was never close enough to the *real* blues to play them. I needed confirmation of my talent but was too frightened to sit in with players who came through East Lansing and Detroit. Didn't help that my bandmates were named Trevor and Steve and came to the blues after several viewings of *The Blues Brothers*. No brothers and sisters were stopping to see me either. So, two months shy of graduation, when I'd been offered a job by Loomis and Pratt, a marketing firm in Cleveland, I was confident I'd take it and keep a harp at home to play along with my Chess records on weekends.

Then came the audition announcement in the *Detroit Metro Times*, calling for harpists to try out for a spot with Brother Ben. I owned but didn't listen much to his and Bucketmouth's first album, *The True Delta Blues*, but like I believed Bessie Smith died because she wasn't allowed into a white hospital and believed Tommy and Robert Johnson sold their souls at the crossroads and believed Blind Blake shot a dog and alone could ride the New York City Subway system with ease, I believed the story in the liner notes about how twelve-year-old Ben was arrested for stealing a Stella from a pawn shop, then sent up before some stern, but sentimental cracker who asked why Ben had committed such an awful transgression. "To play the damn thing," young Ben is purported to say, a response that so tickled the judge, he said, "Then let me hear what you can do." Naturally, Ben shook those strings so well—without even a lesson—that the charge was dropped. I believed all those stories and more, as if by learning them I might make up for my assimilationist experience and play the blues as if I'd *lived* them. I'm sure the twenty white cats I auditioned with in an Auburn Hills Hilton believed this tale, too, only I was chosen to play with the man. My confirmation. And my introduction to a world as much defined by manipulation as music-making. Still, backstage at our first show together, I asked Ben if the story about him and the judge was true. He didn't even say a word right away, just tilted his head and squinted as if I were indeed the rawest negro on the block.

Now, five years later, I hold the notes of "Good Evening Everybody" as long I can before letting them go. This morning, flying from New Orleans to LAX, when I first read the polls, I believed things had turned my way. We'd finally get more than just a nomination at the Beale Street Blues Awards. I'd flash these polls before Ben and he'd agree: "You're right, Pete. Let's just play."

Thank God I couldn't hold on to such notions for long. Thank God the Last True Delta Bluesman showed me once more that this is his show and will be until he says he's through. That he knows much more than I, as a businessman, a musician, a bluesman, a man born black in these United States. Without that, I might have believed I had the answers. I might have believed it was my time to go it alone.

# 2.

**BECAUSE NEITHER BEN NOR I KNOW LAS VEGAS,** we don't follow our usual pre-show routine of checking into the hotel and waiting for fans to find us. We're touring Las Vegas Blvd, looking among casinos, hotels and family-friendly extravaganzas for the newest Jump and Jive Juke Joint, a chain with franchises in Columbus, Denver, Orlando and right next to the Mall of America. "Jump and Jive" reminds me of swing music, not the True Delta Blues, but the promotional literature promises you can eat "authentic Dixie-fried victuals" or

# Take Your Hand Out of My Pocket

"soak up the southern hospitality of our full bars" and, most of all, "stomp your foot to the best roots music." And the owner, a former ad agency president from—get this—Hamilton, Ontario, simply cannot open the Las Vegas Jump and Jive Juke Joint without Brother Ben and me there to christen it. To the man he believed was only our manager, he said, "Brother Ben's the only performer who can provide the genuine roots music experience we try to provide our customers." In his guise as Wilton Mabry, Ben agreed, then told this fellow, Kent Bollinger, he'd see what he could do. The delay doubled our typical appearance fee and assured we'd be there to kick off the tour. Call Brother Ben a con man or a capitalist, Ole Br'er Rabbit and Ralph Ellison's Rinehart have nothing on him.

Ben parks the Brougham in walking distance of the miniature skyline of New York, New York and the mammoth MGM Grand, across from the Jump and Jive Juke Joint, which squats solidly on Las Vegas Boulevard South. When Ben and I get out, a man in gray slacks and a blue blazer walks forward, arms spread wide.

"Brother Ben, Silent Sam," he says. "Kent Bollinger." Bald head shining, he shakes our hands. Mine hard, Ben's gingerly. Then he steers Ben toward the wooden steps that lead to a porch so country I expect yawning hounds stretched out by their masters' work-booted feet. "Buffalo, 1972," Bollinger says. "That's when I saw you with Bucketmouth. I liked Cream and Hendrix and the Stones then. But once I heard the real thing, I was hooked."

"Do tell," Brother Ben says, interrupting himself with the broken, rusty cough he's been experimenting with lately, the one that scared a thousand dollars away from Mr. Habib. Sounds like a lung just shut down, it's so racked and wet, and Bollinger looks on as if what Ben's got might be catching. Still, he's doing a lot better meeting the legend than I did. I'd already met him at the audition as Wilton Mabry, but when I saw him in his plaid suit next to a Grand Prix the color of a bar of Irish Spring, I gasped, "You're Brother Ben!" Today, it's easy to see Ben in Mabry and Mabry in Ben, but that's only because I, unlike nearly everybody else, know to look.

Now Bollinger grips Ben by the arm, helping him up the steps. "Best concert I ever saw," Bollinger says. "I mean, even though it was freezing outside, I could close my eyes and believe I was somewhere like this place."

Vegas? I want to say, but Sam's no smartass. I wipe my hand over my mouth and mustache, which I'm still getting used to, as I only grow it for tours. Bollinger's gold buttons clatter on his blazer as he turns, arms and open palms directing us to take in the surroundings. "You know, when Luther Johnson played the Minneapolis opening, he said it was too real. Gave him the chills." Bollinger smiles, smoothes some stray hairs over his wide, bald head, a man pleased with his enterprise. And he's met plenty of other bluesmen: Guess that's why he's relatively cool around Ben. Now he's encouraging us to reply in kind with Houserocker Johnson. Or is it Guitar Junior he's talking about? Lots of Luthers out there. Whoever it was, I suspect he might have been messing with this Canuck. Then again, I think everyone's messing with someone in this world I live in. Sonny Boy never told a writer the same birthday twice. "They don't know me," he reputedly said.

Ben steps away, winks swiftly at me with the eye farthest from Bollinger. He bends over slowly, as if inspecting the floor, then wearily straightens, only to stamp his heel against the yellow wooden planks. The thump resounds while Bollinger looks on astonished, unable to process just what the bluesman who changed his life is doing to his faux jook's porch.

"Too firm," Ben says, then fashions another tubercular cough. He stoops, hands on knees for a moment, then rises to his customary slouch. "Ever' porch from Friar's Point to Marianna so flimsy folks had to tiptoe." The pantomime he then executes makes him cackle and smack his thigh with his porkpie hat, which establishes it's time for me to smile, and I do, Jemima-big.

"I think it was that night in Buffalo where I had the idea," Bollinger says, reaching for Ben's arm. "To build these clubs that gave people a chance to experience a real life juke joint." He pauses, drags Ben along the porch and resumes. "With nothing to get in the way of their enjoyment."

I wonder if Bollinger's made it to the Delta, been inside a real jook. Many a blues lover flies to Memphis, rents a car and drives down 61, though I hear now Tunica and its casinos sits there like a juggernaut, keeping most from even making it to Clarksdale, let alone Rolling Fork or Alligator, or across the river to Sonny Boy's town, Helena. Truth is, though, Bollinger must have hired some good people to construct the building. Much study of old photographs and newsreels went into the work, maybe even a visit or two to Junior Kimbrough's place near Holly Springs. I allow my eyes to follow Bollinger's hand pointing to the Nehi, Jax and Falstaff signs, artificially rust-spotted and rakishly hung on the exterior walls, which are made of a material that looks as faded and ready to fall apart as the warped and rotted shingles of a genuine jook but is surely as sound as a dollar and will probably be around for hundreds of years. Bales of cottons are piled around the entry, with scythes and sickles and scales hung here and there. New laminated posters are tacked to the wall, advertising shows with Little Milton, Bobby Rush and Latimore, while reproductions feature Mud, Wolf and Little Walter. There's even an empty sack of Sonny Boy corn meal next to the checkerboard atop an old wooden barrel. I try to jump a white piece with a black piece but they're all lacquered in place.

Bollinger's holding open the door for Ben and going off on how the executive chef, though trained at Johnson and Wales, was born and raised in Nashville and fuses classical technique with southern staples. "But it's still down-home cookin," he says and rubs his paunch.

In "No Tellin' How Long," Ben sings of how much he likes pig feet and did claim once, in a radio interview, that he'd made many a meal of Saltines and Vienner sausages, but in truth he's one of the more rigid adherents to the food pyramid I know. Right now, for instance, the wrapper of a protein bar lies crumpled in the Brougham's ashtray. Four years ago, along with red meat, he gave up coffee and soda—both of which I drink steady until nightfall—and started drinking green tea. However, as we all three step inside the Jump and Jive, the old fraud licks his lips and says, "I hopes we gets to sample some."

"Sure," Bollinger says, his hand still clamped on Ben. "You too, Sam? You can order anything you want on us."

I nod, say, " 'Preciate you," then add a "suh," because after years of practice my Midwestern tongue has managed to shape that syllable with ease.

The interior, as artificially rustic as the outside, smells somehow of creosote and spent tobacco juice, but located in the back of the first level is an elevated stage. In the two Arkansas jooks I visited—so Ben's second harpist, Heywood "Razor" Sharp could teach me how to play harp without an amplifier—no stages existed. We took up space at the rear corner of the dance floor, near enough an exit in case some shit got started. No true jook would contain all the high-priced paraphernalia that covers the walls here either. Bollinger holds Ben by the arm, tolling the costs and telling the story of how he got this and that. Considering he's been listening since as far as the Bucketmouth days, I guess it's Ben's ears alone he wants to fill. I slip off and view all the signed guitars, photos, album covers, trinkets, clothes, and other pieces of the blues as well as soul, bluegrass, folk and country memorabilia. I now read the small plaques authenticating this axe was played by T-Bone Walker, that one by Scotty Moore, this banjo by Grampa Jones. I'd kill for something of Sonny Boy's, though I'm sure all his derbies, ventilated shoes and harps were tossed out in the Helena trash the day he died. I find nothing but smile at the signed photo of Mr. Cotton and Mojo Buford's belt with enough loops to hold a dozen harps.

In all, the first floor impresses. I could do without the Blues Brothers and Slowhand on the jukebox and the taxidermy alligator behind the bar. Still, as I inhale the soft dust, I think of what Ben demonstrated earlier: It is too sturdy. Plus, it's in the middle of Las Vegas, and I doubt you could order a fried bologna sandwich here, even with Dijon and a tapenade instead of pickles and Plochman's. Then again, I recall from my marketing classes at State that there's no need for the genuine if your clientele believes what they're getting is real. I've learned that same lesson from Ben, who could have been tenured in the business and music departments and taught the best black studies class you could take.

But here's what I can't figure: Will we go over tonight? I want to believe we'll have a huge crowd of converts to Brother Ben and Silent Sam. The other B.B. lives here, though I suspect his horn-heavy shows haven't prepared anyone for us. Even played by impostors, true Delta means acoustic guitar and unamplified harp, minimal solos and some songs that will depress the shit out of you, like our version of "Stones in my Passway" and Ben's "My Mother's Crying Face." Here at the Jump and Jive, I suspect Buddy Guy could kick ass, as could some of the skinny white boys with three names and long hair and tiresome solos. But us? Shoot, if I were visiting Vegas with my fellow ophthalmologists or oral surgeons and had a choice between strippers and two preservationists of some obscure and ancient musical form, I'd be folding tens into g-strings and telling Lexus I loved her.

"Admiring the décor?" Bollinger says, clamping a hand on my shoulder, his grip so firm and sudden a "What the fuck" almost rolls out of my mouth. I chew my mustache instead. Beside him, Ben has shrunk an inch shorter than his customary slouch. "I was just telling Ben here how much we paid for that." His gesture is vague and I don't know if he's talking about Ray Charles's sunglasses or Mance Lipscombe's false teeth. It's a little dark, too, but soon I see the acoustic guitar encased in glass. Its plaque reads, "Once played on the streets of Atlanta by Blind Willie McTell." It is a twelve-string, yet—and this could be the play of shadow and my own poor vision (who would know Silent Sam wears Bausch and Lombs to correct his myopia?)—it doesn't look played enough. No nicks and scratches that would inevitably result from playing on street corners. The guitar Ben will play tonight was purchased from a pawnshop in Portsmouth, New Hampshire, near the end of last year's tour. It has a nickel-sized hole in the body and a pear-shaped patch beneath the sound hole where somebody's pick wore away the lacquer. Nonetheless, when I turn to Bollinger and see his reverential eyes and fingers tapping the glass, I keep quiet my doubts about its original ownership. Man probably paid a grand for the guitar. "Purty," I say. Bollinger says, "I told our designer that no matter what else he did, put that guitar up in a prominent place." He turns to both of us, beaming. Only way his smile would be bigger is if Blind Willie's corpse lay in that glass, and I wouldn't be surprised to learn Bollinger had a hired man prowling the south's unmarked graves for that acquisition.

"Folks still listening to Blind Willie?" Ben says.

Wicked. Pretending he doesn't know the answer, which is of course no. Unless you're David Evans or Robert Crumb and your office is full of 78s that you never take out of their original sleeves, you might know the name McTell from the Bob Dylan song, but not the man or his music. I maintain a good collection, mostly CD's now, and I bought Blind Willie's entire works on a German import last year. I liked it the first time I listened, as I did with Gary Davis, Blind Blake, and Blind Deacon and the Professor, but I never connected with that Piedmont stuff, always sounded too bright and busy for my ear, nowhere near as lowdown as I like.

But why's Ben digging Bollinger about Blind Willie's obscurity? I shoot him a look, but he keeps his eyes on Bollinger, who stammers and says, "I don't know." Then he rallies and rubs his hands together, saying, "Upstairs? Two more levels to go, the smoking and non-smoking dining rooms."

Now Ben looks at me, and his eyelids droop while he yawns and shows off those sleeves he wears to give the appearance of gold teeth. He claims his Biloxi dentist took a photo of him smiling, to display to patients the fruits of good hygiene. But unless they're dentures, a full set of pearly whites doesn't correspond with songs about evil-hearted women and good old gin. Now he says, "I doan know bout my partnuh, but us old folks thinkin' 'bout a little piece a nap."

"Right, right," Bollinger says. "Wouldn't want to keep you. " Either the man knows his stuff or just finished reading a chapter on Ben in an encyclopedia of the blues. I read *The Blues's Who's Who* back when I was a college sophomore and never dreamed I'd know the man, and it re-told the legend of young Ben and the judge and how Ben's asleep before his head hits the pillow, any time, night or day. Once he's asleep, boy, you'd better not trifle with him. It went on to detail the famous incident where he found Sleepy John Estes in his cot backstage at the '68 Ann Arbor Festival. Mississippi Fred McDowell *and* Big Joe Williams had to pry Ben's fingers from Sleepy John's thin neck. In that same book, though, Sleepy John was reported to possess the ability to sleep standing up. Right now, Bollinger's probably worried *Ben* might fall asleep standing up. He says, "Sure you don't want anything to drink?" He reaches behind the bar, pulls out an ice-covered bottle of Bud and jabs it in Ben's direction. At no time has Ben even pretend to drink what he calls that St. Louis swill. He shakes his head. "Sure?" Bollinger says. "On the house."

"Thank you but no," Ben says. "I be tired enough already."

Head down, Bollinger leaves the full bottle on the bar, then sticks his hands in his jacket pockets and escorts us toward the exit.

Ben tries to push open the door, but winds up coughing, so I finish the job, which hands me an eyeful of glare and heat tightening the skin on my face. We walk to the porch and don shades, then shake hands with Bollinger. Bollinger says, "Show starts at seven sharp, just as Mr. Mabry requested."

"We be here at six then," Ben says.

"You'll need to do a sound check?"

Ben shakes his head, takes his time to wipe his lips with a slow-moving tongue. "No suh," he says. Bollinger waits a moment, as if expecting some salty axiom after all the lip-licking preliminaries. He gets nothing, only Ben walking slowly toward the steps. Bollinger rushes forward about the time Ben grips the handrail and positions his body to descend. I start in that direction, but wait, as Bollinger says, "No warm up act, right? I remember that from the show in Buffalo." He pauses, his eyes gaining the reverence he had inside. "What did you say then? 'I smoke dynamite, drink TNT. I can do all the heating up myself.'"

Bollinger smiles as though he made up for his sound check gaffe. Then again, how would he know the schemer of schemers doesn't really need a sound check because of his near-perfect ear and because he doesn't want people to think, after forty years of performing, that he's become too professional? Sideways, Ben maneuvers down the steps, pretending to slap away my aiding hands. When we reach the bottom, we turn and wave, then make it inside the car and get it and the AC cranked up.

"Bet he tells everyone that shit," Ben says.

"What shit?"

"Best concert ever. I don't think I even played Buffalo in '72," Ben says, steering us into the flow of traffic. "Maybe that's just me growing old, though." He sighs. "Getting forgetful."

I wave my hand near the brim of his hat. "Who you trying to kid?" I say.

Behind the wheel, Ben faces me and grins, showing off the gold sleeves on his upper and lower teeth.

"What about that guitar, though?" I say. "Think it's real?"

"Pardon?" he says.

"Don't go pretending you're deaf."

"I didn't understand what you meant."

"Blind Willie's guitar," I say. "You think that's the real thing?"

"Hard to tell, hard to tell." He unwraps another protein bar and tugs at it with his teeth. "But I doubt it."

"You watch, though," I say. "Bollinger won't let you leave tonight without something he can tack up next to Solomon Burke's conk comb or Big Joe Turner's shoeshine kit."

Ben laughs, puts down the protein bar. "Practically stuck that bottle down my throat." He pulls out a tape from his inside pocket, plugs it in the player. Miles Davis: "Kind of Blue." We lean back and let the frosty AC bathe our faces, forgetful of all else for the moment. Then, at a red light, Ben raises his hand to his mouth and works it there until he says, "Think he'd like these?" and shows me the gold sleeves in his palm.

• • •

Back in the hotel, two hours before the show, I'm barbering Ben. I only know one haircut, a straight baldhead administered with clippers, but neither of us ever spends much time without a brim on— porkpies and fedoras usually—and Ben started losing his hair in the seventies. Not that hair loss bothered him. Going bald spared his having to get a jheri curl like Bobby Bland and the other B.B. and damn near everyone else.

Ben's eyes open when I cut off the clippers. "That's nice," he says, rubbing the top of his head. Silver and black hair falls as light as cigarette ash. "Razor it for me, too, Pete. Fear I got a shaky hand."

I blow stubble from the clippers' teeth into the pile of hair on Ben's sheet-covered lap. In a voice not unlike Sonny Boy's, I sing, "Razor my head for me. I fear I got a shaky hand."

"Sounds good," he says. "Been practicing?"

*Been* practicing? Man, I'm always practicing, my harp, my Delta accent, trying to make it all sound true to the blues. But Ben doesn't need to know. "Naw," I say. "Just trying to make you realize you're talking in twelve bar cadence."

"Occupational hazard. Two weeks ago at the Waffle House I said, 'Two strips of bacon, na-na-na-na, nice and lean, na-na-na-na, put it on an English muffin, na-na-na-na, or you'll see a man get mean.'"

"Waffle House doesn't serve English muffins," I say, lathering up his head with aloe-scented Barbasol. "And I've never seen one strip of swine on your plate."

"The pig is an unclean animal. Part dog, rat and cat and not fit for eating or even to touch," he says, affecting the stern and clipped speech of one of Reverend Louis's boys.

"How much for a copy of *Muhammad Speaks*, Brother Shabazz?"

In the mirror, he looks me up and down. "I'll give you a two for one, 'cause you look like you need all the help you can get, brother."

Here in the Ramada, it's fine to laugh like Mrs. Owens's boy. Razor in hand, I have to wait a minute. Don't want to lop off Ben's ear. Bollinger might have someone nearby to bust in and snatch it. When I'm composed enough to razor a clean stripe through the white foam, I catch a tiny glimpse of myself in the mirror and look away. On tour, I depend mostly on Ben's eye to measure if I look the part of Silent Sam. Or I'll concentrate on one feature at a time. Mustache ok? Any sleep in my eyes? Hat tilted at the most rakish angle? But I never go out of my way to examine a head to toe reflection. Like now: Even though I'm in my underwear with my stage clothes sprawled on the bed, I don't risk another glance.

● ● ●

From backstage, the crowd looks ok, maybe three, four hundred. Definitely more than I expected. Problem isn't that they're all white—I *expect* that kind of crowd. What we've got tonight are young, Soloflex types, tanned and dressed in bright colors and eager to toss each other around a dance floor. The blues faithful come to exalt in the presence of an authentic artifact of some quasi-southern, quasi-African past. Tonight's crowd would make Jimmy Buffet happy. Backstage, I'm tugging at my clingy shirt, which is less the color of motor oil, and more like a pigeon's neck, when Bollinger comes over, asking if we want anything to eat or drink. I shake my head and Ben says no. "You sure?" Bollinger says. "Chef Davis's catfish just melts in your mouth." Disappointment lines his forehead a minute, but he wipes his hand across his face and comes up smiling. "Say, do you remember the series of diaper ads that featured 'Born Under a Bad Sign?'" he says.

"Sho, sho," Ben says, seated in the folding chair he'll remain in during the show. "Had them dancing babies in them, didn't they?"

"That was one of mine," Bollinger says, the gold buttons on his blazer rattling as he touches Ben's arm.

While my hands part the stage curtains, I remember those commercials like a bad night of drinking. I was in my last bar band, Jack and the Dull Boyz, in East Lansing then, and everybody wanted to hear that song and flail around like the babies in the commercials. One night I got so agitated I yelled, "Albert fucking King. Know who he is?" Someone tossed a full can of Stroh's at me. I ducked just in time.

"Anyway," Bollinger says. "I wanted to get one of *your* songs, Brother Ben. For GM. Either 'Old Black River' or 'Leavin on My Mind.' But Mr. Mabry and I couldn't agree on a price."

I pull back from the curtain, pleased to hear Ben, in his managerial guise, said no to the commercial exploitation of our music. At times, I feel his attitude is that after all those years of bluesmen getting shafted, including him and Bucketmouth, the only color that matters now is green. His saying not to a sure-fire profit reassures me somewhat.

"Well," Ben says. "He won't give up nothin' to nobody 'less he get what he want. But he a good man."

"A good businessman, sure." Bollinger bends down for a face to face with Ben. He clutches Ben's wrist and says, "But you don't mind the money for tonight was transferred to his account in Jackson?"

Which explains why he brought up Mabry in the first place. Most people think he's ripping us off, Mabry, which is expected from managers, but made even more mean in our case because he's a brother. Though Mabry is the name on Ben's birth certificate, he's as much a fictional character as Uncle Remus or Bigger Thomas. Ben thinks our dependence upon him makes us seem even more pathetic, which he uses to his advantage. Bollinger's present gesture seems gracious, though his schemes to acquire some object of ours for his wall are shameless, and he has no clue that the man he's talking to with such admiration and deference is also the scoundrel he mistrusts and couldn't agree to terms with all those years ago. Kind of funny, you ask me.

Ben says, "Doan you worry none. Mr. Mabry, he take good care of us. Ain't that right, Sam?"

I nod, stick my harp in front of my mouth and play, "Take Your Hand Out of My Pocket," to warm up, watching to see if Bollinger knows the tune. He stares at Ben, nods, then backs away. I look toward the audience again and note their restlessness as well as their uniform lack of anything that signals we'll be among devotees of Delta blues. A team of security guards takes up places before the stage, and I'm pleased that of the six, two are black, ensuring there will be four living African Americans present in this building constructed in part to honor the musical contributions we've made to this great nation of ours.

● ● ●

Eight months is a long time to go without playing with your partner. Still, after we hit the stage—no James Brown-length intro, just Ben's backwoods one liner about smoking dynamite and drinking TNT to explain the lack of a warm up act—I feel I'm in the one place in the world I belong. I don't expect us to sound as good as when we were bringing last year's tour to a close, when our hearts practically beat the same time. But Ben hasn't varied his set list since I came on, and we catch up with one another like old friends who know each other's stories. Anyway, I'm not here to draw much attention. No Blues Blaster amplified glissandos from these ten holes. I'm here for sweetening, my harp like Henry Sims's fiddle for Charley Patton or Washboard Sam with Bukka White. I echo his turnarounds, punctuate a phrase or two, shape train sounds, and on "Back to Jackson" and "Mind Me Woman," rip solos you can time with a second hand.

About six songs in, my lips stop tingling and I'm feeling good. After a dozen, I'm sweaty under the lights, my G harp warm in my hands and my eyes shut with the effort of so many concentrated breaths. Meanwhile Ben slides that brass pipe on his pinkie over the strings, syncopated, sharp and stinging. Every backstage glance at Bollinger reveals a man clapping his hands together in ecstasy, but the Las Vegas Jump and Jive Juke Joint's first concert is lost on the people who've paid to be here. Most look on as if they know they should be respectful, but that doesn't jibe with what they consider blues, a soundtrack to beer-drinking and shaking your ass. Maybe they think since Ben's seated in his padded folding chair, his skinny body hunched over his guitar, they should also stay in their chairs. They perk up when we play "Leavin' on My Mind," likely because they recognize the opening riff as similar to "Sweet

Home Chicago." When we start "Mind Me Woman," I'm glad we play no encores. With this dead ass crowd I want to get back to the hotel soon.

Still, we need to get our first performance out of the way, so we'll be better off and ready for the next. Since Ben doesn't tell stories between songs—he's all music—we're some three numbers away from the finale. After some tepid applause, I hear someone yelling a request. I always hear such voices clearest, the rare ones belonging to those who feel we haven't done enough and that they have the right to demand more. The only album Ben and I did together, *Blues At Your Request*, contained one original, "Take My Chance," while the rest were covers we were always asked to play, like "Stones in My Passway," "Death Letter Blues" and "Bottle Up and Go." No such requests are hollered now by this fool, who sounds like a victim of the bar's concoctions. With names like "Rattler Juice" and "Swampwater," they all contain at least three liquors and cost ten or twelve bucks apiece.

But fuck if he's not hollering for "Soul Man." The Sam & Dave version is smoking, you ask me. The one Belushi and Ackroyd did featured some of the same Memphis players like Steve Cropper and Duck Dunn. I even know the words, having performed this song at least a dozen times in bars and frat houses for drunken white boys who played air guitar and jumped behind a mic to sing along. Now my contacts shift and settle into place over my irises as I try to locate the body attached to the voice in the crowd. Everyone's dressed alike, so it takes a few minutes to spot him. Wearing Bermudas, a Hawaiian shirt and sunglasses, he's clutching a sloshing glass the size of a goldfish bowl. His other hand's cupped against his mouth for amplification, and the people around him seem more amused than annoyed. Security's keeping an eye on the relics that decorate the walls. Ben counts down to "Take My Chance," but it's no use. Already other elements of the crowd have caught this bug and they're chanting "Soul Man." I can barely hear Ben's voice over the din and at one point put down my harp and glare at Bollinger, who stands in the wings backstage, hands jammed in his pockets. Applause accompanies the increasingly louder chants of "Soul Man." When he closes out "Take My Chance," Ben shakes his head. "Time to go," he says, even though we're one song short. We bow and make our exit in time to hear the boos.

• • •

Bollinger stands between us and the performer's exit, wiping his bald head. "I'm so sorry," he says, backing up as we bypass the dressing room. "I thought we'd have the right kind of crowd, but . . ."

"Ain't yo' fault, suh," Ben says, stooped but purposeful, holding his guitar by the neck. I'm behind him, carrying his empty case.

"But you'll come back again, won't you? Vegas is still new to what you both do. But it'll catch on." Bollinger looks behind him. With a few feet between his backside and the door, he stops. His hands come up before him and he's smiling.

"Might not be no next time," Ben says. I turn to look at him, but he winks, a sign it's all just talk.

"You'll tour again," Bollinger says, his voice pitching higher. "And when you do, can't you at least think about coming back?"

"You kin call Mr. Mabry," Ben says. "But after I talks to him I doan think he be sendin' us here no mo'."

Bollinger reaches out and his hand rests against the neck of Ben's guitar. He doesn't flinch, as would anyone who'd heard what happened to Elvin Bishop when he grabbed Ben's guitar. Instead, Bollinger stands there smiling. Now he says, "Again, I'm sorry." He pauses, one hand fondling the guitar's headstock, a Sharpie clutched in the other. "Could you perhaps leave us something to remember you by?"

I step closer and mumble, "Better open that do', Mr. Bollinger."

Ben's picking fingers find my wrist and clamp. The strength in them shouldn't surprise me, but it does. He wants me to keep cool. So I do for now. "You gon have to wait on that," Ben says, gently pulling the guitar out of Bollinger's grip. "Mebbe when I die you kin ask Sam for this here glass eye of mine. I plans to donate it to him in my will." He blinks and somehow manages to keep the pupil of his right eye fixed while the left eye fidgets about. Bollinger's hands rise slowly to his mouth. I can't tell if the gesture's from shock or if he's determining whether he should keep such an item near Ray Charles's sunglasses or near Blind Willie's guitar. Either way, Ben and I pass him and walk outside to the Brougham. Ben's straight face remains for at least a minute, far longer than I manage. When we reach the Jump and Jive parking lot, he says, "Always liked that song."

"Which song?" I say.

"You know," Ben says. "Do-do-do-do-da-do-do-da-doo, I'm a soul man."

Though my harp's in my hand, I can't make any noise but laughter.

# 3.

**SOMEWHERE ON I-25, I WAKE IN THE PASSENGER'S**
seat, certain I hear "Take My Chance." I rattle my head and wipe my sticky mouth. Can't be a tape. Ben never listens to us. He's more likely to listen to books on tape or jazz, with Miles Davis, Coletrane and Bird big on his playlist of late. And Wyoming, like the rest of the nation, has no blues radio stations. Even if we're passing through while some campus station's featuring a blues hour, "Take My Chance" isn't the song anyone would play. "Where I'll Die," "Back to Jackson" and

## Going in Your Direction

"Old Black River" are sides Ben's famous for. They're the ones, according to a reviewer, that "combine the angst of Robert Johnson with a surprising yet satisfying outlook of hope." "Take My Chance" isn't really that much of a blues. It begins with the almost nonsense verse of, "Some folks says she's from Louisiana, some say she come from Paris, France./ Some folks say she's from Louisiana, some folk says she's from Paris, France./ But when it comes to lovin' that woman, I'm gon take my chance." It's the only original Ben and I recorded, plus I love the tricky octave riff I blow in the intro and close.

Now, in the Brougham, I say, "What was that?"

"What?" he says, both hands on the wheel. His hat's between us and I can tell he needs a haircut soon.

"Thought I just heard us playing 'Take My Chance.'"

"Go back to sleep. You're imagining things. Look." He lifts his right hand to point at the stereo: The radio light is off. No cassette sits in the player.

"Damn," I say, rubbing my face, staring out the window at a world of desolation, asphalt and speeding tractor-trailers. "What's hearing things a sign of?"

"Sign your mind's too busy. And that ain't right, Pete. You need to get yourself together."

I'm quiet for a moment, which is too long for Ben. He says, "Want some advice? You need you a hobby to keep your mind active and balanced. Golf, for instance."

"Ok," I say, then close my eyes before any more unsolicited advice keeps me awake. Ahead of us is a TV interview tomorrow in Laramie, followed by some Nebraska, Iowa and Wisconsin dates, plus the academic conference in Indiana. In these places we might be the only blacks in the county, let alone the concert hall. But I'd rather think of the two-and-a-half successful weeks we spent in the Pacific Northwest, a territory we're more familiar with than the plastic sheen of Vegas. Like I told Mr. Habib, things went purty reg'lar: Sold out shows in Eugene, Corvallis, Portland, two in Seattle. Only a few empty seats in Spokane, Moscow, and Missoula. Last night in Billings—another sellout—we hung out with an army of cats carrying acoustics and wearing patchouli-scented denim. Got my palm scratched nearly every time I shook hands, what with so many fingernails grown long for delicate fingerpicking. "Doesn't anyone play bass?" I wanted to say, but I was Silent Sam, collecting pints of Old Crow we don't drink and fat doobs we don't smoke. There has been some strangeness, though, like the wet kiss I got from a plump earth mother who also handed over an expressionist painting of Ben that's presently rattling around in the trunk. She was in her fifties, claimed she'd seen Ben play at Newport either in '67 or '68 and since had carried around the vision she set down on canvas last year. In it, his guitar's all swervy and the colors in his face and hat are sky blue, ochre, maroon and maybe vermilion. And next year, she promised, she'll have one of me.

At such shows our respectful fans sing along but don't bray and never demand tunes that aren't on our list. They want to jam backstage, and that can get dull quick, though most are solid technicians, at least. After these gigs, though, Ben sometimes admits he fears our base could be diminishing. Youngsters appear in the crowd, probably dragged to the gig by their parents or black studies instructors. Saw ten Af-Am kids in the theater lobby in Eugene standing around a graying white cat with a gradebook but couldn't see them under the stage lights. Must have ducked out after getting their ten extra credit points. Eventually, Ben has said, the numbers might shrink to the point where no promoter will agree to Wilton Mabry's pricetag, and it won't be worth our while to tour. But we don't talk about quitting the road much. Too depressing. In "Last Drink of Liquor," Ben vows, "Whiskey'll keep me standin, long after my friends start to fall./I'm gonna keep on drinkin, probably outlive them all." But even he can't believe every lie he tells.

• • •

"You thinking about tomorrow?" Ben says, a little farther down the road.

I yawn, squeeze my shoulders up around my neck. "Nope," I say.

"You should." Ben smiles, puts his blinker on and exits the interstate. "Been a while since you've faced some questions. And we've got the conference soon." He pulls the Brougham beneath the canopy of a gas station, shuts the car off. We both get out, stretch. While Ben pumps gas, I slide to the driver's side, ready for a moderately fast getaway.

"Why Laramie, though?" I say. "TV station's had plenty of chances to interview you."

Ben shrugs. "I'm more concerned about those scholars. They're gonna want to talk to you. Mark my words."

I open the driver's side door and nod, though he didn't answer my question, and I'm not convinced about the scholars. No one wants to talk to Silent Sam, not with the Last True Delta Bluesman around, friend to Little Junior Parker in some stories, enemy of Honeyboy Edwards in others. I don't share my belief with Ben—I don't tell him three-quarters of what passes through my head—but I can feel his clear eyes focused on me. "Don't think anyone's gonna talk to you, huh?" he says.

I chew my mustache, burned because I'm either so transparent or he is gifted with something like second sight. "They never have before," I say. "Heywood told me all he ever said to anyone was, 'There go Brother Ben.'"

"Heywood said that?" Ben smiles, shivers a little. Without the gold sleeves on his teeth, he appears genuine, a man experiencing a true moment of pleasure, not performing one for an audience. He pulls the nozzle out of the tank, points it at me like an oversized pistol. "Maybe that's why he's teaching high school in Pine Bluff." Then he turns and walks to the station.

While Ben pays, I warm up the car, and play a few bars of "Going in Your Direction," wondering if he knows of some novice harpist who might take my place. Folks think Heywood "Razor" Sharp lost his job when he showed up late for a gig—Brother Ben won't tolerate tardiness—and saw me on stage playing in his place. From there, you either believe Heywood fought me or fought Ben, then went home to Pine Bluff to sulk. Truth is, Heywood did go back to Arkansas. He was tired of the touring and ready to start giving something back. He finished a Masters at Arkansas State and has twice been named teacher of the year in his district. I know his is the only music class in the Delta in which the students hear equal portions of Stravinsky and Sonny Boy.

Ben returns, enters the car and I drive away, the force of the engine still startling even after several turns behind the wheel. I have to ease up on the accelerator and tighten my grip. "Do me a favor, Pete," Ben says. His shoulders are slumped and his hat tilted down to cover his eyes. "Just start thinking about some good answers. You got a lot of questions ahead."

I nod and say, "Will do." Around is a rural darkness that makes me wish I was home in the Garden District. People up here say they live in God's country. He can have it, you ask me. There's no place for a brother to hide, and I'm worried Ben and I resemble crack dealers. Plus, I suspect there's some militia movement or Klan activity not too far from the interstate. So I put my foot in the tank, but ease up when the needle reaches the speed limit, let the Brougham find our way to the next stop in the line.

• • •

Just as he believes we must look the part of bluesmen, Ben believes we must also talk the part. And this means more than how we speak—dropping g's and sprinkling our speech with rural aphorisms—but *what* we say. As with his lyrics, we have to adhere to what's been told and retold in the past, yet not too closely: There's got to be some variation, lest we appear as though we showed up in costume from Central Casting. Last interview I faced was a month after the end of the last tour, when we were visited in Jackson by a knowledgeable Helsinki documentary crew. The reporter asked if Ben could talk about some of his mentors, which isn't as simple a question as it sounds. A hack—like me—might reach too highly and claim Robert Johnson or Muddy Waters. Not Ben. He's been on this job too long. He claimed he learned much about playing from Son Thomas and this advice from a one-time meeting with Son House: "Never let them touch your guitar, boy." The Finns then blinked like he'd strewn dust in their eyes and went on to the next question, why he never played Europe. To which, Ben shook his head and pointed his finger upwards, saying, "Ain't goin' up in the heavens 'til the Lord call my name." When they turned to me to learn if I felt the same way, I said, "Man tell me where to go, I go."

This morning, though, at the KWYO studio, a series of blocky buildings and satellite dishes outside the city limits, I'm wondering if Ben agreed to today's interview as a way to shake me up. Around this point during last year's tour, he accused me of sleepwalking through the shows. I didn't agree with his assessment then and still don't, but my protest now won't keep Ben from parking the Brougham in a visitor space or leading the way to the entrance. Once inside, we startle a receptionist. "Oh," she says, a single syllable of pain and shock. Unless some varsity athletes from the university are also scheduled to appear, I'm sure we comprise the total of African Americans she'll see today. Ben's wearing a tan leisure suit and a burgundy shirt with the head of a sphinx on the left breast. Mine is mostly dark green, but when I move yellow highlights emerge, like the feathers of a starling in a patch of sun. Ben keeps a humble distance from the reception desk and makes a big show of scraping his soles on the mat. Head down and hat off, I hide behind him. "We lookin' fo' Miss Sonja Hutch," Ben says, and we both step back.

"One minute," the receptionist says, her eyes still round behind her wide frames. Red blotches form all over her neck. I expect she's clutching her purse in both hands as she looks left, right, and even under her desk, until a cat with a crewcut, polo shirt and khakis passes near. "Randy. Is Sonja in?" she says, fanning her face with her hand.

"Sure," the man says, looking toward Ben and me, both of us bent like beggars. "Come on. I'll show you her desk."

We follow, hats in hand, Ben nodding and saying "Ma'am" to the receptionist, who steps toward the exit with a trembling Virginia Slim between her lips.

"First time in Wyoming?" our guide, Randy, says.

"No suh," Ben says. "We comes least once a year."

Randy slows, rubs his chin with his hand. "I thought this was Sonja's first year here."

"Might could be," Ben says, scuffing his soles against the carpeted floor. "But me and Sam perfome here reg'lar."

Now Randy stops, turns and faces us both. "Oh, you're the blues guys. I thought. Never mind."

He moves forward again and we follow, only I can't catch Ben's eye to be sure of what just went down here, if I should be concerned. When we enter an office with no people but plenty of cubicles, file cabinets and silent TVs, Randy points to a desk at the far right and says, "There's Sonja's desk. Need anything else?"

"Where the facilities, suh?" Ben says. "I needs to make some water."

I cough to keep from laughing. What a line. I doubt it's even true, though the old trickster did drink a lot of green tea this morning.

"This way," Randy says and Ben and he head out, Ben saying, "You be all right, Sam," in a way that keeps me from knowing if it's a question or command.

The smallest desk in the room, Sonja Hutch's is also tidy and orderly, her cup of sharp pencils next to her stapler and her computer keyboard as white as if it just came out of the packing material. Next to her keyboard lies a worn book in a scratched dustcover with a public library stamp. *Blues for Beginners*, it's called, with a subtitle of *From Johnny Ace to ZZ Top*. A napkin from Wendy's marks her place. Was a time I could read such books without laughing. Now I want to see just how far from the truth this one is, as well as see if I get a mention. I pick it up and it falls open to the entry on Ben. "BROTHER BEN," the heading reads, "b. circa 1923, in Coahoma County, MS." So far so good, vague in both birthdate and actual birthplace. I read on: "Widely considered the last living link to such pioneers as Charley Patton and Robert Johnson, Brother Ben is virtually unknown outside the world of traditional blues fanciers but for over four decades has performed and recorded his distinct brand of authentic DELTA BLUES.

"Little is known about this curious figure—including his surname—until he and his first harmonica accompanist, Reggie 'Bucketmouth' Carter (b. Clarksdale, MS, 1921, d. 1983), were discovered in 1959 by Louis Mankiewicz and Morton Stern on a Clarksdale street corner. Several subsequent recordings and festival appearances established the duo's reputation as purveyors of the 'True Delta Blues.'

"An adept slide-guitar player as well as a powerful singer, the rough-hewn Brother Ben has never recorded electric blues or branched far from his Delta roots. Just prior to the death of Carter, he was joined by a new harmonica accompanist, Heywood 'Razor' Sharp (b. 1960, Pine Bluff, AR), in 1982. Brother Ben still performs and records today."

I skim the rest of *Blues For Beginners*, noting Ben's entry is much shorter than Elvis's but longer than Blind Deacon Roland's. The book neglects such interesting facts as Ben's good grades and college aspirations, the five years he spent with his factory worker father in St. Louis, where he learned of swing, Charlie Christian and single string runs. Doesn't say either that the summer of his and Bucket's discovery he was in Clarksdale courting one Martha Grange, who was ready to enroll in nursing school in Memphis in the fall, and that he added ten years when Mankiewicz and Stern asked him and Bucket how old each was. And that the one and only time he'd been called Brother Ben was the moment he called himself that, knowing Wilton Mabry would not impress these strange white men. Now that Martha and Bucket are gone, the people beside Ben who know this story are Heywood and me, only I'm not concerned about that now. Too pissed I didn't get mentioned in the entry, though the copyright page shows a publication date of 1995, Heywood's last year. This date also proves the Laramie public library doesn't have a large selection of blues books, or Sonja Hutch picked up the first she saw. I am mentioned in the books that count, *The Blues Who's Who* and this massive and wonderful British volume, *Jug Bands, Coon Cans, Bottlenecks and Criers: Blues and its Performers*, if only to mention I was born in Natchez in 1969 (two facts that confound my mother, considering Detroit and 1972 are the locale and date she recalls). And Ben claims that right now, out there among the blues faithful, somebody's starting to compose my entry. He says it's up to me how the entry unfolds.

I close the book and place its worn bottom edge just above and parallel to the bottom of her desktop. When I look up, satisfied I returned it to its place, I turn to hear Ben's cough, followed by a sympathetic female voice, though I can't make out the words. I lean in the direction of the open door, just about the time Ben appears on the arm of a tall, young sister, medium-complexion and glossy good hair. "That man thought we looked alike," he says, pointing behind him. "Think he thunk we was cousins?"

"Brother Ben," she says, swatting close enough to brush the shoulder of his tan sport coat, "You're old enough to be my father."

Mine too, I should say, only Ben turns and says, "Here mah partnuh." He stops, points to me. "Miss Sonja," Ben says. "This here mah good frien' Samuel Stamps."

Miss Sonja smiles and I blink at such an attractive black woman. If her presence was supposed to assure I wouldn't sleepwalk tomorrow night at the Laramie Civic Arena, Ben guessed right. I'm wide awake when she reaches for me with a well-manicured hand. Don't see a wedding ring, but I'm not exactly dressed for flirting. My mumbled "Ma'am" doesn't capture her interest, and I doubt my limp handshake or sunglasses worn indoors help.

"Well," Sonja says, releasing my hand and stepping back. "This is going to be wonderful."

She removes her purse from her shoulder, hangs it on the back support of her swivel chair, while I direct Ben's bright eyes to the well-worn library book on her desk. He winks. Shuffles forward and waves at the book. "Oh no, Miss Sonja," he says. "This here book full of nonsense."

"It was the only one in the library," she says, confirming my suspicion. But she's too slow to block

Ben from plucking the book off her desk, as if his next move is to toss it to me in a game of keepaway. When she reaches for Ben, smiling and protesting, I admire her long, graceful neck, as well as note her generic TV voice. Sounds like she hails from a suburb not unlike my own. Once Ben gives the book to Sonja, she directs us to follow her to the studio. As I brush lint off my jacket with my hat, I look over my shades at the reflective surface of my shoes. It's foolish to speculate on any romantic potential. We'll be out of town tomorrow after the gig, and the only memory Sonja'll have of me—if she remembers me at all—is how pitiable I appeared. Since I moved to New Orleans, I've dated several women: black, white, biracial, a Chinese/Jewish woman named Alison who kept me up at night. No relationship progressed further than a few okay trips to the bedroom, as the women I've attracted all wanted me to play some role for them—a daddy, a money-maker, a wimp to push around—and I've got roles enough already. Last relationship of any length I had occurred during my last two years at MSU. Another Detroit suburbanite, Dierdre was eager, like me, to prove to the campus's black community that she was down. Her route to acceptance was through AKA, a knowledge of urban fashion and dance steps I never mastered like the Cabbage Patch and Smurf. Of course, she hated blues. Every time I played a record for her—even Bessie and Koko, Sippie Wallace and Etta James—she'd say, "Turn off that old-timey shit," as if she'd grown up on stoops instead of cul de sacs. When we broke up, she told me her new man—a Q-Dog with a jheri curl and a Benetton wardrobe—was, get this, a "real brother." I didn't know what to say but good-bye.

Now, in the small studio behind the news soundstage—Ben won't allow a live interview—we sit in three uncomfortable, modular chairs, Sonja next to Ben, with me on Ben's right. Still, I'm close enough to inhale her perfume, which is so spicy I nearly start huffing like a kid with a kerosene soaked rag. She says the interview won't play until tomorrow's evening news at six, an hour before our seven o'clock show. If we can't catch it, she says she'll send a copy to Mabry. "Right, Dan?" she says to the cameraman, who flashes a thumb and hunches behind his camera.

Ben leans forward and says, "Oh, I trusts you, Miss Sonja. You gon make me and Sam look good." He pats her hand paternally, falls back into his seat, his head sunk low, his brown fedora at an angle that should make him dizzy. Around my chest and shoulders I feel a little tight, so I flap my arms. I don't fear any questions Sonja might ask—especially after learning her resources. Most will be directed to Ben, and those posed to me will be, no doubt, about Ben. I'd like to ask Sonja some questions. I thought my upbringing in Troy was bad enough, but Wyoming? Damn.

I slump my shoulders as Sonja tells Danny to start taping. Behind my shades, I envision the close up of Sonja, her enunciation even more precise as she welcomes Brother Ben and me. As the camera pans to my left, including all three of us in the shot, Sonja says, "Where were you born, Brother Ben?"

"Mississippi's where I was born," he says. I expect him to sing, "Mississippi's where they'll bury me," as he does in "Where I'll Die," but instead he says, "Coahoma County. Out in the countriest part."

"And what year was that?" Sonja says, hoping perhaps to scoop the editors of *Blues For Beginners* by coaxing from Brother Ben an actual date of birth. Poor girl. Might be able to flummox a city councilman on the take but doesn't stand a chance against the Last of the True Delta Bluesmen. He shakes his head and laughs a few stage "huh-huhs" before saying, "Now you know good and well, Miss Sonja, that they's things a man mah age cain't 'member. And age is one of them."

A twitching grin mars Sonja's studio-serious face. Ben's working his magic, only she doesn't know. No one ever knows. I wonder if he reminds her of an uncle or grandfather from down south. My mother's people were Northern and proud of it—I never saw an act like Ben's until I met the man himself. Now Sonja blinks and she pulls out some new index cards. "All right," she says. "Next question."

From here, things go as if Ben typed the questions and ordered them. Nothing pushes us far from the legend he's worked so hard to maintain. The TV viewers who don't know already of Ben will tomorrow learn of his early days in Mississippi, the diddley bo he played on his uncle's barn, the discovery of him and Bucket by the Yankee college professors, the records and festivals, Bucket's death, Heywood, then my arrival. At this point, Sonja asks me how long I've played harmonica, and Ben says, "We call it a harp, Miss Sonja." Which is my cue to stammer about my large and poor immediate family and asking Santy Claus for something small—an invention of Ben's that always earns us sympathy and wonder, as if the world from which we claim we hail is one far distant from the blues lovers of the U.S. Meantime, the tightness in my shoulders and chest has faded, and the heat from the lights relaxes my face. Sonja really is beautiful and pretty smart. Is this her first job out of college? Is she on her way to bigger and better places? I wish her luck at getting somewhere warm. That's one reason I like New Orleans: I don't worry about sub-zero temps and snow, which was never a good background for a brother trying to avoid notice.

After about thirty-five minutes, the interview's drawing to a close, when Sonja leans forward and says, "This one's a toughie. I'm warning you."

"Go 'head, young lady," Ben says. I nod, open my mouth then clamp it shut as Sonja reviews her cards, then looks up, smiling at the camera. She turns to Ben. I'm wondering if she's going to bring up the one question I fear, the one I know I can't provide a satisfactory answer for: Why don't you have any brothers and sisters at the show? But her question's this: "Why do people like the blues so much? Don't people just get so depressed? Listening or playing them?

Clearly, the discs she played to prep for this interview weren't Hound Dog Taylor or Slim Harpo, who both make the dead shake a leg. And if I've heard this tired question a hundred times, then Ben's heard it a thousand. Still, Sonja looks on, smiling smugly, as if she has indeed posed a toughie. I lean back, knowing this is going to be the best part of the show. Should be paying admission, you ask me. Ben's scratchy inhalation sounds full of phantom phlegm. And he reaches two trembling hands forward, clenches them, and leans down. "I been playin' blues a long, long time." He coughs, licks his lips and grins. "But I bet you somethin', Miss Sonja, the first blues man, the fellow what started to play that music, he wasn't tryin' to make no folk sad. I bet you he a man who got tired of workin' all day and was lookin' fo' a way to stay out them fields. He picked him up a guitar or a drum or a jug, or maybe just his hands." Ben's own hands, artificially and artfully gnarled, rise as if on their own. For a moment, he examines them, turning his trembling palms toward Sonja then back toward his own face. Then they lower and grow nimble, snapping out a hambone rhythm on his tan knees. "He found him his music, then he got a song to go with it. You know, I bet he was a preacher one time, but lost his faith. Or just one them men who can get folk to do what he want, even when it ain't good for nobody else. One them, them, them. I doan know what to call them fellows." The hambone stops. I'm watching closely, but not nearly as close as Miss Fine Brown over there. Eyes wide open, Sonja leans forward, placing her thin fingers atop Ben's bent ones. "Do you mean a con man?" she says.

For a moment, Ben seems less infirm. His spine almost straightens. "Right," he says, and I know he's got her hooked. He's got me, too, and I knew he was as phony as Piltdown Man all along. Ben continues: "But this man, he played that music for the folks who had a lot to be blue about. Them that worked too hard, didn't get much pay. Them that loved those who didn't love them. And them folk wanted to hear him some more, because the song he sang said 'I got them blues, too.'" He coughs again, dipping his head, while Sonja says she can edit out the cough. Ben sits up a little straighter, smiles. "So you got to see it my way, Miss Sonja. A man feelin' good, he gon listen to blues and say they's sad. And that's all right. He doan need to hear no blues. But a man feelin' bad, he gon feel better, because the blues man sayin' he got them blues too, maybe worse than you. Ain't that right, Sam?"

Startled, I lean back, lick my lips, and say, "That's right, Bro' Ben."

Sonja signals the cameraman and the red light dims. We all three stand, Ben taking his time to arrange his slouch, and Sonja shakes my hand, thanking us both. Ben tells her there'll be two tickets in her name at the Will Call booth, but I think we all know she'll pass on tomorrow's gig. She's seen enough of a show already, even if she thinks she got the True Delta Blues on tape. As I hook a hand under Ben's shoulders and steer us toward the door, she lopes over and hugs Ben, then kisses him on his cheek. With her eyes closed, she doesn't even see the wink he gives me.

Outside, I still can't believe how good Ben was. I take off my hat, smack it against my thigh, then plant it tight on my head. If the scholars at the conference get half a performance like this, they'll be writing books about Ben for years. I open the door to the Brougham, say, "Nice performance back there."

"'The first duty in life,'" Ben says, sliding in the driver's seat, " 'is to adopt a pose.'"

I know he's quoting, though I can't summon the source. Warily, I say, "Who said that?"

Ben opens the passenger door for me, then buckles himself in. Near a venue, he'll undo the strap to demonstrate his hellbent ways, but he's safety first when it's just the two of us. "My man Oscar Wilde," he says.

I smirk and thump the roof of the car with my fist. Don't even leave a dent. I say. "What part of Mississippi was he from?"

Ben doesn't blink. "Up around Glendora, I think," he says, starting up the Caddy. "Like your man Sonny Boy."

• • •

Back at the Ramada, we change into track suits, and I lose the coin toss to see who'll take the Brougham to Jiffy-Lube. Ben's job is laundry, and he slings our bag of polyester, Orlon and Dacron over his shoulder, as merry as a black Santa. After I drop him off at a laundry, I make it to the Jiffy-Lube, and prowl around the waiting area. My Styrofoam cup of scorched coffee is barely made brown by a big helping of powdered creamer. The limp newspapers are smudged, while none of the magazines has a cover. Fortunately, I discover a payphone, even if the cord doesn't stretch far from the receiver. I haven't gotten a cell yet—Ben's owned one the last three tours—and a payphone is getting as rare as black blues fans. I punch in the numbers of my calling card, then the only number I know in Pine Bluff: Heywood Sharp's. After Ben's performance, I need to talk to someone, if only to share my praise of the man. Most of the blues faithful would be downright shocked to learn Heywood and I—I never call him Razor—speak at least every other month, but he is the person with whom I can share anything meaningful. He taught me how to be Ben's sideman, onstage and off. He's only twelve years older, plus, I respect him, what with his decision to go back to school and teach. Thanks to Ben's advice, he's got a sizeable portfolio and secondary income from rental properties, so he's not hurting for money. Still, I can't help but admire his aims in remaining at a public school in one of the poorest parts of the land of plenty.

On the fourth ring, as I'm about to hang up, Heywood answers. "Sharp," I say, a finger in one ear against the hydraulics and shouts from the oil change and brake-check bays. "Where you at?"

"Pete," he says. "Where you at? Seattle? Missoula?"

"Try Wyoming," I say, then relay an account of the interview, Miss Sonja and her kissing Ben. "That's nothing," Heywood says. "I saw a Miss Missouri rub up on him like she couldn't get enough his stuff. A white girl, now."

I laugh, knowing the rule concerning all stories about Brother Ben: They're true, even if they never happened. "Anyway," I say. "Man was in rare form today."

"This was 21st Century Ben, right? Not the burned bluesman with all his grudges?"

"More like *Uncle* Ben. Only time he got a little huffy was when the girl asked about the blues being so depressing."

"Damn," Heywood says, his voice rising. "Haven't heard that one in a while. How old was this girl?"

"Younger than me, probably. But not by much." I press the black receiver closer to my ear, turn to the picture window to monitor the progress of the work on the Brougham. The hood's still up and half a worker is visible. My coffee doesn't taste any better cold, so I pitch it in the trashcan. "But you know how it is," I say. "Sitting there wishing you could applaud."

"Man does good work."

"Then he pulls out Oscar Wilde on me in the parking lot."

As if reading it off a cue card, Heywood repeats the quote. "Yeah," I say, suspicious. Heywood is, I know, a living, breathing human being, but it's hard sometimes not to view him as a total creation of Ben's. I suppose the two could have consulted between the time I dropped Ben off and now, but I doubt they're in that tight. "But you know what?" I say. "Sometimes I wish we could tell the real story." I really haven't been thinking this at all, though as soon as I speak, it sounds somewhat real.

"Not that story," Heywood says.

"The legend's bullshit. The real story's . . ."

Heywood cuts me off. "But you may as well quit thinking about it because the man won't allow it. You know what he told me? 'Don't let the truth get in the way of the story they want to hear.'"

"Sounds like Brother Ben all right."

"So when did you think start thinking you know what's best for the act?"

A good and bad thing about Heywood: He won't let me talk shit. I can see him now. A well made brother, shorter than Ben and me, but with wide shoulders and a linebacker's chest, light eyes and a caramel complexion. Dressed in natural fibers, he's got to be smiling with that mouthful of straight, white teeth—none of them fake, despite the many rumors of Ben's punches and mine. He knows me pretty damn well, once even suggesting I was drawn to blues because of my fatherlessness. That I idolized these men because they possessed knowledge I wanted but couldn't find at home. I was playing harp, he said, to prove I was black *and* blue. Whenever he brings this up, I remind Heywood of his C in psychology, but I don't doubt there's some merit in what he says.

Now I try to speak but wind up stammering, as though my Sam persona's threatening to take up residence full-time. Tangling my fingers around the metal coil of the phone, I watch a worker in a blue uniform shut the hood of the Brougham. I could use this and Heywood's distance to end the conversation, but I brought us here. And I know I'll be talking to him again, and he'll remind me of this conversation until I answer. I try him with this: "The reporter, Sonja, she'd never heard of us before. Had to look us up in *Blues for Beginners*."

"Kids in my classes don't even know CeDell Davis," Heywood says, "and he lives here."

I look at the Brougham and three workers surrounding it. Are they admiring it for the well made piece of Detroit steel it is or trying to figure out who might be the driver of such an obvious mack-daddy mobile? No one's joined me in the waiting area, but even were it full, I'm sure after one look the Jiffy-Lube boys would know I belonged to that automobile. "You should see the car we're driving," I say. "Exactly the kind of mess that keeps the brothers and sisters away. They don't want a reminder of what people already think about them."

Heywood sighs, just as I hear my name called out. My real name, that is. I fish out the credit card, a gold Corporate Amex, with Peter Owens typed under Mabry Enterprises, Inc. Wondering if I silenced Heywood for a change, I tilt the card up and down to reveal and obscure the hologram. "Got to go pay the bill," I say.

"Hold up, Pete," Heywood says. "It's cyclical, blues. Always has been."

"What?"

"You'll see. Black folks'll come back to the blues. Trust me."

"To the true Delta Blues?" I say, the phrase so comical, I hardly say it anymore.

"You never know," Heywood says, laughing a little bit too much like Ben. "Never thought afros would make a comeback either"

I laugh louder than probably that statement deserves. I say goodbye to Heywood, hoping his prediction comes true, but now I need to get the credit card receipt, because Ben never keeps anything but the tidiest of records, and the last thing I want to do is disappoint him.

• • •

"Now this is what I like to see," Ben says. He sets down a laminated brochure on the dresser in our Ramada room and strips off his tracksuit. Doesn't look a day older than the day I met him. In fact, he might look younger.

"What's that?" I say, turning my attention to the TV set: We get six channels, four of them fuzzy, and none shows anything but happy white faces. I switch it off.

"Twenty-four hour exercise facility," Ben says, stepping out of his shoes and searching through his gym bag—an item he keeps hidden in his battered suitcase. Out of it, he snatches his New Balances, black compression shorts and a white tank top and short set. Clothes in one fist, he passes by me on the way to the bathroom, talking all the way: "Trouble with online reservations. Descriptions of the facilities aren't always accurate. This time, they were right on the money."

"Really," I say. Five years ago I had an email address and he didn't, but since he's lapped me technically. I still get by with a G-3 while he's onto some Gateway laptop—he's always been a PC man—that he almost brought along for this tour but decided against. If someone discovered his running clothes, he could lie around their presence easily: "Doctah said I needs to do some walkin fo' my high blood pressure," he might say. But a computer? Especially one with all the frills of his? That's why he also eventually dismissed the idea of setting up a homepage: Though Mabry would have been the webmaster, it just didn't seem the blues faithful would appreciate logging on to LastTrueDeltaBluesman.com.

Dressed to run, his spine erect, eyes bright and smile unmistakable, Ben says, "You coming?"

Never before has he asked me to work out with him. Told me I *should* but never asked me to join him. I turn down the volume of the TV, feign my own spell of deafness. "What did you say?"

"You heard me. Come on. You already got that track suit on. Walk on the treadmill next to me. I need some company."

It's going on eleven and my eyes drift to the Subway wrapper in the trash can. Only an hour ago a double-meat BMT was my dinner, followed by two black and white cookies. Each earned from Ben a scornful look. Now he's got another lesson, this one on empty calories and the disadvantages of a sedentary lifestyle. I sit up on my elbows, watch him grab the doorknob and say, "I'm not asking, Pete."

Though my rebellious spirit weighs me down—along with the junk food laboring toward my intestines—I rise and walk toward him. He opens the door a space, sticks out his head and looks both ways, always checking for that one hanger on who might upset the charade. "We'll take the stairs," he says, as together, we creep past the closed doors of the third floor.

Downstairs, I'm a little winded but not letting Ben know as I step on the treadmill. Facing a mirrored wall, we're side-by-side, me nearest the entry to the exercise room, which contains in addition to the two treadmills a stationary bike, a Stairmaster and a weight machine. A smell of bleach and perspiration emanates from the damp towels in the hamper and reminds me of high school gym class, the last time I had a regular exercise routine. "Just get warmed up, first," Ben says, his stride long and his hands moving easily, the MPH display reading 4.5. I notch my speed a mile slower but that doesn't keep my feet from tangling together. My legs move along jerkily and unwillingly and I decrease the MPH until I'm comfortable at 2.9 and hoping Ben can't see how slowly I'm traveling.

"Nice, huh?" he says, facing forward. "Get that good air in your lungs"—he inhales, his chest expands broadly—"then let it on out." Exhaling, he makes a hissing sound while bringing his hands up closer to his ears with each stride. He's got a towel around his neck and he keeps sneaking looks toward the entrance. Now I know why I'm here: My width makes me a good barrier should anyone pass by. The beeping music of his increasing speed accompanies us as I try to decide if I should look straight ahead or watch my feet. Either way, I suspect I'll fall off the damn machine. Plus, I recall you shouldn't exert yourself at a level that makes speech difficult. Ben hasn't demanded a reply, yet I fear when he does I'll not be able to say a word. So I pre-empt him and say, "You think Blind Deacon Roland and the Professor are keeping up with us this way?" Pleased I pushed out that sentence without gasping, I punch the MPH a tenth but don't like the rhythm my shoes are making on the treads.

"What made you think of them?" Ben says. The soles of his shoes are starting to slap the treadmill louder as I hear his MPH increase again. "Still carrying around those polls, aren't you?"

I haven't thrown them away, that's true, but I don't look at them more than, oh, every other day. I say, "Man, I got better things on my mind."

"Like what?"

There's plenty I could tell him: of fine Miss Sonja and my conversation with Heywood. How I think we've found that relaxed groove on stage. Or how I wonder if he and I will ever record again. Or whether he ever fears, as I do, that the music, no matter how good it is, is always secondary to the act. But the many ideas clogging my mind aren't the reason for my silence. The sweat stinging my eyes and dripping from my mustache, the knots of flame in my calves and the rattle I hear in my lungs have quieted me, even after I slow the pace of the treadmill to a poky 1.8.

"You know they're going to give it to him," Ben says.

I grip both bars with slick hands, try to get my feet in synch again. "Give what to who?" I gasp.

"Blind Deacon. With Ott and Henry gone, he'll win easily. Voter sympathy. People are surprised he's still alive."

"You too," I say, then swallow and risk the security of my hands gripping the bars to wipe away the sweat on my forehead. Should have gotten a towel before I started. Should have gotten two.

"Naw," Ben says, raising his voice so I might hear over the pounding of his feet against the treadmill. "They just think I'm broke down and a little feeble. I'm too evil to go away quietly."

The cackle that follows sounds ominous enough to be genuine. It makes me want to ask him another question, because I'd like to hear more. Just between the two of us, he's never shared a word about mortality. With his diet and physical regimen, I sometimes think he plans on outliving me. "You," I begin, but it's too much to try and speak while maintaining any kind of pace. I lower the MPH to zero and step off clumsily, landing with too much weight on my heels and waving both arms to avoid a fall. I grope for a towel, embarrassed to discover that even with the many years between us, even with my MPH slower than where he started, I can't keep up with Brother Ben.

# 4.

**AFTER BEN TOLD ME WE'D PLAY FOR THE UPPER**
Midwestern Blues Appreciation Society, I had some questions: How many members does the Society have? How long has it been around? And why would they hold their annual concert in March and Wisconsin? I'm always relieved when we leave the Badger State, a bad place for bluesmen, you ask me. Otis Redding died horribly here, as did Stevie Ray and Luther Allison. According to Ben, though, the UMBAS made an initial offer that tripled our going rate. Which is why I'm driving east

## Keep It to Yourself

on I-90 wondering where is the Tomah interchange that will take us to 94 and Eau Claire. Snow, that's right, *snow* slows our progress but doesn't fall heavily enough to threaten peril. Living in New Orleans, I haven't seen a flake since that freak May storm hit Nebraska two years ago, when Ben and I were in Omaha so I could fly to Detroit for my mother's wedding. Never made it out of the airport. Still, I'm more than acquainted with the white stuff and am now visited by memories of snowsuits and damp mittens, the season's first snowman awaiting his carrot nose and button eyes, a frozen pond or a chilly rink, where I deflected many a wrister and slapshot, secure behind my goalie's mask. Many a member of the Upper Midwestern Blues Society shares such memories, I'm sure, though none would expect Silent Sam Stamps of Natchez could reminisce along with them.

In the Brougham, Ben sleeps next to me. I nudge his shoulder and he snorts, then opens his eyes. "Snow," I say, both hands secure on the wheel.

"I see," he says, stroking his chin.

"Remember Nebraska?" I say.

"Twelve inches in twelve hours, wasn't it?" he says, his offstage voice particularly un-Delta today. Makes Colin Powell sound like a gangsta passing around a forty.

"Was a time when I liked it. Snow," I say.

Ben rolls his head toward each shoulder, wipes clear his eyes. "Used to get some now and then in Clarksdale. St. Louis, too. Always a surprise, though. And it was white, pretty and gone by the next morning."

"Puts me in mind now of Sonny Boy. You know, 'Nine Below Zero.'" Were I in Ben's seat, I'd play the first few bars. As it is, I have to settle for humming.

"Everything puts you in mind of Sonny Boy," Ben says.

He's got me there. Sometimes I think it's a good thing I was born when and where I was. Had I actually crossed Sonny Boy's path, my admiration for him would have made me run his errands, break up fights between his ladies, pretty much walk off of buildings to keep that man happy.

Ben sits up straight, yawns, then dials down the heater. "Makes me think of Bigger Thomas. The morning after he killed that girl." I glance from the road in his direction. Eyes closed, he taps a long finger against his upraised chin. "What was her name? Mary something?"

"Dalton," I say, recalling the name easily though it's been years since I read *Native Son* in Dr. Jeffrey's Black Studies class. I got an A-. The scene Ben's talking about is easy to visualize: Bigger waking up to a world full of white, an actualization of what he's felt most of his life. As I consider sharing this wise reply, Ben says, "This is too grim." He opens the glove compartment, rattles a cassette in its clear case. I can't see the title as he punches it in the player before I agree or disagree. "Here's something more appropriate," he says. In the brief silence, I try to guess his selection, keeping in mind the many surprises he's capable of. I'm expecting jazz, maybe some Basie or Ellington, since he's worn out Miles Davis and usually goes backward. But when Nat King Cole's silken voice croons, "Chestnuts roasting on an open fire," I shake my head.

• • •

Two hours later, it's still snowing, but we're in the Eau Claire Holiday Inn. Ben's showering and I'm drinking a grande coffee and staring out our window at the white streets below. Seems the local chamber of commerce is trying to spruce up the downtown with wider sidewalks, benches and wrought-iron light poles, but the only storefronts open are consignment shops, a few taverns, a diner and an adult bookstore. Still, the falling snow and the few inches on the ground give everything a festive appearance, though at the same time it spurs in me recollections of tips about steering into skids, following tire tracks and looking out for black ice. In New Orleans, we all fear a hurricane—"the worst of all," St. Louis Jimmy sang (to be true he was singing about Florida). Whenever some Gulf depression gets named, my mother phones, frantic, wondering what it will take to permanently remove me from the city that, to her, always seems in the path of destruction. She doesn't just want me out of Louisiana, though. She wants me living somewhere closer to her, but I can't. Might run into folks who know me as Peter and will want an explanation why I never keep in touch with the Troy High alumni association or haven't attended any MSU Homecoming games. Also, I feel I got out just in time. Sonny Boy and Robert Jr. Lockwood lived in Cleveland a mighty long time, Mud, Wolf and Willie Dixon lasted in Chicago for decades, but the record for many bluesmen living north of St. Louis was not good. Take Pat Hare. That brother may have been a little crazy to start—his most famous side was titled "Gonna Murder My Baby"—but I've always believed his eventual move to Minneapolis did him in. There he did indeed murder his baby, a cop as well, and died in the pen at St. Paul. Much could explain his crime, I'm sure, though I don't doubt he felt like Bigger Thomas some mornings, like I did: He didn't belong in this place. Though as for me, where I belong other than the stage is still an open question.

Don't know why I'm stuck on such a riff. I pull back from the window, take out my harp—the remedy I trust—and blow "Nine Below Zero," in time for Ben to come out of the bathroom, a white towel around his waist, his broad shoulders and wiry arms shining with lotion. I change the tune to "Keep it to Yourself," as Ben enters the kitchenette area, where he fills the four-cup coffee maker with water, then drops a tea bag in a mug. He walks over to the table, sits down across from me, staring, then shaking his head. From his Dopp Kit he retrieves a host of pill bottles, uncaps them, then starts filling his weekly pillbox with Vitamin C and zinc lozenges, glucosamine for his joints, and gingko boloba for his memory, which has never erred or disappointed him, you ask me. A few tablets appear as big as the paper footballs I used to make in study hall, but I don't know their function. I always tune out when Ben starts listing their miraculous capacities and why I should be filling a pillbox of my own.

"Sounds nice," he says, which makes me stop playing. The coffee pot bubbles and hisses as Ben caps all his bottles and his weekly pill organizer. I keep my harp near my mouth, waiting for whatever his next statement might be, only he takes his time pouring hot water into his mug. Humming, he glides from the kitchenette back to the bathroom, emerging from there in his drawers and a tank top and his socks in his hand. Sitting on the edge of his bed, he unrolls his socks and pulls them up to his knees. A funny picture, this is, the Last True Delta Bluesman parading in his socks and skivvies, made even funnier when he purses his lips to blow the steam off his cup of tea. This is the image I'd like all the blues faithful to see, but for what? I don't want this show to end any more than he does. Hell, if I keep playing as well as I've been, I might be moving up higher on next year's top ten list.

"Pete," Ben finally says, bringing his tea with him back to the table. "Looks like you lost your best friend."

"For real?" I say and place my harp on the table. I sip from my coffee. Ben's smiling, looking above the rim of his mug. "Want some advice?" he says. "This tea's better than all that coffee you drink. Try it."

My head nods though I don't know if I'm agreeing. "Here," he says, handing over the remainder of his tea. I look up and he predicts my question. "I'll make some more," he says.

I put down my coffee, sniff the tea but find no odor. I'm sure it's fine, yet I pause until Ben says, "Good for what ails you. Trust me."

• • •

Tonight's gig's in a local performing arts center, typically home to community theater and regional symphonies, according to the brochure in the Holiday Inn. As Ben drives there, snow falls, lightly now, but the roads are scraped clear and salted. After my years away, I've forgotten the effectiveness of Northern clean up crews, and we arrive without incident, earlier than we planned. No one lingers near the performer's entrance, though and no crowd gathered earlier in the hotel lobby. Since Vegas, we've always run into some folk who want to jam. Still, we are early, and I'm not sure what to expect from the UMBAS folk. Will they show up with their Martins and National Steels after the show? Will there be at least fifty?

Ben and I exit the Brougham, tip over to the performers' entrance, holding on to each other like the warm-weather Mississippians we pretend to be. Ben's teeth are genuinely chattering and I feel the tremor of his body with his arm crooked in mine. Even I'm cold, though it can't be much cooler than thirty, a temperature I once would have worn a sweater and down vest against. Plus, I'm trying not to view the snow as a sign of bad luck, considering what happened last time. Ben can't control the weather, but I don't doubt he knows the phone number of who can.

Inside, we rub our hands together, while noiseless dry heat flows from overhead vents. Ben says, "Remind me never to travel here in March again. Shoot."

"I grew up with this weather," I say. "But that's not helping tonight."

"All those years down in Louisiana," Ben says. "Thinned your blood."

We look around but find no one here to greet us still. Ben even calls out, "Hello," and I remind him we're early. To our right stands a door marked Performers. It's unlocked, so we snap on the lights, survey the room. The usual director's chairs, low sofas and lighted makeup tables, along with some posters of plays performed of late: *Biloxi Blues*, *The Iceman Cometh*, *Cats*. No *Fences* or *Dutchman*. I toss two empty pints of Old Crow in the wastebasket, then take one out, set it near the can to suggest we're interested in emptying the bottle more than its proper disposal. Ben's opening up his guitar case. Next I hear him strumming chords, a G, C, then an F. I'm no guitar expert, but judging by where his fingers are on the neck, I'd swear he's in standard tuning, which he never plays in when we're on stage. Now a jazzy run travels fluidly down the neck. I don't know enough players to compare him to, though he says Charlie Christian took hold of him like Sonny Boy did with me. Another cluster of notes streams from his nimble fingers, then a series of bright chords you never hear in songs about lonesome travels or mules in and out of stalls. My harps lie in their case, as I could never keep up with him now. A chromatic might do the job, but I lack the improvisational skills to weave in and out of the range he's messing with. Once, early on, I asked him why he didn't drop Bucket and the true Delta Blues for a career in jazz. "I wanted to make a living," Ben said. "And I didn't want to move to Paris to do it."

Now I say, "New composition?"

Ben stops playing, wipes finger grease off his strings with a rag. "Just getting in tune," he says, turning down the top pegs.

I'm about to say more, tell him to accept a compliment for once, but there's a knock at the door. It opens a space and in walks two white women who don't wait for an invite. The taller one walks straight toward the seated Ben. Judging by her black hair and the turquoise that chokes her skinny neck and wrists, she'll likely claim some fraction of Indian heritage. Trailing a few steps behind is a short red head with curves whose smile appears as my neck cranes for a glimpse of her ample backside. "Ma'am?" Brother Ben says, standing up wearily. I might be mistaken, but I hear creaking bones, though most of my attention is fixed on trying to not to get caught staring at this other woman. "Brother Ben," the brunette says, surprising him with a hug. In his affected slump, he's shorter than this woman, who I realize is wearing leather pants, the source of the creaking. I stand, walk closer, but put a director's chair between me and everyone else.

"I'm Audrey," the woman says, licking her already shining lips and rattling her bejeweled wrists. "One of the founders of the Upper Midwest Blues Appreciation Society."

"Mah pleasure," Ben says. "There go mah partnuh, Mr. Sam Stamps." I remove my hat but find it best to stare at my shoes for awhile. Audrey says. "Brother Ben, Silent Sam, I want you to meet April Lynn. April?"

"Hi," the redhead says, her voice not as confident as Audrey's or as loud. I find myself moving closer to listen, then stopping short. What's going on here?

"April loves blues," Audrey says. "She's only twenty but she's an old soul."

Ben assumes a Delta courtesy, doffing his hat and shuffling back a step. "Miss April," he says. "Pleased to make you 'quaintance." No handshake or hug from him. But Audrey keeps closing in and gestures for April to do the same. "We were hoping to get a chance alone with you two," Audrey says, looking around. "May I?"

Ben nods. I don't know what she's requesting until she takes off her long jacket and folds it over a sofa. Her shirt is white and nearly translucent, unbuttoned well past her flat chest. Those leather pants creak again as she sits down. I've never seen a pair on a live human being before. April removes her coat, a little rushed, and joins Audrey on the sofa. Tiny sunflowers dot her low-cut navy dress, short at the sleeves and rising high above her plump, stockinged knees. Neither wears shoes appropriate for a Wisconsin snowstorm. Ben says, "Ladies," in a questioning tone, a rare moment when he doesn't appear comfortable with the course of events around him.

"I see you've been admiring my jewelry, Sam," Audrey says.

I haven't. Still, Silent Sam knows it's his place to be polite, especially to very forward white women. "They nice, ma'am," I say, turning my hat with both hands.

"From Santa Fe," she says, holding her bracelets up. "A Navajo artisan's work."

"They is nice," Ben says.

"I'm Anishannabe myself. One quarter."

I look to the door, so she won't see me laughing. I'm also hoping for some other members of UMBAS to join us, as well as wondering what Sonja Hutch or my mother might make of this scene.

Audrey unsnaps a small black purse, fishes out a crooked joint. She puts it in her mouth, snaps a flame from her Bic. "Interested?"

"No ma'am," Ben says. "Not before no performance."

"Don't be so shy, Sam," Audrey says, leaning back against the sofa, one bare foot rising from her sandal's straps. She drops the unlit joint and lighter in her shirt pocket. April pats the sofa next to her, sitting up straight but watching Audrey, as if awaiting her next cue. I'm not completely naïve, though it has taken me longer than it should to recognize what these two are. Only question is do we have to pay. Ben says, "Ma'am, don't take this no wrong way, now, but much as I'd like to keep on visitin', it be time we gets ready."

Smiling, Audrey rises, April following a half-second behind. "We totally understand," Audrey says. From her purse she extracts an envelope as thick as a poker deck, hands it over to April. "Meantime, here's something for you both to think about while you play."

April gets up from the sofa, smoothes her dress with her empty hand, tottering from the height of her platforms. She keeps her balance, though, and when I recognize it's me she's walking toward, my heart lunges in my chest, and I chew my mustache with my lower teeth. "We've got copies," she says, handing over the envelope, bending forward to expose better the white tops of her breasts, which I study briefly before looking away. A sweet, powdery smell lingers, even after she turns around, and I don't know whether to watch her curvy bottom or check out the photos in the envelope. I choose the photos and receive a few glimpses of bare bodies, one unmistakably Audrey's angular and lengthy self, another perhaps of April, though I can't be sure, even after the eyeful I just got. Without fail, the men in the photos are black, and I see some faces, too, of famous bluesmen who should be ashamed. Largely because they're breaking marriage vows, but also because they should have known better than to let a camera into the proceedings, and shouldn't have tried to arrange their aging limbs into such awkward positions as these.

"Told you he'd like them," Audrey says. I look up and she's waving. So's April, who then blows two kisses and closes the door. Ben's at his full height beside me. He snatches the photos, tosses them into the wastebasket without looking at one.

● ● ●

The lack of hangers-on before the gig is explained by the UMBAS members surrounding us afterward. Fortunately, it's Ben they want, and I duck into the restroom, upset at my playing. Technically, it was pure and precise, only it lacked heart. No grit. No gut. Even after all the titillation in the dressing room, it had no groin. Sonny Boy would have walked on stage, snatched the harp out of my hands and planted one of his vaunted and ventilated size fourteens in my behind.

After I wash my hands and return to the dressing room, I see the room starting to fill, Ben perched on a sofa, alone, his guitar by his feet, looking far shabbier than the glossy six strings carried by the middle-aged white men who take up places on the rust-colored shag. I say no to a joint, try to see if Audrey and April are around, though I haven't decided what I'll do if I see them. Ben will say no, that's for sure, and I don't know if I want action in the sheets with these two blues-groupies. Ben occasionally plays us up in interviews as hounds, but he's too practical and health-conscious for anonymous and frantic couplings. To my knowledge, since Martha died, he's avoided paternity suits and STD's, though there are supposedly some ladies in his condo community who invite him over to change light bulbs now and then. I've stayed clean, but few have thrown themselves at me. Plus, I've always feared I'd get to talking during the act, and my hard vowels would betray me as the Midwesterner I am.

Now a bearded someone asks Ben where he learned how to play slide. He's got a lighter touch than most of the masters and there's never that buzz or clink of slide against frets you sometimes hear. "Son Thomas," he's saying. "That man showed me mo' in two minutes than I could learn y'all in a year."

Nice story, and the praise for Son's talents is real, but Ben's talking shit. Son's a good choice for a mentor, being dead and all, but he's also obscure, known by scholars, but not by your fan turned on to the blues by Jagger and Richards. Bucket knew Son, played many a house party at his side. By the time Bucket introduced his new partner to Son, though, Ben had already incorporated the styles of the slide players before him and snuck in the precision of Christian and other jazzbos. But along with a few moments of jamming, the UMBAS members crave to be transported back to a time before CD's, when the other B.B. didn't do commercials for diabetes prevention, and Ben's taking them there with his talk. "Y'all better buy you self one his records if you ain't got it already," he says. "That man knowed how to work them strings."

I stalk the perimeter of the room, say no to another joint, autograph a ticket stub—a shaky, slow maneuver that pains the guy in a leather jacket who asked, I can see it in the way he looks away after I cross the T in Stamps. No sign of the ladies yet. Audrey claimed they'd be back, and she seemed the kind to keep a promise. A young guy in a down vest asks Ben to sign his guitar, a handsome Gibson that shines as if it's never been played. After Ben labors with his signature—taking more minutes than I did—the kid holds the guitar by the neck. "You can play it now, if you like," he says, grinning.

Wearily, Ben reaches for his own. We don't know the maker, as the brand name had faded to incomprehensibility, but the guitar looks particularly shitty next to this sunburst masterpiece. "What you mean?" Ben says, striking a chord. "They somethin' wrong with mines here?"

Amidst the laughter, somebody offers me a beer, which I accept, wondering when was the last time I authentically drank an alcoholic beverage. The brand's Leinenkugel, some local brew, sweet and crisp going down. I tilt back the brim of my hat, roll the cool aluminum over my forehead and thank whoever gave it to me, but find no one to accept my gratitude. That's when I see April, alone by the doorway, looking over her shoulder, her coat folded over her arm. I take another swallow, try to block out the drones of detuning as some younger players realize it's Open D Ben plays in, not standard. I lean forward, take a breath and another sip of beer. Saying hello isn't the same as posing for one of those photos. If cameras appear, I'll *leap* out of the room. By the time I get my calfskins moving in her direction, though, she's joined by Audrey, who's not alone. And I'll be damned if on her arm isn't a brother, a dark skinned fellow with a part shaved into his close-cropped head. The sweater he's wearing is thick and Cosbyesque, multicolored oblongs scattered across its front. He and Audrey then collect April and they scan the room. Where I'm standing is the worst or best place to be, as the crowd's in the center and no obstacle prevents Audrey from spotting me and pointing. "Sam," she says. "There's someone you've got to meet."

A foursome? Serves me right. Wanting all the time to have another brother around and here's how I get him. The man's presence makes sense, though. Some photos showed the two women wrapped around a single bluesman, and the intensity captured suggested no one was pausing to set up a tripod. I drink more beer, my biggest swallow yet. My eyes close as my head tilts back, and my hat nearly slips off. I catch it, settle it in place and open my eyes to see Audrey, just as she comes in for a kiss. Her lips find my cheek and a corner of my mustache, while I grip the can with both hands. She still hasn't let go of the brother with her. "Sam Stamps, you must meet George. George Njoku," she says.

Even with my surprise at meeting an African in Eau Claire, I'm able to resort to Silent Sam. "You ain't from up around here, is you?" I say, as George reaches for my palm with his wide, salmon-pink palm. Damn, I'm getting good at this.

George laughs first, a booming rumble that opens his mouth wide, showing off white teeth and dark gums. He smells of Polo, while Audrey reeks of pot. "No, I am not, Mr. Stamps. I live presently in Superior, but originally come from Nigeria."

While I shake his hand, I keep my eyes dull, prop the can before my mouth. It'd be too much to ask if Nigeria was anywhere near Milwaukee, and I want to find out what the attraction is here. I try to spy April's sweet round face, but George has blocked her off. "Africa, my brother," he says. "Where the blues was born."

"You met Brother Ben?" I say, an escape line Heywood taught me. After George lets go my hand, though, he shakes his head and doesn't demand the chance to meet the legend. He says, "I see he's busy right now. I can wait."

"We didn't know George was coming," Audrey says, hanging on one of George's shoulders, reaching under his sweater with her other hand. "Did we, April?"

She steps slyly to George's other side, smiling at him and not me. "No," April says. "But he's here now."

"How could I not come down?" George says, raising his arms to encircle both women and pulling them and their exploring hands closer. "When I heard that Brother Ben and Silent Sam were going to be in Eau Claire, I rushed to the computer and purchased my ticket."

I nod to George's kind words, a little jealous he's fetched all of April's affection. He can have Audrey. Meantime, the guitars have started up, and I detect Ben's instructed them to play "Cherry Ball Blues," a Skip James tune that often frustrates novices into quitting early. He doesn't sing the lyrics, as if offering someone else the chance. No one takes that opportunity. George is saying, "Last year, the Society invited Benny Walker. You know of him?"

"I think so," Audrey says, obviously grabbing a little of George's flesh underneath his sweater. He flinches but isn't distracted enough to stop talking to me. "Mr. Stamps, did you hear me?"

I blink and nod, recalling one particular photo in April and Audrey's stack. Thought that was Big Town Walker. I'll have to tell Ben.

"He can be quite entertaining but he's too much a clown, I fear. So many obvious double-entendres. Those falsetto imitations of women distract from the sincere talent he has as a vocalist and pianist. Because of him, I did not attend last year's concert."

"So we had to be extra nice to Benny," Audrey says, nipping George on the ear. At that, he waves his hand as if at a fly, while clutching April closer to him. She sighs throatily. A few players keep up with Ben on "Cherry Ball Blues," but I also hear mumbled curses and the kid in the down vest sets down his beautiful Gibson and opens a can, as if beer seems a more tolerable alternative.

"Nevertheless," George says, his narrow eyes nearly closing. "I appreciated your show tonight. Brother Ben has always seemed to me so true, so genuine. A protector of blues and its African roots. Like a griot, he is. Tonight's performance convinced me of this impression. Do you know what a griot is, Mr. Stamps?"

My eyes dull, I keep my tongue lazy and heavy while I sound out the word phonetically and blink. George begins a definition that I could have gotten from an online encyclopedia. He must think I'm stupid or he's not too certain himself. And if he believes Ben's a griot, George needs to get back to Africa. I'd almost suspect he was running some con himself were his skin not darker than onyx. Still, I'm sure he's gotten a lot of white girls, playing the role of the exotic African. Ben strikes a few bell-like tones, usually an intro to "Special Streamline," by Bukka White, another tricky number. A few players pick up the tune and follow him. Ben sings the opening words, "Got that fast special streamline, leavin' out of Memphis, Tennessee." George leans closer, whispering, "I'd love to continue this conversation back in my hotel room." He smiles. "Which happens also to be in the Holiday Inn."

But I'm done with George, happy to let him, Audrey and April conduct whatever acrobatics they desire. "Next time," I say and turn toward the center of the room.

"There won't be a next time," Audrey says. "Not with you and Ben."

I pause, turn around. April and George continue to gape as if they've never been turned down before "What you mean?" I say. What does this fake Indian Princess know that I don't?

"Next year," Audrey says, shaking out her hair. "Blind Deacon Roland's supposed to be our guest."

"Oh," I say, then shrug and walk away a few steps. A strange wave of relief passes through me, and I pause, eye the trio over my shoulder. After a moment or two, they turn and exit the dressing room. April's behind is lovely, but I'm glad I won't find her next to me, naked, flushed and eager to depart. She's sampled so many others, I'd be the first bluesman to disappoint. Besides, over there among the guitarists, Ben's led them to the part where Bukka talks about the Special's air brakes, and I've always felt a harp mimicked far more effectively the whooshing sound. I finish my beer, head on over to see if I'm right.

# 5.

## INDIANA NORTHERN UNIVERSITY APPEARS ENTIRELY

made of concrete. My alma mater wasn't Harvard, but we had green places to meet, toss the 'bee, and ogle ladies. Here there's no quaint office of the registrar built at the turn of the century, no frolicking squirrels and tree-lined, undulating brick paths, just a series of sidewalks connecting utilitarian cubes. There is, however, a big sign stretched across the doors to the host building, a Hilton hotel, featuring the conference's jive title: "WHAT IS BLUES?/ BLUES IS WHAT?" And in red letters beneath it reads: "INU welcomes Brother Ben!" I can't say I'm fine with the omission.

## Don't Start Me Talkin'

I crease the brim of my brown fedora, then put it on. Earlier, when I was waking at seven and Ben came back from his four miles—completed under forty minutes—I asked if we could stop between the Comfort Inn and the campus. That way we could at least start the day in natural fibers. Either the synthetics are so slippery you can't sit straight in your seat or so coarse you feel body hair slowly abraded. Ben came out of the bathroom, wrapped in a towel, his gold sleeves in. He sat on the edge of his bed, crossed his legs. "Nothing between here and there," he says. "So for now"—and here he assumed a pimp's mincing delivery—"we gon spend time with the finest of ladies. Poly and Esther."

At six stories, the hotel's the tallest building on campus and isn't institutionally gray. Inside the lobby, I console myself with the small sign that welcomes Sam Stamps in addition to Brother Ben, but there's little time to admire it. We barely get our hats off—courteous southern gents that we are—before a mass of white men in their forties and fifties, nametags encased in plastic pinned to their lapels, turn our way. Like lions sensing a crippled wildebeest, they regard us, the old and young representatives of the True Delta Blues. Keys to a past that probably never was.

Two emerge from the pack, one a wide-set fellow with comfortable shoes, a blazer and an Albert Collins t-shirt. Albert the Iceman's smiling face is in silhouette, stretched by the wearer's broad gut. The slimmer of the duo holds a clipboard and appears like the English profs I recall: bow tie, tweed jacket, wide wale cords and black and white saddle shoes. Together, they walk toward us, and the older guy extends his hand. "Deeply honored, sirs," he says. His British accent throws me. I step back, a perfect Silent Sam gesture. Ben offers his left hand and says, "Glad to be heah. And who I makin' a new 'quaintance with?"

"Sorry, so sorry," the Brit says, releasing Ben's hand and clasping mine. "Rodney Graham. Co-organizer of the conference, professor of American Studies here at good old INU. My partner, in more ways than one"—at this, the bowtied dandy steps forward—"Dr. Lowell Hardy."

"A pleasure," Hardy says, bowing. Then, to Graham: "Rod, we do have a panel on Field Hollers in fifteen minutes and no slide carousel." He taps the face of his watch while his saddle shoes scuff the carpet.

"My younger colleague is insistent on promptness," Graham says, patting his hand on his stomach. "As I know you are too, Brother Ben."

"Folks got a right to 'spect the show gon start when it say on the ticket." Ben shuffles forward, shrunken and bent already. I've seen this transformation many times yet still check my urge to applaud. Earlier, just out of the shower, he looked like one of those old-timers lapping thirty-year olds in the Ironman Triathlon. Now he looks as though someone removed his spine.

"Gentlemen," Hardy says, another slight bow following. "And whatever you call yourself," he says to Graham, who blows a kiss that Hardy catches before racing to the center of the conferees. I don't know what to make of this brief introduction, other than to remark on how odd a combination they are. Hardy

I've never heard of, though Graham has written two books I remember. Too fond of casting every blues player as ass-kicking brawlers—*"Tell Razor Totin' Jim": Bad Men and the Blues* is one of his titles—he is knowledgeable. Some of the other men—and there are nothing but—are also dressed in blues-fan gear, the older your concert t-shirt, the better. Others, like Hardy, appear in outfits designed to wear when talking about Edmund Spenser. Walking backwards, Graham says, "I should probably make an appearance at the Field Hollers panel. You gentlemen are welcome to attend, but I imagine you'd prefer, ahem, a bit of rest before four."

"Thank you, perfessuh," Ben says and Graham walks away a few steps.

In a Sam Stamps voice, I say, "Thought the concert at seven-thirty."

"Is," Ben says.

Graham turns around. "And oh yes," he says. "If you get hungry, feel free to call room service. And if you need some, ahem, libations, we'll be sure to dispatch a graduate student, if you wish." He winks, turns with a chuckle, and joins the other conferees squeezing into the elevator lobby. "What's this four o'clock mess?" I say.

"Four o'clock mess," Ben says, musing. "Good title, but a little too close to 'Three O'clock Blues,' don't you think?"

I shake my head, flex my fingers over the taut muscles of his arm. My lips are close enough to his ear to kiss it, yet I put up a hand to shield my mouth, lest anyone from the conference be skilled in lip reading. I'm too upset to speak in any voice but mine now. "Seriously, what's going on at four?"

Ben groans, turns to face me and straightens up. We look as secretive in our communication as a pitcher and catcher. Ben says, "A little question-answer session. An hour tops. I told you."

I say, "But that was." I pause, try again. "I thought you were talking about some before and after show bullshitting."

"Didn't I say it was formal?" he says. He actually scratches and shakes his bald head like that old noggin ain't keepin facts straight no mo'. "Getting old, like I said." Bet he'd know to the penny how much we have in the touring account. Bet he knows the interest rate and how his Wendy's and WalMart stocks did yesterday. "Don't try to con me," I say. "Not this time around."

"Tell you what, Pete," Ben says. "These are some persistent dudes. Worse than reporters or regular writers. The folklorists want your stories. You know, hard time livin', that sort of stuff. The musicologists want to know whether you copped your chord progression from Ishmon Bracey or Roosevelt Sykes. And I don't what the hell the English professors want."

I let go his arm but still feel blindsided. "What if I say no?"

"Pete," Ben says. "Don't talk that mess. I forgot to tell you. An honest mistake."

"Honest," I say. "That's not a word you should use too much."

He kneads my shoulder. I shrug away. "Let's get checked in," Ben says.

We advance to the reception desk, staffed by a young brunette with braces, whose red tag on her black vest reads, "Tara Bruns, Class of '02." She hands over two white key cards and Ben says, "Thank you kindly, ma'am." She blushes and smiles, ducks her chin near her chest. Probably the first time in this college sophomore's life she's been called ma'am, let alone from such a respectful old gent of color. I turn away, surprised to discover I want a drink. Maybe it's the one rebellious thought I can summon, like getting drunk before the Q & A could keep me out from under Ben's hand. Yet I would only confirm the scholars' suspicions. Can't even get drunk without remaining a part of the act.

· · ·

Ben's rep for promptness is well earned, and we show at the conference room at 3:57. While he shuffles forward, I'm holding on to one of his arms and wearing sunglasses, which hide my contacts and, according to Ben, look good on a shy country boy in front of all these smart folk. I doubt any question will be directed to me, beyond: Name, home state, and harp maker. We enter the room and survey its gray carpet, auditorium style seating, buzzing florescent lights. Ben tips his hat to the crowd, says, "Y'all must be blues people." This knocks every one of the scholars out. Not only recognized for the blues lovers they are, but told so in authentic Delta dialect. A long table sits at the front of the room. Two chairs with our names taped to them greet us, as well as a pair of bespectacled students setting up microphones and checking their recording system. Ben whispers, "You'll like this," then says aloud, "No tapes, goddamnit. You got to get Mist' Mabry's approval."

Hardy steps forward, still resplendent in his bow tie and jacket, though the creased flesh around his eyes shows fatigue. "Problem?" he says.

"Never said nothin' 'bout no tapes," Ben says, jabbing a shaking finger at the mics.

"In the past," Hardy says, "we've always . . ."

Ben says, "I doan care 'bout no goddam past. This is today and today Brother Ben says no tapes." Wheezing, he gropes for the tabletop with his hand and says, "Sit me down, Sam."

I get him in a chair, then take my seat, watching the rest unfold behind the safety of my lenses. Everything appears dim and green, as though I were submerged in a still pond, but nothing obscures my enjoyment as Ben stands up and says, "You want my voice, you buy you a goddamn record." This is the burned Brother Ben Heywood talked about, he who signed performance contracts that paid him pennies, who's still trying to collect royalties from record companies that swindled him, who swore long ago he'd never let someone make another nickel off his name unless he made a dime first. He and Bucket did get caught in some tangles early on—Mankiewicz and Stern fucked them out of some serious change—but that's precisely why he resurrected Wilton Mabry, an imposing and intelligent cat who didn't drop his g's while speaking the language of cash-up-front, and allowed Ben and Bucket to never fear for their finances again.

Nonetheless, it's a rare opportunity for everyone, including me, because this side of Ben doesn't get seen much. In this new century, as he's neared his fictive eighties—he's only sixty-six—he's become more of a diplomat, eager to, as he says it, hand on his heart, "Show folks how happy I is just to be alive." Now I keep my hand in front of my mouth, so no one can tell just what a fine time I'm having while Ben lists past injustices—how many are real, I have no idea—and Hardy keeps tapping his pen against his clipboard. The conference participants have moved away from the front rows. No one wants near Ben's manufactured fury, yet none looks away. Then Ben says, "Gimme a quarter, Sam. I'll call Mist' Mabry. He clear this up right quick." Now he coughs and Hardy jumps back, expecting, no doubt, a shower of sputum. Ben collapses into his chair and his head lolls close to me. He whispers, "Tell him to get me some water. Might get some more bills after that tirade."

I nod, then ask Hardy for water, wondering whether Ben knew about the taping and planned on this little performance or was it entirely impromptu. I'd prefer it planned, otherwise he's too scary to be believed. And when Hardy returns with two bottles of Evian and an apologetic look, he tells the students to remove the microphone, then says, "No taping. Brother Ben, you have our deepest apologies, both for our presumptions and the past wrongs you suffered."

I want to grin but open my mouth instead, a good response for a Natchez boy unused to so many syllables. "We ready," I say, once my spell of incomprehension passes.

"Wonderful," Hardy says, dragging his sleeve showily over his dry forehead. Then, to the crowd—slowly filling in those empty front seats, now that the storm has passed—he says, "Can we now get everyone seated and let this afternoon's Q & A commence?" He takes a seat and suddenly Graham appears beside him. In his seat, Ben slumps, his fedora tilted back and the collar of his lime-colored shirt spread like wings, same as mine. The first time I saw him shape himself into this mysterious relic of a distant past, I wondered how he could transform back to the fellow he was in everything but the blues. I wondered as well if he ever feared, as I did and still do sometimes, that one day he might not be able to flip that switch.

No question poses much of a problem, as they're directed at Ben and concerned with the legend he's gone to such lengths to establish. These university profs want to know if he and Bucketmouth *really* met at a church supper, drawn together by a visiting minister's sermon against the blues? Did the events described in "Put Down that Pistol" transpire as he sings about them? Had that feud with Honeyboy Edwards ended, or was Ben still claiming Honeyboy hadn't been there the night Robert Johnson died?

(Sonny Boy II claimed to have been there, too. Then again, he claimed Charley Patton died in his arms. Always good to know someone told more lies than I can muster.) Ben says, Yes, Yes, and No, though he still doesn't think the night of Robert's passing went down as Edwards tells it, he just concedes Honeyboy was likely there. Behind my sunglasses, I scan the rapturous and genuinely moved faces of these white men, watching Ben spin. Unlike Sonja Hutch, they all know the stories. Some jot down notes, while others mouth words with him, or nod knowingly when he's about to reach some high point in the telling. Likely, this is the closest they'll ever get to such experiences, which is why they make so much of the music, want so much to understand it and its makers. Ben says if it wasn't for white men like these fellows, and Lomax, Charters and Strachwitz, blues might not be alive, even in the precarious position it occupies today. Still, I wish somebody darker than Tony Orlando were trying to prop it up.

"Why did you never go electric?" someone asks.

Ben cocks his head, fits a curled hand behind his ear. "What he say, Sam?"

Deafness. That and the cough seem to be his new wrinkles on this strangest of tours. You ask me, it worked for Reagan, why not the Last True Delta Bluesman? I repeat the question, far louder than I need to. A smile stretches Ben's lips and he holds up his right hand, rubs his thumb against his fore- and middle fingers. The laughter in the room is almost complete. From Graham and Hardy, seated as close as sweethearts in the front row, to the late arrivers in the rear of the room, all seem entranced by the charlatan next to me. Ben says, "Them electrics did costed a lot of money." He coughs into his fist, his throat rattling. "Thought I'd buy one by and by, but that day still ain't come."

"But you did consider switching?"

"Considered. But considered and buyin' is two different things, my frien'."

A number of pens scratch across paper as a younger guy, curly-haired and thin, like a Q-tip, stands. "Plus, I'm sure, it's a question of tone," he says. "The early electrics didn't quite have the brightness one can get with an acoustic."

He's got calluses on his fingertips. A shiny Martin undoubtedly waits in a case in his hotel room.

Ben agrees and spurs other players to share their insights on whether a brass slide, like Ben uses, elicits as eerie a sound as a bottleneck, shot glass or Case knife. All the divisions are starting to show. I could point to the Piedmont lovers and the champions of the Texas sound, the standard- and open-tuning camps, those who swear Skip James or Lightnin' Hopkins should be elevated above Robert Johnson, and those who maintain, despite his bloated corpse, Elvis was far more than a white boy copying a black man's groove. Some point during this conference, there's going to be some hollering among them, and I hope we're out on the road when it heats up.

As I envision such a ruckus, some fellow in a denim shirt and a bolo tie stands, hitches his trousers. He says, "I'm Dane Connor, editor of *Good Rockin' Tonight*." He pauses, looks fore and aft, as if waiting for a deferential hush to fall. It doesn't, but he presses on. "I wanted to know why we've heard so little from Silent Sam?"

Ben grins at me, pats my knee as Graham stands—Dane Connor hasn't seated himself yet—then tugs his t-shirt over his stomach. He says, "Naturally, Dane, his very nickname might indicate why this is so." Still seated, Hardy reaches and tugs the tail of Graham's blazer, his clipboard hopping on his bouncing knees. I feel like a man with a savior, though Connor crosses his arms, looks my way, and says, "I'm sure he wouldn't mind answering a few questions."

Ben says, "Sho he doan. But when he got somethin' to say, lissen up. Won't say it mo' than once."

I am prepared. Able after many years to freely share Sam's knowledge: Mississippi—its weather, staple crops, how that noisy nuisance of a mockingbird is the state bird. I can tell you the high school curriculum of the Natchez City Schools, can share the charming anecdote about playing harp outside Gilmore's barbershop while the one and only Brother Ben was getting his head cut. But neither Graham nor Connor speaks, and a man heavier than Graham says, "What would you attribute as your key influences?"

I lean forward, slide my sunglasses down and stammer, "Attribute?"

Ben, slouched in his chair, winks, then covers it with a blink and a yawn. Only one in the room to see that rapid wink, I also know it's a sign of teacher praising the pupil. He shouldn't be surprised. I stole that gimmick from him.

The questioner's t-shirt features a photo of R.L. Burnside, another legend whose years left seem few. "Who'd you listen to growing up?" he says.

Too easy, only I need to remind myself to add a "Mr." before everybody's name. Learned that from Memphis Slim on *Blues in the Mississippi Night*, where he jokes with Big Bill Broonzy about asking for *Mr.* Prince Albert tobacco because of that white man on the can. In my head, it sounds a bit ridiculous, still I say, "Mr. Big Walter Horton. Mr. Little Walter Jacobs. Mr. Sonny Boy Williamson." But that's Silent Sam, a deeply grave young man who finds little in the world of the blues to laugh at.

"I or II," someone says.

"Mr. Sonny Boy Williamson what played with Mr. Robert Johnson some and taught Mr. Howlin' Wolf to blow harp." I pause, toss out another "Suh."

"You're such a young man," Dane Connor says, standing again. "I would think that at your age you wouldn't be interested in such players. I'd even think you'd be more interested in R& B, soul. Even rap and hip-hop."

"Is there a question among all that supposition, Dane?" Graham says, seated. Hardy gently smacks Graham's broad belly with his clipboard.

Hands on his hips, Connor stares at Graham, then at me. "Did you listen to any hip-hop or rap growing up?"

Overhead, the florescent lights buzz. I drag my low heels over the carpet, unprepared for this question. Ben says the best thing is to tell the truth when you're stumped because we can always somehow work it into the act. Let slip some telling detail about my Michigan youth? We'll invent an uncle who worked at Fisher Body and let me visit some summers. Details like that, he's convinced, are ignored by the fans in favor of the stories they already expect to hear. "No suh," I say. Then, because I can't resist and think I can pull it off: "Them rap fellas talk a lot about nothing and cain't none of em play even a juice harp."

And fuck if for the first time in my performing life I don't get a big hand for something I've said. Ben pats his hands together, too, while Dane Connor sits down. I don't know how to respond so I go back to an old stand-by: shut up and duck my head low as if I believe I've said too much.

Ben leans in, whispering in his off-stage voice, "Want me to leave you alone with your adoring public?"

I scrape my lower teeth over my mustache, shake my head. "You know they're yours," I say.

• • •

In all the time I've been on the road with Ben, no one's ever said or done anything that revealed suspicion I wasn't who we insist I am. We selected 1969 as the year of Sam's birth—making Sam three years older—because that year in Rodney, the tiny hamlet we chose as a birthplace, the county hospital's records were lost in a fire. A Samuel Murray Stamps did go through the Natchez school system, but as far as we know, that cat's never been called by anyone to find out if he blows harp with the Last of the True Delta Bluesmen. And to be even safer than we probably need, one of Ben's properties in Jackson—he owns two apartment buildings in Meridian and just bought another in Oxford—is a duplex the utility companies attest to be our residence. (He's in 1408 A S. Jefferson. I'm in B.) Another reason why New Orleans is a good place to live: If Ben needs me, I can fly Southwest to Jackson and at the duplex we two can greet those who've arrived to learn about the True Delta Blues.

Only one time did we have a close call, when we were in Phoenix after the sole blues festival we played together. (Ben demanded the promoter call Wilton Mabry and explain why instead of cash they had a check made out to Brother Ben, then called Heywood, who had fun playing along.) In the airport, we were walking to our gate and a girl I went to high school with, Melanie Keys, breezed past. Still blonde and pale as paste, she looked good in Top-Siders and Lacoste, which is what she wore when she won my heart back in ninth grade. "Peter?" she said, and I froze, largely because of that terrible crush. My body ached for the hug she looked ready to give. "Peter Owens," she said. That's when Ben grabbed me by the arm and pulled me along before I could answer her. "Keep movin', Sam," he said in a voice Melanie must have heard. "Lady be thinkin' we all looks alike."

Hasn't always been easy as Sam, though. A lot of Razor's fans weren't happy to see him gone. Those first few years, most claimed Razor was a better player. A crueler number called me Simple Sam, as I didn't speak much, for fear no one would believe my accent placed me any further south than Toledo. Folks talked a lot of shit my first two tours, but Ben made it clear I was not to reply. I had to be like Jackie Robinson in 1948, holding still my tongue in a mouth that wanted to chew those people up.

Yet what ultimately makes Sam such an easy figure to fake is his lowly status. Save for his talent, there's absolutely nothing about him anyone would want to emulate. Those caught passing are trying to improve their station: the nouveau riche pretending they're old money, the gay acting straight, the black playing white. Why would a college graduate—*cum laude*, no less—pretend to be the lowliest of low, a near-illiterate man of Mississippi, nearly frightened of his own shadow? Makes no sense at all. Which must be why it works

• • •

An hour before the show, we're in the lobby listening to requests for interviews, to which Ben says, "You gots to talk to Mist' Mabry." We pass up many chances to ride over to the Performing Arts Center, which is within walking distance, and take the Brougham. Waiting outside the entrance are Hardy and Graham, who offers us a pint of Old Crow and says, "I'm sure you came readily supplied. Nonetheless, thought you might enjoy another."

Behind him, Hardy rolls his eyes and holds flat the clipboard against his chest. In "Leavin' on My Mind," Ben sings, "Ain't gon follow no highway, I keep on followin' that crow," which once lead him, in an early concert with Razor, to say, "You know that old crow I'm talkin' 'bout." From that aside, word got around that this was Ben's preferred distilled spirit, and since he's received thousands of pints from people trying to show they knew what he was really *talking* about. According to Heywood, Ben used to pour that nasty-ass shit out and fill the empties with Hennessey to soothe his frayed voice after a show. I've seen nothing of the kind, as if with me Ben needs to be sharp and sober all the time, can't look away for a minute.

"Why, I thank you, suh," Ben says now, handing me the bottle. I place it in my harp case with the three empties I brought to scatter in the dressing room as evidence of a pre-show debauch. I've also got a flask filled with caffeine-free Diet Dr. Pepper and the least smidgen of Jim Beam for aroma, which Ben will call his private stock and not share with a soul except me. I'm hoping for a beer or two after the show. Just then, Dane Connor walks by, tugging on his string tie. Graham stops and Hardy keeps escorting us to the dressing room. Ben says, "Them's two mens who doan like each other."

"Tell me about it," Hardy says, shaking his slim head.

I feel a little slow on the uptake, remembering the exchanges from earlier. I believed Graham was on my side, not against Connor. Ben says, "What the problem, perfessuh?"

Hardy pushes open the door of the dressing room and Ben shuffles in, grumbling about sore feets. They should be pained, hemmed in by those boots he bought in the store off Crenshaw. I follow and Hardy says, "Do you really want to know?" Still tapping a saddle shoe nervously against the floor, he clutches his clipboard against his chest with both arms, looks both ways, and before we agree to hear him, he says, "Graham's been dealing with Dane forever. Swears he's a homophobe. And Dane's new to blues. He did much of his early work on Appalachian folkways. Anyway, his stuff is pretty paternalistic, all this talk about how the black community has abandoned the blues and how well-meaning whites like himself are doing the most to keep it alive. But even for all his talk about how much he loves our music, he doesn't seem to like black people very much. Sometimes he won't even talk to me."

I thought Hardy and Graham were lovers, and what Hardy's said seems to confirm that, but the transition to Connor's bigotry and what that's got to do with why he won't talk to Hardy—I'm confused.

Behind my sunglasses, I look at Ben who looks sage and says, "Hurts my heart when I hear that mess still goin' around."

"I know," Hardy says. "But I do a number on him in a chapter from my book."

Ben sits down on a low couch and I sit at the other end, hand him the flask. He thanks me, uncaps it. I can smell the bourbon as he sips from it and makes a face. "Your man down in Vicksburg brew this, Sam?"

"Yessuh," I say, shifting my attention to Hardy. I study his close-cropped hair, his slim nose, his green eyes to determine if I've been in the presence of a brother all along. Whether he is or isn't, he seems all right, and after Ben caps his flask and makes another face, I say, "You study blues, too?"

"Yes. Well, no. But. Let me explain." Seems I'm the first person who asked him a question about himself during the conference, instead of demanding A/V equipment or reimbursement for mileage. He pulls up a director's chair, sets the clipboard on his knees and says, "I deconstruct . . . . Well, I really rigorously examine what writers have previously written about the blues. Graham's publisher is already very interested."

"Pardon?" Ben and I both say at once.

Hardy drops the clipboard, holds out one hand above his knee. A pen's still between his forefinger and thumb. "Take, let's say, Charters, and his romantic, overblown descriptions from *The Country Blues*." He sets the other hand down on his other knee. "Then bring in the more down-to-earth, gritty readings of someone like Bill Ferris in *Blues From the Delta*. Are the writers really responding to what they witnessed among the musicians and their audience, or are they actually revising what their peers wrote, giving us this endlessly self-reflexive body of work that might not really be as much on the subject itself, blues, as versions of the subject itself, the writing about the blues?"

"What you callin yo' book?" Ben says, to my surprise. I could barely repeat what Hardy said, and I'm supposed to be, as Ben's said many times, the educated one.

Hardy's palms press together and he shakes them. " 'Sittin' on the Outside': White Misrepresentations of the Blues."

"But your book ain't about the music," I say.

"In a way, no, but what I'm saying is that most writing isn't about the music."

"But you like blues, right?" I say. The answer's obvious, I think. Why else would he be here?

But Hardy leans back and makes a face, appearing to shake his head. With a start, he consults his watch and springs from the director's chair. "I need to leave you two be," he says, clipping his pen to the clipboard. "Break a leg!"

I look at Ben, who passes me the flask. "Need something stronger than this?" he says, then takes out his guitar to get us in tune.

• • •

It could be said if you've seen one of Ben's shows, you've seen them all, especially when you consider the consistency of his playlist and that he hasn't recorded since *Blues at Your Request*. But judging by this crowd—and it's full, another SRO—people look old enough to remember Heywood and Bucket. With my two predecessors, Ben had a different show, more quiet and country with Bucket—half the time, Ben claims, they were pretending to be folkies—and a bit more lively with Razor. They had an on-stage rapport that was two parts profound and one part profane. We're somewhere in between, ordinarily, but not so mechanical we produce the same show every night.

Take this performance. Ben's aware, probably in a way I can't quite claim, of how these people, rightly or wrongly, see him as the remaining link in a chain of performers that stretches back past the giants to those true ciphers like Robert Petway or Garfield Akers, men about whom we know next to nothing except they wandered into makeshift recording studios and left behind a sound so pure. And Ben gives it to them, as best he can, this sound, this history, this ideal, the True Delta Blues. He snaps strings between his fingers and growls like Patton, offers the occasional Tommy Johnson yodel, slashes strings and keens like Son House, and on "Stones in My Passway," his voice and playing resembles

Robert Johnson's so much you better not close your eyes too long. You'll think Ben's been to that lonely crossroads in Coahoma County, had his guitar tuned by the same big, black man.

He's giving them all the great Delta players, making up for the fact that the only one they may have seen perform was Son House, and even then near the end of his life, when he had to be more or less shown how to play by Al Wilson of Canned Heat. (I've always mistrusted that story, though. I think Eddie was having a little fun with those white boys. Lord knows, he needed it.) Ben's playing like Delta blues won't be heard again in these parts for some time and it's his responsibility, as a person who belongs to this lineage (even if he does drive a Volvo and shoot scratch golf) to play them as best as they can be played, and in so doing keep them alive until he comes around again.

Me, I'm trying hard not to get caught up in the reverie, trying hard to forget what went down in the dressing room or the Q & A before that, and hear once or twice my playing get a little behind. Ben slows down while keeping his eyes shut, his mouth open, even when he's humming, so the lights catch the gold on his teeth. His boot sole slaps the stage and the echo travels my spine and tingles in my hands. Feels like we've got a hold of something and I don't want to let go. Which is why I should endure the off-stage performance. Hard to believe it, but we sound so true together. I savor the rusty taste of my harp, feel the notes shaped by my hands and breath right before I hear them. My shirt's wet under the arms, as are the backs of my knees, but it's a good sweat that loosens me up, keeps me right on time with Ben. Sadly, the end of the playlist is coming. No matter how loud the hollering for more gets, when we finish "Old Black River," that's it. I've heard two answers to the question of why Ben doesn't play encores. One from a surly Ben: "If you wants mo' music, you gots to pay mo' money." The other from a kinder one: "I gives all I can till there ain't no mo' in the tank."

But tonight he surprises me, surprises the crowd, too, because after "Old Black River" fades out, and I drop my G harp in my pocket and prepare to tip my hat, his slide slips down to the bottom of the neck and he's playing something lively on the thin strings. Could be "Dust My Broom," could be "Highway 49," but out of that riff he pulls "Don't Start Me Talkin'," a little slowed down and less rowdy than Sonny Boy, but I'm still happy to play along. The scholars, to a man, jump out of their seats and try to clap the same beat Ben's boot slaps out on the stage. For a second, as Ben and I wind up the intro, I almost think he nods, a gesture signaling that I should sing. It would be a first time for that. I've never even spoken on stage. Then, as I blink and near my mic, my harp in both hands, he sings, "Well, I'm gon down to Rosie's, stop at Fannie Mae's." I doubt anyone can hear me above all the ruckus, yet I get to it, sucking air from my harp as if it's the only source of oxygen in the room.

• • •

"Amazing," Rodney Graham says. Followed by Hardy, he's the first to enter the dressing room, and unless he's got wax paper and a comb in his pocket, he holds no instrument. "You threw in what the Cajuns call a *lagniappe*," he says, an unfamiliar word before I moved to New Orleans, where I hear it about every day, from the dry cleaner, the butcher, the barista at Starbucks.

"Caught me out, didn't you?" Ben says.

"But why that number?" Graham says, scratching a grizzled eyebrow with his thumbnail. "Seems a bit, how should I say, modern, for you." He turns to Hardy, who nods fiercely, though his eyes seem blank.

Ben gets seated, holds his left hand out like he's wearing a papal ring meant for kissing. "That's just fo' a frien' of mines," he says, then sips from his flask to end that line of questioning.

I step away, size up Hardy. Maybe he is a brother, but he's got a white parent. I figured neither of these two were players, though plenty are streaming in, their guitar cases banging against the door frame. I wouldn't mind another harpist—I could use the competition—but none appears tonight. Cats sit on the floor around Ben, who keeps his guitar case open, sipping regally from his flask and offering his left hand for shaking. Then, just as I wonder if he's going to arrive, Dane Connor walks in, case in hand, only it's not big enough to be a guitar. Everyone's tuning up and looking toward Ben, who hasn't yet dropped his flask, and doesn't have his guitar resting on his chartreuse slacks. I take off my leisure suit jacket, look around for anyone holding a six pack of beer. No one matches that description. Connor unlocks his case and pulls out, of all things, a mandolin. "Christ," I hear someone say, and it's Graham, whispering pretty damn loud to Hardy. "Of all things." Then, aloud to everyone, he says, "Dane. The bluegrass jamboree is held in Tennessee next month. This is a conference on the blues."

"Yank Rachell," Connor says, so sudden he had to have walked in intending to say that man's name. "A fine blues mandolin player."

"Another?" Graham says, waving away the hands of Hardy, who looks at me and mouths, "Told you."

I see Connor's lips moving, but Ben shuts his case and caps his flask. "Enough's enough," he says. His head droops as he mimes drunkenness or fatigue. "The spirit willin', good people, but mah flesh weak." He raises his head to me. "Come on, Sam. He'p me up."

I collect my jacket and weave through all the players, taking Ben's guitar case in one hand and his elbow in the other and lead him, with all his mock-infirmity, to the door. The players have stopped tuning up and flexing their fingers. Dane Connor, whose name is getting muttered with a lot of venom, stands alone near the doorway. Ben tips his hat, says, "Perfessuh," and flutters his eyelids, as though he can't for a minute more keep them open.

"I didn't mean any offense earlier," Connor says. His skin's so pale it takes on a blue tinge. "I just was wondering about something that's been bothering me for quite a long time." He pauses, looks down at his mandolin as if it's somehow the reason for Ben's abrupt departure. He looks up, blinking, but then he starts nodding. The silver ends of his string tie clink together as he says, "You know, there's just not a lot of your people who listen to the blues anymore. Why do you think that is?"

Your people. This chump probably is a bigot, like Hardy said, and must have been waiting since the end of the Q &A to get his shot at this question. I'd like to bust that mandolin over his head. Yank Rachell wouldn't mind. Ben shakes his head, which inspires me to start working my lips, as if to avoid the stammer Sam's anger often breeds. "Axe some them black folks what doan like blues," I say, with a little stuttering. "If you can find any."

I wanted to stress "you" but lean harder on "find." We don't see Connor's reaction, as we're out the door, keeping quiet until we reach the Brougham. Inside, seat-belted and locked in, Ben says, "That was a good one."

I overlook the compliment, ask why Ben quit before the jamming started. Heywood warned me once that as long as there were two people gathered in his name, Ben would play.

Now Ben says, "I'm tired, Pete. Just like I said." He starts up the car, gets us on the campus roadway, where there's no traffic at all, and lamps on both sides light the way back to the hotel. "You think Hardy's mixed?" I say.

Ben turns to me, his face shadowed but enough of his disbelief visible for me. "You got those contacts in, Pete?"

"It wasn't that obvious."

"Better get to your doctor, tell him you can't see a lick."

I chuckle, blow the opening riff from "Don't Start Me Talkin" again. "You're in twelve-bar cadence again," I say.

"So I am," Ben says distantly. The hotel's just up ahead and he slows down. "You feel like driving some?"

"I need to take my contacts out," I say. "But go on."

Ben turns off the car and we get out to gather our things from the room. Then, as if I'd forgotten all about the performance and only remembered it now, I say, "You played some kind of fine tonight."

At the elevator, he waves his hat at me dismissively. "That ain't nothing. You were two for two with that quick lip. Next thing I know you'll be asking to sing."

The elevator doors open. I step inside. Actually recall that moment from tonight's performance and wonder what I'd do center stage, the mic all mine. Eventually, I wave at Ben with my hat again. "Ain't my show," I say.

"For now," he says and winks.

# 6.

**THIS TIME, IN THE BROUGHAM, I'M SURE I HEAR**

"Take My Chance" on the radio. I'm wide awake, drinking a double-espresso, parked outside a Kinko's in Toledo while Ben checks his e-mail. Wilton Mabry's e-mail account, that is: bluesmgr11@yahoo.com. Trouble is, I've got the tuner on scan and can't hit the stop button before the station switches. Nothing sounds at all like Ben's guitar or voice—let alone my harp—just news, some imitative rap, and soulless country music. I try another scan through the

# Bring It on Home

stations, get talk, classic rock, chipper teens. No blues. The college station, my last hope, features an interview with an animal rights activist. I toss out the dregs of my coffee—the grounds weren't tamped too well—then shut the radio off and look up. Ben stands by the passenger's side door, frowning.

When he gets in, I say, "Heard us again."

"Heard what?"

"Us playing 'Take My Chance.'"

"Doubtful. The station at the university has a blues hour but that's on Saturday night."

I almost gasp. Yes, we've come through the Buckeye State enough times to know when the restaurants close and where Ben can find, among the many meat-eaters here, a veggie burger that doesn't taste like sawdust. Still, I'm stunned by the wealth of info he commands, though I'm able to return to the matter at hand. I say, "One thing I know is the sound of us playing."

"That's sweet," Ben says. "Still doubtful." A second or two passes, then he pokes me in the shoulder with his finger. I flinch far more than I need. Physical contact is so rare between us, except when we're showing the blues faithful how Ben needs my strong hands to guide him from dressing room to the stage and back. When I turn to face Ben, he's smiling. I look away, place my hands on the steering wheel, in time to hear him say, "Pete, nobody's playing *us* on the radio." He chuckles, and I back up the car from the lot, humming "Take My Chance" before I know it. "Still learning, aren't you?" Ben says, then laughs like he hasn't heard anything funny in weeks.

• • •

A casualty of taking me on as his harpist was Ben gave up dates in Michigan. Ann Arbor in particular was a hard town to quit. He'd play the Big 10 cities, Madison, Champaign and Bloomington, then drive to U of M and bathe in nearly universal approval. It's rumored he still gets votes in mayoral elections there, and who can forget Ann Arbor's was the festival where Ben choked Sleepy John Estes? Still, he's always given us a break midway through each tour and since we're usually near the place I call home then, we check into pricey hotels in Detroit's central city, careful to remain incognito while I spend time with my mother and her husband, Grover Streets. This visit, we're in the Atheneum, where Ben's signed in as Robert Johnson, a name so evocative and common at once, but without gold teeth gleaming and all his swap meet clothes in a laundry sack in the Brougham's trunk, no one suspects him of carrying firearms or mojo hands. Some of the young men of color scurrying about, carrying bags and fetching newspapers, might think he's the billionaire who owns BET. Doubtful they've heard of the Robert Johnson from Coahoma County, these cats who've fed on hip-hop as if it's the only form of nourishment available.

To give me some privacy, Ben's paid for two rooms and will be leaving soon for eighteen at The Elms. He'd rather play Huron Hills in Ann Arbor but doesn't want to make that drive. Even if I weren't seeing my mother and Grover, I'd pass on the golf, but it's especially important to see them this time, as they depart for Africa in two weeks. Though I blame bad weather for my absence at her wedding, my mother chooses to find fault with my being on tour in the first place. I hope my paying for their air fare—and booking it through a black-owned travel agency—might give her reason to forgive, but I'm not hoping too hard. Main thing is, during the next forty-eight hours, I need to be Peter Owens, who doesn't worry about perfectly mismatching his shirts and suits, doubling up his negatives, and doesn't care whether he and Brother Ben will defeat Blind Deacon and the Professor at next week's Beale Street Blues Awards.

● ● ●

"Calendar says it's supposed to be spring," Ben says, scowling at the local weather forecast. His v-neck sweater might keep him warm, but I'm suggesting raingear. It's not as bad as Eau Claire but is a typical Midwestern April: raw, gray and windy, with the consistent threat of rain. After a shower, I'm lounging in a bathrobe on my bed. I just shaved, too, removing all traces of my mustache for my mother, who said it made me look like one trashy negro.

Ben checks his watch, a Timex Ironman. Watchless when he's in character, he has pretended to tell time by the position of the sun. "They's some Osage in mah family," he told a writer once. "On both sides." On the TV screen, the local meteorologist summarizes the daily forecast, predicting a three-hour dry window, which is all Ben needs to get in nine holes. He picks up his gloves and spikes and calls the concierge to confirm his tee time and club rental. I say, "Sure I can't interest you in some quality time with the family?"

Ben shakes his head. "You know I was breaking eighty after I got those new Calloways." He gazes at a point between his shoes, draws back his right arm. "I hope I can keep a little of that momentum going. But do give my best."

I nod. Though they've only met once, Grover and Ben get along pretty well. The two aren't more than fifteen months apart, and each shares the uncanny ability to select the right stocks or get out of bonds and into mutual funds or real estate at the right time. My mother, though she's never said an unkind word to Ben, holds onto some resentment. In addition to blaming Ben for my absence at their wedding, she deplores the amount of time that passes between visits. Most of all, she's none too thrilled about the men we are to the blues faithful. The daughter of teachers who themselves were the children of teachers, she worked up the line of administration in the Detroit Public Schools and now directs the secondary schools' curriculum. As her folks did for her, she always tried to instill in me the sense that I had much more than myself to worry about when I walked among the world. I had to promote a positive vision of my family, my people and my history. Now her eyes narrow when she chooses to talk about Ben and how he and I make our money. In my youth, that gesture, along with the slight flaring of her nostrils, as if she's smelled something horrible but is too demure to admit it, confirmed when I was about to do something that would not please the many who'd fought so hard to allow me the privileges I presently enjoyed.

I leave the bed, shed the robe, and drag out my suitcase. My mother's face would register far more than narrow eyes and flaring nostrils at this display of colors and fabrics, especially in the combinations that suit Silent Sam best. Beneath these piles, I locate my Owens wear, change into a blue Polo and a pair of khakis. I slip a lambswool sweater the color of merlot over my head and feel my smooth cheeks. I've got my contacts in but debate whether to trade them for glasses. My mother always liked me looking studious. While I step into my oxblood loafers, Ben returns, a golf tee between his teeth. "Damn," he says. "If I had a daughter, I wouldn't mind seeing you on the front steps."

"Mr. Huxtable," I say, holding out some of the artificial flowers from a vase on the dresser. "Is Denise home?"

"Ever wonder how two brown-skinned parents turned out such light daughters?" Ben says.

"What's Lisa Bonet doing now?" I say. "And the other one? The one that played Saundra?"

"I always liked Rudy best," he says. And with that, he's out the door.

• • •

I'm playing along with Sonny Boy's "Bring it on Home," when the phone rings a few minutes before two. It has to be my mother and Grover in the lobby. Still, my heart knocks against my ribs, and I nearly swallow my Marine Band. An unreasonable sense tells me somebody—maybe George or Audrey, maybe Dane Connor or the intrepid Sonja Hutch—has tracked us down and is about to discover our masquerade. Even though we've followed the same path, more or less, this tour hasn't been like any of the others. Don't know what to expect but the unexpected. When I answer, though, I hear Grover's voice and tell them to come on up. Slip my harp case deep in my suitcase, close it, then stuff it in the closet. Check my upper lip for patches my razor missed. After a few minutes, my mother and Grover appear. He's wearing a blue blazer, a Munsingwear polo and Dockers, as if he were meeting Ben on the links, while my mother's more formal in a navy suit and sensible heels. Her embrace is sudden and strong. Grover grips one of my hands and slips inside the room. It's been a year since we've been this close and that was during their one and only visit to New Orleans, where the temperature stayed steamy enough to make most activity sound oppressive. We waited for evenings to go out to eat, watched TV with the sound off, not talking a whole lot for five days. Now my mother says, "Baby." I feel her nails on my ears as she straightens my head so she can get a good look. Her face softens as if she's about to say more. Instead, she massages my neck then lets go.

"Been in the lobby here once," Grover says, hands in the pockets of his Dockers, playing with his keys and change. "To meet a client." His neck cranes and with his bald head he resembles a turtle as he slowly inspects all the amenities: phone in the bathroom, wet bar, enormous TV, impressive view of downtown.

"Your employer is paying, I hope," my mother says, crossing her arms and breathing sharply through her nose.

Along with big hands, big feet and a wide behind, I inherited from my birth father, my mother says, a willingness to laugh at things. An orphan, he had no other brothers for me to know along the way. My mother passed on her sense of duty, as well as fast-growing hair and a chocolate bar complexion.

Neither was at all musical. Never played an instrument—not even a song flute. Both sang in choirs, but that was compulsory in church and school. My mother claims she only ever moved her lips while all others lifted their voices in praise. At our house on Apple Blossom Court, a few Motown and Aretha records were stacked neatly in the high-fi but played rarely. After I bought my first Marine Band—making me and Stevie Wonder the only harmonica players she knew—my mother encouraged me to practice but believed it was simply a hobby. For my profession, she had the far-ranging but limited ideas assimilation-minded and upwardly mobile parents usually imagine: doctor, lawyer, a businessman who didn't cheat the common man. Once, however, she invited a young black man named Jarvis to stay with us for a couple nights. He was traveling around the country with an enormous Christian vocal group, Positive Voices! Young and charismatic, he was filled with the spirit, and his fro was so big it scraped doorways. I knew how to play "Battle Hymn of the Republic" and "When the Saints" then, but after my mother and I endured all the evangelical nonsense of the Positive Voices! concert at Cobo, Jarvis asked me if I cared to play anything for him on my *harmonica*. I lied and said I'd left it at school, when even then I was carrying my *harp* everywhere.

Now, in my hotel room, my mother examines the results of her encouragement of my harp-playing, her eyes roaming for some item she won't approve of. That's why I took the precaution of hiding everything. In this room nothing of Silent Sam is displayed, that no account bluesman she either tolerates or loathes. Which means that, except for the furniture, the room's pretty much empty. I'll let her impose her vision of who Peter should be on the blank screen so she can walk away feeling she, a single mother, did what she needed with her only child.

"Y'all want anything to eat?" I say, grabbing a room-service menu from the sturdy, walnut writing desk.

My mother turns. Her nostrils flare. "Did you just say 'y'all'?" she says.

"Occupational hazard," I say, sounding more like Ben than myself. Thinking of him, I say before I forget, "Mr. Mabry, Ben, that is, passes on his best."

"How is that old rascal?" my mother says. She's one of the few people in the world who knows some of the truth, yet, unlike Grover, she refuses to see Ben as Wilton Mabry, businessman, and prefers to believe the myth of Brother Ben.

"Bet he's on the links," Grover says.

I nod, hand him the leather bound menu. "I was just about to order."

Grover grins as he inspects the menu, then hands it over to my mother. Her head tilts back and her arms stretch forward, partly out of her uncorrected eyesight, though also, I'm sure, out of astonishment at the prices. "It's on me," I say. "We'll write it off as a business expense."

My mother says, "He should pay for it. I mean, why is it you're staying here anyway?"

Her voice worries me, as there's a quality to it that sounds as though she's arrived this afternoon with something to say and is warming up to it with sharp asides and questions. I explain why we don't play Michigan—even though she knows full well why—and claim we need this break, especially with so many gigs forthcoming and a long drive to Florida soon. I avoid contractions, let all my g's ring at the end of words, and don't repeat my earlier mistake with Y'all. Grover nods and plays with his keys and pocket change, while my mother sits on a sofa and won't move her boxy purse from her knees, a gesture that seems perhaps more hostile than she intends. She says, "Uh-huh," when I finish speaking. I call room service and order a grilled chicken sandwich and fresh fruit to impress my mother, who'd agree with Ben that my diet shows no regard for health. "Sounds good," Grover says, making it easy. Saying she doesn't want to trouble me, my mother refuses to eat.

"It's no trouble," I say, knowing now that it's not a question of will she turn on me but when. I could ask what's her problem, but she raised me to acquiesce to her wishes, whether she's stated them plainly or indirectly hinted at them. "Sure you don't want anything?"

She shakes her head. I repeat my order and room number, put down the phone. From her purse she digs out a neatly folded handkerchief, dabs at her nose with it. Never would she, with an audience of anyone, blow her nose without reserve.

"Which course is Ben playing?" Grover says, seating himself on the arm of the sofa. He puts his arm around my mother, but she sits too straight to ease into the warmth of this loving gesture. I've seen them hold hands and kiss, but the contact of their lips never lingered past ten seconds. Grover's also trying to small-talk his way around the imminent blowup, so I humor him and name the course.

"Good choice," he says.

"You know how much the membership fees are at that club?" my mother says. "Not to mention the years they didn't even allow Jews to join, let alone African Americans." She laughs wryly, turns to her husband, keeping both hands on the straps of her purse. "And you know good and well the three blacks they've let in are all card-carrying Republicans."

In a brief instant, Grover and I regard one another. His eyes apologize and his eyebrows rise, as if to communicate he can't do anything to quiet or comfort her now. Still, I try to steer us somewhere pleasant. "Less than two weeks and you'll be in Africa," I say. "Excited?"

"Did you say y'all again?" my mother says.

Before I can answer—I'm sure I didn't—she says, "Any more of these 'occupational hazards' I should know of?"

"What time is room service coming?" Grover says.

Not soon enough, I'm thinking, as Grover springs off the sofa's arm. His hands digging through the coins and keys in his pockets is a welcome annoyance. "I'll check," I say, grabbing the phone as if it might turn this day around.

• • •

When I first told her about my gig with Ben, my mother was excited. She'd witnessed how long I'd practiced, knew how much blues meant to me, but believed my touring with Ben would be temporary. In a year, two or three at most, I'd get the travel and excitement out of my system, then drop the stage name and act and work in some building named after a prominent and philanthropic family, earning my keep in one of the vaunted professions. Not only did she learn I had no intention of working nine to five, she tried to deal with the consequences of my joining Ben, namely my being far from home much of the year, the new name I answered to, the fact she couldn't even tell her family of my success. Ben flew her out to Portland, Oregon to see my first concert, gave her a front row seat. Hers was the applause I listened for, and after each song I heard her, and felt I had her approval. Then, afterward, the three of us dined in a dark, Ethiopian restaurant, and it was the first time I saw my mother's narrowed eyes and flared nostrils directed at what I was wearing: a pimp hat at an angle, polka-dotted faux silk shirt, and a suit the color of Heinz 57. Had I a sibling, making money in a doctor's white gown or an attorney's Brooks Brothers wardrobe, I imagine she would have let me be, but I'm her one son, her legacy. And though she smiled through the rest of the meal, I knew a day like the one I'm experiencing was coming. I hoped I'd survive the assault.

• • •

Room service arrives and the chicken's flavorful, the fruit fresh and firm. If nothing else, it keeps my mouth full, and I can't, in my mother's presence, talk at the same time I'm chewing. Her lessons still emerge whenever I sit down to a meal: don't smack your lips, don't lick your fingers, know which fork is for what. But even now as I chew each bite to pulp, time isn't elapsing fast enough. It's a bad thing to want your annual visit with your mother to be over in less than two hours, but you ask me, I didn't start this fight.

When our plates are empty, my mother says, "When is this tour over?"

"Another two months," I say. I take a sip of water, wishing I hadn't emptied all our prop bottles of Old Crow.

"And then what?" she says, dabbing at her nose again with her perfectly folded handkerchief. She won't even sneeze in front of her son and husband, such is her self-control. Still, I think I have a way to earn back at least some affection today. "Hold on," I say, heading to Ben's room in search of his homeopathic stash. I don't know how far along my mother's cold is, and, according to Ben, no remedy works unless you're in the early stages. Should call my mother in to show her there's no John the Conqueror Root or gris-gris, like they call it in down in Louisiana. Instead, I return to my room with a tube of Airborne and a bottle of Echinacea, find her and Grover sitting on the couch together, so close they could be plotting. They definitely were whispering and now move apart as I say, "Here's something from Mr. Mabry's private stash, to help with that cold."

My mother makes no move toward me, though Grover says, "Heard about this on Larry King the other night," and puts on his reading glasses to inspect the Airborne label.

"Ben swears by it," I say.

"We ran into Perry Monroe," my mother says suddenly, her delivery too steady to be impromptu. "You remember Perry?"

"Sure."

"Well, we saw him just a little while ago. Had a good talk. He asked about you."

This I don't doubt. Perry was never quite a friend of mine, as he went to school in Detroit. Also, Perry was a member of the choir and knew it, though I didn't care and apparently wasn't his type. Whenever we got together, it was usually with other kids on the upper floor of some teacher or principal's house, while parents indulged in mixed nuts and stiff drinks in the furnished basement. These were the few occasions I'd be around groups that were entirely black, yet I didn't know the girls or boys, wasn't included in their kissing games, didn't care much about their gossip or listen to the same music. Which left me, the oreo, with Perry, the sissy.

I haven't heard from him since I attended his college graduation party the week after mine, but I'm trying to figure out what he's doing in my mother's side of the conversation. I'm sure he did recently encounter my parents somewhere in the Detroit Metro area, though what I expect now is some comparison, where I won't wind up feeling flattered. "How is Perry?" I say, louder than I need.

"He is doing very well for himself," my mother says. "Lives in Southfield, works for an AMEZ church there. As choir director."

I try not to smirk and be so damned homophobic, but choir director sounds a perfect job for Perry. Always did have a wonderful voice, one that sounded best when he praised the loving deity whom he firmly believed had shaped it for him. We didn't go to the same church as Perry's people. My mother complained there was always too much whooping and hollering when what she needed was sober reflection upon God's Grace. She found that among the Episcopalians, whose church we never officially entered, though we did follow the lead of the congregation and attended only on Xmas and Easter. "But he was concerned," my mother says, sniffling. "He wonders why he never hears anything about you."

Nodding, I look at Grover, still engaged by the tiny print on the tube of Airborne. My skin feels dry from all the warm air and my clothes aren't sitting right. I push up my sweater sleeves. Push them back down. Ben's right about my blood: It has thinned since I left behind the Midwest. Now I want to hear what my mother said to Perry. The line she's supposed to answer inquiries about my profession with is that I work for Mabry Enterprises, Inc., a small, black owned marketing firm in the south. I use it myself for the few people in New Orleans who've conversed with me. Never heard of it before, is the most common response, but I don't do much to clarify. "What did you tell him?" I say.

My mother's shoulders rise as she lifts her sharp chin upward. For a moment, I think she's about to say she told him the truth, and I wonder what Ben and I will do to keep that news from spreading. "What I always say," she says. At last, she drops her purse between her feet.

"Thanks." I nod toward Grover, who has just taken out one of the tablets—they're as big as a half-dollar—and cautiously extended his tongue toward it.

"They're effervescent," I say. "Put it in a glass of water. Here."

While I'm reaching a glass toward him, my mother says, "You know how tiresome it is to tell these lies?"

And that's what she came here for. I hang my head. "I do appreciate what you're doing."

"But they are lies, all the same." My mother sniffs again, this time to make a dismissive sound as well as relieve her blocked sinuses.

"Not too much longer," I say, though I don't intend to stop touring or allow her to start yakking about how it's her son backing up Brother Ben. My mother would never make that admission. In her crowd—responsible, prim women for whom seddity is too mild a modifier—most would say, "Who on earth is Brother Ben?"

Grover leans forward, sets the glass and the Airborne down. "What do you mean, Pete?"

I shake my head. "It's just," I begin, then turn to my mother, who leans forward, turns her head as if to hear better. I say, "It's just, I don't know what it is."

With a chuckle, my mother leans backward, her eyes rolling ceiling ward. All her strict lessons about precise diction and this is what I've become: a mumbler who can't say what's in his heart, likely because nothing's inside, just the raucous wind I save to blow through that infernal instrument. She snaps forward, groaning angrily, and jams her handkerchief in the open mouth of her purse. I'm not too upset at such motions, because they signal she's about ready to go home. When I knew I'd be in Detroit, I had no timetable in mind. We could have made a whole day of it—the Atheneum offers plenty of entertainment to its guests. Now I want my mother gone. I wipe my hand over my face, surprised by the smoothness of my upper lip. A mustache is a fine thing to chew on when you don't have much to say, or you know the people around you don't want to hear what you're willing to share. Next thought I have isn't too generous, but it seems time to remind my mother Perry Monroe's not so perfect. I say, "Perry living by himself, is he?"

"No," Grover says, leaning back his bald head and pondering. "He's been married since . . . "

I have to interrupt. "Perry said he was married?" I wouldn't be surprised to learn he had a lover—"a friend," women like my mother are fond of saying—and that the two of them shared a life and love that was enviable, but Perry must have lied to my mother, who'd always overlooked the swish of Perry. Or she and Grover misinterpreted his terminology—partner or companion—and assumed he meant bride.

Snapping his fingers, Grover says, "Since two years ago, right?"

"Yes," my mother says, smiling at Grover then scowling at me. "Right after our wedding." I didn't think she'd forgotten, but now I know the Ghana trip won't make up for my absence.

"Girl named Regina," Grover says. "We even sent a present, didn't we, dear?"

My mother nods. "*She's* a loan officer. At Banc One," she says. When she looks at me, her face is hard, but quickly, the muscles in her cheeks soften and her eyes look damp. "And she has a sister, you know. Pretty as a picture, too." No longer is anger controlling her, it's anticipation. She wants me to ask if I can meet this sister, start a more conventional life. My mother wants a son with a job she can share with her friends. A son who pushes a mower on Saturday afternoon, hauls the kids and his pleasant wife for visits to grandmother's no fewer than twice a month. Who never worries if his actions, appearance or outlook sends the wrong kind of message about his people. "Is that what you're so upset about?" I say, aware my mouth has eased into a smile. I still can't get over the idea of Perry with a woman. Almost need to see that for myself. "You wish I was more like Perry Monroe?"

"Y'all," my mother says. "You said it again. You have become that man you pretend to be." She stands, opens her purse and tugs out her fluttering handkerchief. This time, she dabs it at her eyes. I should be reaching to comfort her, but first I have to scan my memory to see if I slipped into Sam speech. Further, I wish to rewind the whole visit, start over with pleasantries and attempts to maintain an illusion that no one's angry or anguished, that we don't need time under a therapist's watchful eye. I close my eyes, but when I open them, they're directed toward the window. Some pigeons roost on the still and the glass is streaked with rain. Gray clouds loom. That dry period promised by the weatherman is over. My mother says, "You make it so hard on us, Peter. I want you to be happy but I wish you'd try to see things my way."

Grover steps between us, leaning mostly in his wife's direction, while eyeing me. He licks his lips but doesn't speak. Trying to please us both at once and discovering just how difficult such a task is. "Don't you have anything to say?" my mother says, crying now. Fat tears streak the powder on her face, revealing her slightly browner cheeks. She could be talking to me or Grover, who turns his back to me and pats her on the shoulders, though she says, "I am all right. I am fine."

What I want most is my harp. The words that exit my mouth do little good, especially when compared to what I can shape through those ten holes. Though she lacks the ability to say what's the difference between Sonny Boy I and II or Little vs. Big Walter, I want for her to hear how good I am now. I want her to know I'm in the top ten list of players, but the magazine's in my suitcase. Anger stabs at my palms and I open and close them, open them again. "Perry must be the most unhappy brother in Michigan," I say, surprising myself with the heat and volume. "He's not who you think he is. But I bet his parents don't care. As long as they can show off baby photos." The next sound out of my mouth is laughter, and it sounds like Ben's stage laughter. "I can't do that. I can't be who you want me to be."

"Even if it tears me up inside?"

"This is what I'm good at." I say. I mean this. I believe it. Shit, I'm getting better.

"Come on now, Pete," Grover says. "Your mother's showed me your transcript from State."

I laugh again, huh-*huh*, and say, "You know, I'm helping keep something very important alive. Doesn't that mean anything?"

My mother raises her head, showing her narrowing eyes. "If you took a good look at *yourself*," she says, "you'd stop."

A long moment passes, then another. No one says anything. Rain sounds louder against the thick glass of the hotel room window and my fingertips dig into my palms. Were music playing, you might think Grover and my mother were dancing, as close as they stand, but I've never seen my mother dance. Even though I wasn't at the wedding reception, I know they didn't hire a DJ or a band. But as I watch her and Grover, the connecting door between our rooms opens, and Ben enters, shaking his head like a dog. "Whoo," he says. "Momma didn't raise none of her chirren to stand outside during an electric storm with a piece of iron in his hand." Was he out there timing his entrance to be the worst moment possible? His delivery and intonation are pure Delta, which, in this case, is about as useful as a ukulele when we're playing "Back to Jackson." Were we alone, though, I'd join in like some Kingfish and Andy act. Instead,

I nod toward my mother and Grover, arm in arm now, unified against Ben or me or both of us. And I don't have to tell anyone who's staying and who's going.

• • •

Ben showers and changes, giving me a little time before asking what he walked in on. I say it was the usual and turn it around, ask how many holes he played before quitting, as I expect he was still chasing the white ball after the second or third thunderclap, given as long as he's been away from a course. He describes a dog-leg tenth, requiring a shot that laid up near the hinge and then, as he says it, "To get to the green I needed to bring the ball in from left to right. Rain was just starting then and I only had a five, seven and a nine in my bag." He stops. "Pete," he says. "You aren't interested in this."

"I am," I say, turning my face toward his and lifting it from my palm. I widen my eyes as evidence of interest, but who am I fooling? This is Brother Ben. He knows me better than my own mother does. I'm still wearing my sweater, polo shirt and khakis, and although they feel far more natural than anything I'd wear on stage, I'm in more of a hurry to get them off than explain all that happened. I say, "I don't even want to talk about it."

"Don't then," Ben says, reclining on my bed and snapping on the TV.

I yank the sweater off, pitch it to the floor. "It's just," I say, standing and kicking away my loafers. "She doesn't know who I am." I flop back on my bed, but sit up to wriggle out of my khakis. "I don't know who I am sometimes," I say.

Ben gets up, grunting a little. "How about this?" he says. "You're the best damn harp player I know."

"What?"

"You heard me," Ben says, reaching in his white robe's pocket and walking my way. "And I'm not the only one who thinks that. Here." I need a few blinks to realize he's handing me a long envelope of heavy, parchment colored paper with a Memphis return address. Inside is a map, a list of phone numbers, and a letter my dumb ass self slowly recognizes is from the organizing committee of the Beale Street Blues Awards. When I look up, Ben's standing above me, saying, "We won't win. I'll just remind you of that first."

Nearly naked, I stand and embrace him, only wondering after I cinch my hands behind his back if we've ever been this physically close. He doesn't back up or push me away, though he says, "Just think of it as another mini-break. We're there two days, then hauling ass to Tuscaloosa."

"Ok," I say, though my stomach hurts. Whether from anticipation of our time in Memphis or from all the noise of my parents' visit, I don't know. Better to concentrate on the here and now. "The best harp player?" I say.

"Don't get a big head about it," he says, tilting back his head to wink. "But yeah, the best harp player around today."

For the moment, neither of us lets go. The Last True Delta Bluesman is the one who knows me. The real me. Whatever that means.

# 7.

**THE CLOSEST I'VE BEEN TO MEMPHIS IS DRIVING** on its outerbelt in my U-Haul when I left Detroit three years ago. I've always suspected it was two cities like New Orleans: one a sanitized theme park for tourists, the other an ill designed, corruptly governed metropolis on the verge of bankruptcy and race war where the locals resided. Yet this morning as Ben and I get in sight of the Pyramid, DeSoto Bridge and the Mississippi beneath, a trembling thrill seizes me. In the city that calls itself the "home of the blues" and "the birthplace of rock

## I Can't Be Alone

and roll," I feel the need to grow as humble and reverent as some of our fans around Ben. We exit I-40 and drive downtown, headed toward Beale.

At a red light, Ben fetches his hat from the seat, hands it to me. "Smooth that brim for me, Pete," he says.

I run my fingers over the brown fedora's stiff and curled brim to flatten it out. Street names and buildings and black and white pedestrians flash past but my mind keeps sticking like a record on the word Beale, Beale, Beale. I know it's no longer the street Sonny Boy may have strolled over. Ben claims he's happy it wasn't completely destroyed but won't fully praise its gentrification. I need to see it for myself. Now, in the Brougham, Ben stops in front of the host hotel, another Holiday Inn, one of the few constants of this tour. Barely does Ben open his door before a nimble Latino valet's saying, "Welcome to Memphis, Home of the Blues." I'm too quick for the other fellow. Grab my garment bag and harp case and lope to the entrance, wondering if we're here early, wondering who might be in the lobby. James Cotton? Carey Bell? Will Bobby Rush remember me from that single festival Ben and I played in Phoenix? Plus, I haven't forgotten the photos I saw in Eau Claire: At least five bluesmen need hassling for their bare-assed antics in the frozen north. Then again, I want to sprint toward Beale and start blowing harp. In fact, I never gave Ben his hat back. I could drop it on the sidewalk to collect coins. My own gray porkpie's tilted forward on my head—we both need our heads cut—and I'm clutching Ben's in the same hand as my garment bag. I turn around, find Ben shuffling forward. I slow down, allow the valet to enter the lobby, then drop the fedora on Ben's head. His breath smells of green tea and the zinc lozenges he's been sucking on since we left chilly Michigan behind. From Columbus to Louisville, he was in particularly good voice, so I guess these prevention methods are doing their work.

He grabs me by the arm and whispers, "You ok?"

I want to shout. I don't know if the city itself has me so wired up or the smell of magnolias and pork barbecue has allowed me to forget what went down in Detroit. Could even be anticipation of the awards show tomorrow. Ben looks over both shoulders, spits out his zinc lozenge. As if reading my giddy mind, he tightens his grip on my forearm, saying, "Remember where you come from, Sam."

The sun's so bright and warm today, I feel I've been shivering since we left Las Vegas, but Ben's reminder snaps a pair of fingers in my head. It can't be Sam's first time here. For a Mississippian, even one from as far south in the Delta as Natchez, Memphis has been the center of the universe: the place to buy shoes and suits, to ride the Zippin Pippin at Libertyland, to see your nanny lying in a hospital bed when the local doctors couldn't cure her. May not have stayed at a hotel as luxurious as the one before us, but these heels have dragged over the sidewalks alongside Union Street many a time. Now Ben's hand slides up to my shoulder, as if to keep me from rising too high.

• • •

Though I may be his favorite harpist, Ben's told me again and again since we left Michigan that Blind Deacon and the Professor will stroll away with the award for Best Traditional Artist. I don't doubt he's right. A recording released in the same calendar year is not required for a nomination in our category, but in the past five years Blind Deacon and the Professor have released three acclaimed CDs, while we haven't re-issued anything or cobbled together a greatest hits. Still, our first arrival at any awards show is sure to cause a stir, and Ben's counseled me to be ready to talk with people who'll want to know why Ben has gone back on a promise of many years ago, to never attend such an event or even accept an award. "Blue ribbons is what you give a steer or a hog," he was quoted as saying. "Some time a dog, too. But not no man."

I wonder if he said this shortly after he and Bucket severed ties with Mankiewicz and Stern, who oversaw the recording of five Ben and Bucket albums, sent them around the U.S., but only upon Stern's first heart attack (and Mankiewicz's IRS-exile to Honduras) did Ben learn how much he and Bucket *should* have been earning. That was the one time in his life, Ben says, he came close to telling all exactly what was what. Now, though, he's glad he didn't because Brother Ben and Wilton Mabry are both still alive and well and letting bygones be bygones. "Turnin' over a new leaf," he claims he'll tell all the inquirers tomorrow night. "Thanks to my good frien' and partnuh, Mr. Sam Stamps."

I convinced him? A new role for Silent Sam, you ask me, yet Ben's plan makes sense—all his plans do. I'm to tell reporters, who'll be here from *Blues Today*, *Stormy Monday*, some of the European mags, maybe even Dane Connor's *Good Rockin' Tonight*, that I wanted to at least try these awards out and that Mr. Mabry thought we had a chance at winning this year. Mentioning Mabry will make any reporter grumble: He's the sentry whom they have a hard time getting past to try and interview Ben and me. As well, Ben thinks we should play him up as opportunistic and disrespectful, positioning his clients for an award when he should be joining the rest of the blues world in mourning the loss of Ott Sikes and Henry Lee Bascombe.

When Ott and Henry were alive, all knew one would totter home with the prize, primarily because of their ages—Ott was ninety-seven, Henry ninety-four—but also due to the obscurity of their styles. Fife and drum and ragtime made True Delta look practically modern. Which is another reason why Blind Deacon Roland and the Professor have an advantage over us. The Piedmont style they play never seized the public the way Delta did. You rarely heard of blues lovers scouring small towns of the southeast the way they pored over every whistle stop and hamlet between Memphis and New Orleans. The other nominee, Henry Taggart, might be the best player of us all, but not only is he white (so's the Professor) and Ivy-League educated, he never sticks with one style for more than one record: acoustic one album, with Texas horns or Leadbelly covers the next. Two years ago, he even did something called *Sacred Steel.*

But our attending the Beale Street Blues Awards Ceremony is not about winning or losing. We're here because Ben thought I needed cheering up after what happened in Detroit: I did need such a happy distraction as these sixty or so hours, and so far I'm hooked on Memphis, or Me'phis, as Ben has instructed me to say. I'm wondering how soon I can get back.

• • •

The Hospitality Committee has gone to great lengths to welcome us "masters of the Blues," as we're called in the letter that accompanies our security passes and programs. Along with comping our hotel rooms, they've invited us to take in the area's many sights and sounds, with complimentary passes and shuttles to Tunica's casinos, the Gibson guitar plant, some art and music museums, as well as Graceland, of all places, and a Redbirds game. Right now, Ben's in the room, on the cell, getting directions to a health food store. Didn't even hassle me about my present destination: Interstate Barbecue. I'm the only passenger on the elevator, and I keep my eyes closed for a minute, just to make it more exciting when I enter the lobby, hoping to see some blues legends or at least another member of the top ten harp players according to *Blues Today.*

When the elevator doors and my eyes open, there's plenty of great players, of all instruments, and many styles, but they're my age or a decade or so older. The elder generation—Cotton, Gatemouth, Koko, Pinetop and the like—must not have arrived or are up in their hotel rooms. Because Ben and I don't play festivals, these aren't cats I've jammed backstage with or sat in with on a record. But I recognize them and they me. I nod at Clay Sampson, who used to be in Luther Allison's band, nearly bump into Mary and Buster Stewart, the "new sweethearts of the blues." They play at least three nights a week at Tip's, a show that's more soul than blues, with lots of corny banter, but they're all right. I scan the room for Blind Deacon and the Professor, though I'm not sure I'd recognize them if they stood right before me. I own one of their records, a vinyl LP, but rarely am I in a mood to hear Piedmont, and hardly ever stray from my CDs and Discman.

Larry "Bottom" Diggs—the cat from Houston who wins best bassist every year—nods at me, and I wonder if he knows me by name or is happy to see another brother. I don't ask because he's walking toward the revolving door, where two white kids stand, the guy with a Replacements' t-shirt and Elvis sideburns, the girl with Betty Page bangs and black Japanese characters tattooed on her milky upper arms. "Gentleman. Ladies," the guy shouts. "Anyone needing nourishment for the soul from Four Corners, Miss Jeri is your driver. If it's the Mid-South's finest Q you want, then come with me." Doesn't even sound like a southerner. He could be from Troy. Along with the New Sweethearts of the Blues, I find myself headed in his direction. I can put away fried chicken and pork chops, yams and black eyed peas, but my eyes tighten and my gorge rises whenever I get in smelling distance of greens, even though Ben sings in "Satisfy My Soul," "I drink potlikker like it's water."

And I'm not the only one this hungry at three o'clock, as there's a wait to get through the revolving doors and out to the two silver vans with Blues City Tours stenciled on their sides. I get my opening right after Clay Sampson and his three-piece band and step outside to wait another few seconds. I wipe my knuckles over my lips and mustache, which is thickening up nicely, though I may have spied some grays among the black hair this morning. I tug the collar of my shirt—I'm wearing the one with the sphinx head today—make sure the points lie like wings atop the collar of my jacket. Then, as Clay steps into the van and I follow, I see seated at the back Henry Taggart, smoothing his long gray-blonde hair off his patrician brow, while dressed like a hired hand in boots, bleached jeans and denim workshirt. Clay sits near him and smiles, as if acknowledging Henry's the most famous of us mid-level acts. No one here has heard his tunes on a movie soundtrack. Most play venues where draft beer's served in clear plastic cups, and outside of festivals and warm-up gigs, we've never seen more than a few grand cheering us. If the van behind crashed into this one, no one's obituary would make it on Yahoo's headlines, and there'd be no appearances in the memorial video montage at the Grammy's.

The only seat left is behind the driver, so I drift toward it, first nodding toward Henry—he plays harp as good as or better than Butterfield and Musselwhite—but he's staring forward down Union Street. The driver jumps in, welcomes us again, and has the keys in the ignition, playing it cool, until he turns to me. "Silent Sam!" he says.

My shoulders shoot back and my head wobbles side to side. Eventually, I nod and have my hand out in time for his to grab with force. "Where's Brother Ben?" he says, as they all do.

"Up in the bed," I say, automatically.

The driver nods, as if confirming what he already knew. "Silent Sam," he says, starting the van. "No fucking way."

I turn and shrug apologetically, then stop, thinking that might be too complex for Sam. As the driver pulls away, I watch from behind my sunglasses the crew of valets and bellmen working outside the hotel, most of them brothers, a few Latinos. I wouldn't dare ask them if they liked Brother Ben and me. I'd get an answer I know too damn well.

• • •

The driver's name is Michael Hunt. He's heard all the jokes, which is really one joke, told over and over again, and it made a Michael out of him instead of a Mike. Two years younger than my real age, he drives this tour bus four days a week for Blues City Tours, though he's disappointed none of his passengers ever inquires about Joe Hill Louis, the Memphis Jug Band or even Mr. Handy. "Half of them don't even know Willie Mitchell still lives in town," he says. He can't drive down Beale, since it's closed to vehicle traffic, and most of his passengers are only interested in the termination of the tour, Graceland, and the opportunity to traipse around the great man's house.

I learn all this and more on the way to the restaurant, as Michael talks nearly non-stop. As long as I don't have to answer questions, I'll endure a monologue, especially one with so much praise for Ben and me. When we enter the parking lot of Interstate, Michael lets everyone know that their meals are gratis, thanks to the good people at Blues City Tours, a sponsor of the Beale Street Blues awards. Taggart, the last one out before me, smiles at Michael, and he might have said, "Sam," as he passed. I'm not sure because Michael's telling me that he's in two bands, one a covers act that plays three nights a week at two airport hotels. "Everything from Bill Monroe to Bob Marley," he says is their introduction line. But that gig—along with the tour bus—supplements what he's doing with his real band, which he describes as a "blues-based quartet" called, get this, The Sons of Sonny Boy. Were I not attracted by the tangy aroma of hickory smoke and pulled pork, I'd ask him why they selected Sonny Boy. Mud and Wolf and the other B.B. make up the trio that intrigues most white boy blues players. But I don't need to say anything to Hunt to keep him talking. As we enter the restaurant, he says, "We're not, you know, some tribute band. We try to capture the spirit of the blues while keeping some, you know, ironic detachment and self-awareness."

Ironic detachment? Self-awareness? That deserves a Silent Sam double take. I remove my hat, scratch my shaggy head. "Sho," I say, then walk to a table and read the menu.

The interior of Interstate Barbecue suits me well. No gimmicks, no cute reproductions of olden days, just black and white tile floors, wobbly ceiling fans, formica tables and plenty of napkins. Requisite celebrity photos hang from the walls, though none of the waitstaff rushes to grab a camera and snap any of us from the Beale Street Blues awards. The other players sit among the customers, Clay and his bandmates in a booth underneath a photo of Willard Scott, the new sweethearts of the blues squabble at a table over who'll sit with his or her back to the entrance, and Henry Taggart all by his lonesome in a booth at the back, the RESTROOMS sign above his regal head. My table-mate is Michael Hunt. I sit angled from him so he won't see my contacts. He recommends I order a wet slab of ribs—I do—then asks our honey-colored waitress for the same and tells me Brother Ben and I should easily win tonight's Best Traditional Artist. Before I fabricate humility and mumble how it's nice just to be nominated, he asks me why Ben and I never play Memphis. "I mean," he says. "Last year I drove down to Tuscaloosa to see you guys. My van overheated around Aberdeen on the way back."

"I ain't got no say," I say. "The man tell me where to go, I go."

"Sure," he says, tugging his sideburns with his thumb and forefinger.

So much of what I say in Sam's voice is a lie, but this isn't. Never have I suggested we try gigs in other places: Why mess with the good thing we've got going? Why think I could tell Ben we need to play Baton Rouge or Austin in addition to our surefire towns? I suspect there's more to Ben's keeping us away from the Awards weekend than his alleged claims of years ago. He wouldn't have been so hard on me about the polls if that were so. And as for why we don't play in Memphis, Martha's buried here, but it's been over twenty years since she died, and I'd never say sentiment got in the way of Ben making a dollar. We also don't play anywhere in Mississippi or Arkansas and Louisiana, these being places that don't need to hear our honest and solemn evocations of Delta life because people like Cedell Davis and Raful Neal rip the joint with jams that sound as though they were made in the same century as the one their audience lives in. None of the brothers and sisters at Booba Barnes's old place in Greenville is going to stand in line to see us summon the ghosts of the past, you ask me. They want something to dance to, not nod quietly and gently tap their feet

I tell Michael Hunt none of this. Instead, I swallow Dr. Pepper and let my eyes grow dull. Our waitress appears with a large platter on her shoulder, filled with overlapping plates of ribs, pulled pork, and sandwiches dripping with slaw. One of them, I hope, is mine. I'll be interested to see if a mouthful of rib might quiet Michael. Large oval plates in both hands, our waitress walks over—she hasn't heard of me or Brother Ben, I bet. She might like something from Malaco Records now and then, but not a whole lot. "Enjoy y'all selves," she says after setting down our plates. I thank her, tug a fistful of napkins from the dispenser. As I turn to my plate, though, I smile when I see Taggart eating ribs, too. With a fork and a knife.

● ● ●

Hunt doesn't make the drive back to the hotel any easier, for as soon as we all get in the van, everyone smelling of smoke and heavier by two pounds, at least, he slips into the CD player *Blues At Your Request*, then cues it to "Take My Chance." I don't mind hearing us play—I'm glad I'm not the only one hearing this song—but I can't say everyone else is as eager. However, I wish Ben were here to see our fan base might be growing. I never believed we attracted such hipsters as Michael Hunt. Few, if any, of our fans talk about "ironic distance" and "self-awareness," when it comes to blues. "Authentic," "genuine" and "real" are their words of choice.

On our return to the Holiday Inn, the only obvious sign of discontent with the musical selection appears when Clay Sampson's keyboard player tosses to Michael a copy of their latest, a live recording, *Let Me Hear You Holler*. Judging by the title, I won't be adding it to my collection. Clay's from North Dakota, though he's got good cred from having backed up Luther Allison many years. I just hope he's not trying to affect a showman's routine. Out of the mouths of white boys, most patter sounds strained, especially when they put on a southern accent. Wind up sounding like Foghorn Leghorn. *I say, I say, y'all feel all right?*

Meantime, after every passenger but me files out of the van, "Take My Chance" comes on again. Behind my hand, I belch, savoring the smoky remnant of the ribs—perhaps the finest I've ever eaten—then push up from the seat, suspecting Hunt has a request. No way was all that praise and attention delivered without something in return anticipated. As my heels hit the sidewalk, I hear him say, "What are you doing tonight, Sam?"

I tilt my hatbrim, run my finger over my mustache. "Gon do what the man say," is my answer, though I only turn around part way, and mumble. Hunt lights a Lucky, blows smoke, then steps next to me. He's not blocking my path but presses in my hand a sheet of purple paper. "The Sons are playing tonight," he says, a little cooler than before. As if we're not fan and idol, just a pair of working musicians. "Thought you might convince Brother Ben to come check us out." He blows more smoke. "You too, Sam."

I open up the folded sheet, peer at it over the top of my sunglasses. On one side of the page is a Xeroxed image of my man Sonny Boy, in his later years, dapper in a British-looking suit and derby and sidling next to a bouffant blonde. Across from that image is a group shot of Hunt's band, mugging in a manner suggesting that each member is tough, sensitive and wise-assed all at once. The name of the club is Turner's J.O.B., though I'm not going to ask what that stands for, as I'm sure Hunt expects I already know it. But I don't know what else to say, other than no way would Ben spend a minute in a club. All that cigarette smoke, the harsh sound of inferior PA systems. The show's starting time of nine would keep him out well past his bedtime. I don't know if I want to come either. Hunt's attention and his present request aren't a fair measure of my fame. If Ben were here, Hunt would be all up in his business. Still, it is nice to be asked. So I face him, press my shades closer to my face, then nod and say, "We see."

And though I start walking immediately after speaking, I don't get far enough away to avoid hearing Hunt say, "Bring your harp, Sam. Don't forget to bring your harp."

• • •

I'm still too full from Interstate's ribs and sides to attend a dinner with the rest of the nominees, and Ben just got back from the health food store. It's now a little past eight and he's unbagging black bean empanadas, tabouli, dried figs and a protein shake. "Found a really good deal on VISUstein," he says, as if I have any idea what the product does. The sofa's comfort makes me think I shouldn't move an inch until it's time to rack out. No need to put back on my jivey clothes, which still reek sweetly of smoke.

Only I'm debating whether to go to Turner's J.O.B., because Hunt asked me to bring my harp. He might not have even meant it, only tossed that request when my back was turned to get me to work harder at bringing Ben out. Groaning, I lean forward, push myself up and off the sofa. Ben strips the recycled wrapper from his fork and knife, settles behind his dinner at a table overlooking Third Street. "Want some?" he says, pointing at the tabouli.

I walk behind him, stretching the fabric of my t-shirt and filling my cheeks with air to show Ben how full I still feel. "You want advice? "he says. "Go with the chicken next time. Pork takes its time going down. These figs might help you chase it out. Five grams of fiber a serving."

"That's all right," I say, lifting my pants off the bathroom doorknob and tugging out from the pocket the flyer for Michael Hunt's band. When I got back from the restaurant earlier, he was asleep. I decided to put off showing him the flyer until he got back from the store. Don't know why I feel obligated to show him now. Do I owe Michael Hunt this gesture? For all his flattery? I wait for Ben to pause in his eating, then hold the flyer before him. "Cat who drove us to the restaurant," I say. "Wants us to come out."

Ben dabs at his lips with a napkin, places it on his lap, then grabs the bottom left corner of the flyer with his thumb and crooked forefinger. I let it go. After a glance, he turns and looks at me the way he did those many years ago when I asked him about the judge and his first guitar. "You really thought you needed to ask me?"

"You never know," I say, examining my pants' cuffs.

Chewing, Ben regards me out of the corner of his eye. "You going?" he says.

In the instant I slip on my pants, I decide that I am. "Just for a little bit."

"Hmm," he says, cutting an empanada in two with his fork. "Bringing your Hohner?"

I stop putting on the sphinx shirt. Do I ever go anywhere without my Hohner? Still, I turn my back to Ben, button my shirt and say, "Naw. Won't be gone but an hour or two." I hear Ben chewing, his breath exiting his nose. I slip my jacket on, collect the white keycard from the dresser, and almost reach the door. "Be careful," Ben says, as stern and tender as a parent. I've got my hand on the door handle. Still an opportunity to stay inside, call off this curious expedition. "I will," I say, and push my way out before any more thoughts cross me up.

• • •

The show's just likely started and Beale isn't that long a street, but I don't walk directly to Turner's J.O.B. Instead, I stroll toward the river, then, at the intersection of Front, cross the street and meander east. Beale's not quite as bad as Bourbon Street: Though pedestrians spill bright colored cocktails from plastic cups, barkers holler in every other doorway, and fortunes get told by tarot-card reading mediums with henna hair and nose rings, at least there's no simulated sex shows and transvestite strippers. A nice mix of people, too. I see more tourists beguiled by Elvis impersonators than I need, but locals are among the throng. Handsome brothers and sisters move about in sharp clothes, trying not to gawk at me in my seventies finery. They shake their heads at shabby members of our brethren, who promise white folk the best of the blues while wheezing through corroded harps or plucking the strings of guitars more raggedy than Ben's. My first time ever on this famous street might be a real pleasure, if *I* didn't feel so strange. Out here in the mid-April night, amid the squabble of people happy to spend money on overpriced menus and souvenirs and mule-drawn tours, I tighten my stomach muscles behind all my flab but can't still the flutter deep within. Can't keep my head clear. In my pants pockets, my fingers curl into claws. It's the feeling I used to have when I was young and had made a decision to do something wrong, like smoke a cigarette, drink a beer or jack off. Almost expect my dick to stiffen, a development that won't be too comfortable in these slick slacks of mine.

I've lied to Ben before, of course, have committed the sin of omission hundreds of times. Yet never have I done what I did tonight, tell him something I knew he knew to be untrue. Still, I want to play with Hunt's band—I realize this now—or at least have the option to do so, and didn't want to explain myself. Ben would have talked me out of going, kept me on that sofa while he enumerated the virtues of his latest supplement. After I cross Beale again near Fourth, I wind up outside W.C. Handy Park near the Father of the Blues' statue. He's wearing a suit and holding a trumpet. If I recall correctly, he was playing marching band and orchestral dance music when he first got close to the blues: Waiting in a Mississippi train station, Handy encountered some brother playing what he later called "the weirdest music I had ever heard." The statue depicts him as genial, courtly, respectable. If he were my employer, my mother wouldn't mind. I start walking again, trying not to think of what she's doing in Ghana. Most likely telling Grover she wishes somebody can talk sense into her only child. I shake my head, wipe my hand over my mustache. A temporarily empty head is what I want most of all, and I hope I find it in Turner's J.O.B. Only way to find out is to get there. I pick up my pace.

• • •

J.O.B. stands for "Just Off Beale." I discover this as I stand outside, waiting for the ID checker. Just below that sign hangs another, reading, "Where Historical Preservation Ends and Good Times Begin." After a dubious glance at my Louisiana drivers license and an equally incredulous examination of my outfit—I almost flash the sphinx head—the ID checker stamps my palm and I'm inside. The doorway's not quite a portal to my past life, but when my nostrils recoil from the stench of cheap disinfectant over spilled beer and human funk, I may as well be in one of the bars I played in East Lansing. The clubgoers aren't dressed as they were back in the early nineties—in all black or fifties' gear. These cats look like truckers and cowboys, with big wallets and chains, sleeveless plaid shirts and straw hats, their ladies in western skirts and ornate boots. I've arrived between sets and don't see Michael Hunt anywhere, though a number of people resemble him and his tour-bus partner from earlier. I count one-Mississippi, two-Mississippi before I walk to the bar to detect whether I'm the only brother here. Even the ID checker was white, and I thought you always stationed at the door massive and dark-skinned linemen whose scholarship eligibility ran out. Though I'll concede it's dark here, and I haven't gotten a good look at the custodial crew yet, it appears I'm in a minority of one. Still, it's time for a drink, and I order an Old

Milwaukee, the closest thing to my hometown's favorite, Stroh's. The bartender fishes for one and hands me a tallboy, says it's only a dollar for another hour, then points to a papier mache bust of Ike Turner and says, "In honor of the patron saint of Friday nights at the J.O.B."

I leave two singles on the bar and open the can, hoist it high in Ike's direction. In musical style, I feel more kindred with Tina's old man than I do with Mr. Handy down the street, though I wonder how many people in here know anything about Ike other than what Larry Fishburne showed them in *What's Love Got to Do With It.* For that matter, what do they know of Sonny Boy, the man whose quote-unquote sons appear to be mounting the stage again, greeted by shrill whistles and raised tallboys. I find my place at the rear of the club, between the Gents' and the Ladies', a slippery paneled wall against my back. Between me and the stage is a dance floor, ringed by tables and chairs, but there's no room for dancing and everybody in the bar is on his or her feet as none other than Michael Hunt appears, in wraparound shades, a sleeveless Public Enemy shirt and tattered jeans. I dampen my mustache with another sip of beer, while Hunt grinds out his cigarette, blows smoke, then grabs the mic. Two brothers pass me by then, each weighed down by a gray tub full of empties. Now that I know that there are three of us—three and a half if you count Ike's bust—I settle down to listen.

Back in the van this afternoon, I could have predicted the noise these fellows would make: It's of the kind our Vegas crowd desired. The drums go boom-blat, boom-blat, the bass keeps a steady but undistinguished pulse, and the guitars chew up rhythm, until it's time for Michael to solo. Sons of Chuck Berry or Keith Richards would be more accurate a name. Better yet, Sons of Grand Funk Railroad. Don't hear any of the "irony" or "self-awareness" he promised in the van. Yet who am I to criticize? Played my share of this shit and now pretend, that's right, *pretend* to be an embodiment of a musical tradition that's as much mine as it is that of Michael Hunt or anybody else in his band. And hell, they at least live here, a claim one Peter Owens cannot make.

Soon time feels as jittery as their sped-up covers, and an hour passes, though it seems only half that. Over the nonstop noise of the clubgoers and through the muffled sound system, the band plays John Lee

Hooker, ZZ Top and George Thorogood, and an original or two, the subjects of which are drinkin' wine and steppin' out. What enlivens the people here most, though, is the patter Hunt manufactures between songs. No surprise after this afternoon to find he's an onstage talker, only now his voice doesn't sound as suburban. Everything he says is nipped from Joe Tex and Peter Wolf, yet it takes on a ragged and Dixie-fried edge that sounds legit when he exhorts the crowd to *Get nekkid* or asks *Y'all feel awright.*

Now he's rapping about the blues and how people in Memphis are lucky to live in a town where so much good music was made. Behind him, the rest of the Sons play a quiet shuffle, keeping it slow and rumbling like a distant storm. I've finished my Old Mil and don't need another. I tune in closer to what Hunt's saying. "I know y'all been to Memphis in May. I know y'all been to Sun Studios. Some of y'all been to Graceland." The crowd boos but quiets once Hunt waves both hands, then yanks off his shades. He assumes a stance and grip on the mic like those of the Marines at Iwo Jima. "But how many of y'all know about the Beale Street Blues awards tomorrow? How many of y'all know the best, I mean, the best of the blues is in town and probably just for another day?" The response from the crowd is mixed, people not knowing if they're being shamed or prodded to act. Meantime, the rest of the Sons of Sonny Boy have picked up the pace with their shuffle, and Hunt falls to his knees. "But we extra lucky tonight, good people," he says. "All y'all visitors to the Friday night throwdown at Mr. Turner's J.O.B." He stands up now, his limbs loose as he points to the bar and salutes. "First a toast to our patron saint of Friday night, Mr. Izear 'Ike' Turner, the founder of rock and roll long before he was kicking Tina's ass."

A lusty shout of approval emerges, nearly from every voice in the club except mine. Might be time to leave, as I can't quite tell if Hunt's delivery amuses or pisses me off. He's swerved into the quasi-black dialect that manages to parody more than praise. I look for a trash can to toss away my empty—don't want to make the two man clean-up crew work any harder than they have to—when Hunt says, "But tonight, like I said, good people, we extra lucky. Why? Cuz, y'all, we got"—he quiets, raises one hand, drops it the same time as the drummer hits his crash cymbal—"we got somebody here tonight. Somebody who's been there. A man from the Delta, where the blues was born. All the way from Natchez,

Mississippi, good people, Mr. Silent Sam Stamps!"

How did he know? I know I'm somewhat easy to find, but not amidst all this dim lighting and cigarette haze. Did he know I was coming when he invited me? Somebody tip him off? The bartender? A spy out on Beale? Ben? Whatever the case, I don't want to embarrass the man, and so far the only request appears to involve me walking to the stage, which I do, tripping over no one, the crowd parting to give room, though no one applauds the way they would had Hunt said, Mr. Al Green or Mr. Buddy Guy. I reach up for my hat brim, touch nothing but the stubble of my recently trimmed head. What's that a sign of? Bad luck if you leave a hat on the bed, what about when you forget it as part of your disguise? When I reach the stage, I see the bassist, who also approximated back up harmony for Hunt's lead vocals, has moved center stage, freeing up a mic. I wave to the crowd, rub my hands together. "Mr. Sam Stamps," Hunt says again, and the applause sounds like rain that might shift from a drizzle to a downpour.

Meantime, the rest of the band steadies their rhythm, with Hunt joining in. No single tune has emerged, just a passable shuffle, easily sped up for Chicago, slowed down for Delta. Hunt's eyes widen and he shrugs, a gesture any musician knows means, What do you wanna play? I haven't even taken my Hohner out of my pocket. Haven't made a motion or said a word. Do need some practice, though, which is what I'd be doing if I were back in the room with Ben. Thinking of him while I shake my harp and bring it close to my lips, I recall one of his tricks. I'll give the Sons of Sonny Boy a tough number, and if they can't find their way in, I'll wave and duck back into the anonymity of Beale. " 'I Can't Be Alone,'" I say to Hunt, just barely knowing the lyrics. I quietly play the intro, then Hunt shouts: "Ain't no way in the world, I can be by myself." Nothing left to do then but close my eyes and blow.

## 8

**MOST MORNINGS, I WAKE AS SOON AS BEN RETURNS**
from a jog or finishes a shower, and today I hear him pouring cereal in a bowl
while humming "Take the A-Train." Only I'm pretending to be asleep, uncertain if
I want to spend much time in his presence until the awards ceremony tonight. A
sheet close to my face, I sneak a quick look. He's in his green track suit, looking out
the window, returning to his bowl of bran in front of the silent TV. His routine's
been interrupted—two whole days without a jog or workout—and he fidgets and

## Your Funeral & My Trial

leaves his seat before he's taken a spoonful of cereal. I feign a
snort, roll over and flatten my face against a pillow, trying to
get back to sleep when I know I won't. When I got in last night,
I thought Ben was doing what I'm doing now but he never
woke. I needed to remove myself from the stage because I damn
near flew all the way back to the hotel replaying the applause
and admiration. The people there may have walked in ignorant
of Silent Sam, but they left knowing who he was. I hadn't even played that well.
Sounded more echoey than I like and bent some wrong notes right. Hunt begged
me to jam some more in his Midtown apartment, but I said no. In the room at
three, I took out my gummy contacts, shed my clothes quietly—they smelled like
I'd rolled on the floor at the J.O.B.—then stuffed them in my garment bag, away
from Ben's fussy nose. Though my body was fatigued, my mind stayed busy, seeing
my hands clutched around my harp, my bent elbows rising past my chin, as if I
might generate enough energy to lift my whole body off the stage.

Recalling these moments while Ben washes out his cereal bowl feels wrong, especially after the compliments he gave me back in Detroit. Especially since he took us out of our way to attend the awards. I haven't thanked him enough. Now I roll back over, try the other side, but my mind's alert and my body is too, though I couldn't have slept more than—what time is it? Five hours. Damn.

That's when Ben goes into the bathroom and the shower comes on. I'll wait for his next move before I let myself out from under the Holiday Inn's smooth sheets. He'll know exactly what I did, I'm afraid, as soon as we're up and about in the same space. Time passing isn't going to remedy anything, but it's the best solution I can summon. I close my eyes tight, pull a pillow over my head, hearing Michael Hunt shouting, as he did when we finished "I Can't Be Alone": "This is the real deal, y'all. Silent. Sam. Stamps!"

• • •

Around eleven, I'm showered, shaved and still not relinquishing my hold on last night. Ben's just back from some errands, but I'm not sharing any news. I sit up in my bathrobe and try not to smile too much—a sure giveaway. "Sleep ok?" he says, and I nod. He drops two slick plastic garment bags on his bed.

"Surprise," he says. I walk closer, read the red lettering on the gray bags: Daniels Formal Wear. Another reason why I'm not in charge. At some time today I would have recognized that we'd need to wear something more than our performance rags, but it would have been too late. Ben took care of things, kept a problem from ever arriving.

I reach for the garment bags, unsure which is which. "Can I see mine?"

"You mean, May I?" Ben corrects. He tugs the one from the bottom so they're side by side. Pointing to the one on our left, he says, "That's yours."

After unzipping the bag about halfway, I pause. "Will I need my shades?" I say, predicting a tux with a metallic sheen, ruffles and a texture you don't see much outside pool tables, something Isaac Hayes may have dismissed as too wild when he dressed in chain for the '72 Academy Awards. The suit I uncover, though, could be worn to a wedding. A proper shade of black, lapels of classic width, the shirt white and plain fronted with black and gold studs and cuff-links. "What's up?" I say, holding the gently flared trousers before me.

"I was thinking," Ben says. "Mabry should be pulling the strings. And cheap as he is, you know he'd rent, and wouldn't allow us the opportunity to choose purple velvet and matching shoes." He picks his up, hangs it on the rack by the bathroom. "So when anyone asks you tonight about your apparel, you say, 'Mist' Mabry picked it out for me.'"

I drop my robe from my dry shoulders, try on the jacket. A perfect fit in the chest, though a tad long in the arms. "Pickeded it out for me," I embellish.

"Perfect," Ben says. "And now, if you don't mind, I'd like a cut." Yawning, he rubs a hand over his head. What's there of his stubble looks more silver now than I've seen.

"No problem," I say, like a Jamaican waiter on a cruise ship, taking off the jacket and zipping it back up with the pants and shirt. We've even got rented shoes in the bottom of the bag, along with a pre-tied bow tie, black and slim, nothing like those I saw Ben and Razor wearing back in the day: I swear, they were big enough to signal Batman.

● ● ●

"Don't get used to this," Ben says, as we wait for the elevator on our floor, identical in our tuxes, though we each spoil the look with a fedora. Can't look *too* good.

Now, as the elevator door opens, I half-expect Michael Hunt to spring out and give me up to Ben about last night, but the car's empty. Earlier, after we'd shaped up our heads and sat around watching the Memphis news, Ben asked me what the show was like. I shrugged and swigged Dr. Pepper, asked if he wanted room service. Nothing else about the show since, which makes me wonder if I needed to be so sly. The elevator now stops at the third floor, and who's standing there but Henry Taggart, resplendent in a black tux of his own. A khenti cloth scarf's around his neck and a Southern Poverty Law Center button adorns his lapel. Man's too good to be true. He steps into the car, says, "Brother Ben. Sam."

"Mist' Taggart," Ben says, stooped and leaning in my direction, one arm hooked around mine for support. I nod, lips clamped shut, eyelids heavy.

We three nominees for Best Traditional Artist say nothing but eye the descending numbers. The elevator doors open and reveal a space so packed with bluesmen it appears no other guests are staying here this weekend. I scan the crowd for harpists and catch Mojo Buford on his way out. Everybody's nined, though few have opted for the traditional black tux Ben, Taggart and I wear. The fellows mostly sport those loud and long suits the BET televangelists wear, the fits loose and the colors guaranteed to leave you blinking through a hazy afterimage. His hand locked around my wrist, Ben shuffles forward, saying how-do to a number of players, everyone's eyes wide open and alert to his presence. The general whisper is "You see that?" or "He ain't never been here, has he?"

As if to be sure everyone sees him, Ben makes a game of being the slowest human being possible. In my pocket, I touch my security pass, the keycard, the Brougham's keys and my harp. Mojo Buford's brief presence assures me of somebody to jam with once the show's over. Doesn't matter if it's onstage at the Orpheum or in a hotel room, after last night at Turner's, I'm looking forward to more. Finally, we make it outside, where Henry Taggart says, "Beautiful evening." I nod. Wouldn't mind jamming with him. Cat might be recording a zydeco album next, but he's learned the lesson Slowhand and a lot of others haven't. Taggart always has a dynamite backing band, not a bunch of studio hacks who can't push him to the places where the best music is made. I'd get out my Marine Band if he asked, but for now he says, "How are you getting to the Orpheum?"

Ben wheezes and coughs, though not his new one—he must be saving it for later. I lick my lips, sense Ben's pretending he's too winded to speak, then secure my tongue's tip behind my lower front teeth. "We drivin'," I say.

"Sure?" Taggart says, hands in his pockets, turning to face me. "I've got a limo. Record company, you now. Seems a waste to sit in the back all alone."

Ben rises to a slouch, his shoulders rounded but his head up. He flashes to Taggart a smile so gold filled I swear he's added a new sleeve. "You do that fo' Sam and me, Mist' Taggart?" he says.

Taggart nods, looks away shyly, as if uncomfortable with Ben's obsequiousness. With bent fingers, Ben tugs my sleeve. "What you say, Sam? Let that Caddy rest till mornin'?"

"Sho," I say and keep my mouth open, breathing but saying nothing else.

"Good then," Taggart says. We three maneuver toward a line of limos, one driver holding up a sign that says H. TAGGART. A tidy and slender Indian gent in a white shirt and black slacks, he opens the rear doors, tells us all what a privilege it is to have us in his limo. He says not a word on the three-minute drive to the Orpheum, a spectacular old theater that I'm sure has only a brief history of allowing blacks entry through the front doors. BEALE STREET BLUES AWARDS lights up the marquee. Underneath it, smokers dirty the sidewalk with ashes and butts. Big Town Walker chews a cigar and I shake a naughty you finger at him, wondering if other culprits of the Eau Claire photos are around. Through the smoke and gossip, I hear the other B.B. sent along several videotaped acceptance speeches to make up for his absence. Dr. John's on his way up from New Orleans, someone says, and Buddy's already inside, as are Delbert McClinton, Deborah Coleman and others. I've seen all these folk and more when they played East Lansing or Detroit, and I was in my cheap seat. I saw many backstage during that festival Ben and I played in Phoenix. Shaking hands and saying hello with people whose music has moved me is always a joy, though regrettably I've never been able to communicate my feelings to anyone, other than Ben. I've needed to sand away my genuine appreciation for all these men and women to the bare patterns of Sam speech. How could I possibly say to James Cotton that he gave me hope? Or tell Otis Rush, the guitarist I love best, that he helped me feel I was connected to something? If you know Sam Stamps's story, as it's told in liner notes and magazine articles, you'd recall his big family in the colored section of Natchez: Why would he ever feel he was the only one?

After the security check, inside the Orpheum's lobby, for which ornate and opulent don't get close, Taggart splits up with us, going over to shake hands with Bottom Diggs and his young Hispanic wife. My palm grows moist in my pocket. I clutch my harp, waiting for Ben to make his entrance. I've never seen him in a situation like this, and I'm anxious to see his performance. Sullen and wary? Or the glad-hander and well-wisher of recent years? When he staggers forward, then gets everyone's attention with a cough, the talking quiets, the drinking stops. A channel in the sea of bodies opens, leading to a corner by the staircase where Blind Deacon Roland and the Professor stand, both of them in khaki suits and matching hats, the Deacon's dark glasses obscuring half of his face and his frame so frail and propped up by the cane he clutches with both hands. No one else notices, but Ben's pace speeds so the Professor, if he's so inclined, can't steer Blind Deacon elsewhere. There's no antagonism between Brother Ben and Blind Deacon, fabricated or real, but I recall Heywood told me that around '82, in a festival in Spokane, Ben waved two lit matches near the Deacon's face. The Professor came in as Ben was striking a third. Ben claims he's not jealous, but the genuine sightlessness of Roland makes him more sympathetic. As they do with the work of Blind Willie Johnson and Reverend Gary Davis, the Deacon's mentor, most overlook the fact that while the strings are shaking out a blues rhythm, the words are full of veneration, a simple but sturdy faith. In "Lord, I'm Ready," Deacon's most famous song, he sings, in his quavery tenor, "Lord I'm ready/Carry me home when you will." Yet tales exist of the Deacon possessing a slightly more earthy side. Before he took up with the Professor, he always demanded to be paid in cash. One night, after a show, he put the bills in one hand and held the other out like a pair of scales, then told the promoter, "Seems a little light, if you know what I mean."

When I catch up, Ben's shaking one of those famous hands. He and Blind Deacon share a few words about old times and festivals past, while the Professor nods nervously at me and I at him. Rumor is he dropped out of the PHD program at Caltech and lived a decidedly hippie lifestyle until the right combination of brown rice and windowpane acid brought to his eyes a vision of Christ, who told the young Professor that he needed to live his life right and start doing so by accompanying Blind Deacon. Right now, I'm looking at a graying cat whose beard doesn't quite conceal the fact he has no chin, who won't meet my eyes. Most of the time it's me who looks away first. Like Taggart, the Professor's a multiple instrumentalist, backing Blind Deacon on guitar, banjo, mandolin, even harp. I think he blows too much on the high end, but that's probably a Piedmont thing.

Ben says, "Deacon, you know my young partnuh, Sam Stamps?"

Blind Deacon's thin fingers claw the air as he says, "Don't think so," his high voice so pure it's unearthly, as I imagine guardian angels sound when they tell you your labor on earth has ended. I take his hand and he grips like he's trying to pull me forward. "Suh," I say.

"Mr. Stamps," he says. A gold tooth gleams when he smile. "A pleasure."

Without looking at the other performers and onlookers, I know their pleasure as they witness two elder statesmen of the blues sharing a moment, neither one guilty, it seems, of corrupting the purity of his craft. Neither has appeared on *The Tonight Show*, nor lent his voice to the marketing of low calorie beer or basketball shoes. If I didn't know about Ben's bank accounts and Machiavellian exploitation of his contrived image, I'd sniff back a tear, fearing this might be the last time these two speak to one another. With such legends, so advanced in age, you never know which moment will be their last. Last year, Ott Sikes, who'd just won Best Traditional Artist, died two weeks after the awards, then Henry Bascombe, the award winner a year earlier, was gone a month later.

But I do know Ben, so I don't get caught up in any reverential nonsense. I wait for him to finish shaking hands with the Professor, who nervously adjusts his string tie and can't seem to steer away Blind Deacon and himself fast enough. I wonder if I should have warned them about Eau Claire. Audrey and April might kill that old man if they get their hands on him. As Ben and I walk over the cushioned and elaborately patterned carpet to the seating entrance, I gaze at the chandelier and golden tiles of the ceiling, then check over my shoulder. "Fake," I whisper, to show I haven't succumbed to his trickery. "You probably got people hoping you win tonight."

"Naw." He looks around. "Next year, though. Just wait," he says and winks.

• • •

Installed in a section of plush Orpheum seats reserved for nominees, we await our category to be introduced. There's a lot of waiting to do, with not only six other categories before us, but several musical interludes, including a fife and drum tribute to Ott Sikes, a trio of local church choirs singing "Oh Happy Day," and Marcia Ball playing some of Bascombe's greatest hits. Ben prefers the gospel act most, clapping and whispering to me that serious money's now to be made in the service of the Lord. "Get you a TV show," he continues, "and talk about your sinful past playing blues, shoot. Hand over fist." He lets his eyelids flutter and slumps in his seat, tapping my foot with his when it's time for me to pretend to wake him. Other times, he snaps awake with a snort and a wipe of his weary eyes. His charade's not too far from true, you ask me. I'm making faces and yawning, shifting in my seat and re-reading the program, happiest when a winner is named so I can stand and pound my hands together. Still, the only surprise is which of the Stevie Ray Vaughn clones will win Best New Artist and I haven't heard of the skinny youngster who wears his Kangol backward and thanks his music teacher in Colorado Springs. From there, you could pretty much recite the results, as best female vocalist goes to Koko Taylor, best female musician to Bonnie Raitt, best group to the Holmes Brothers, best male vocalist to Robert Cray, and best male musician to Buddy Guy. Only Buddy and Koko are here to accept their awards—his twenty-ninth, her eighteenth—and the rest appear via videotape. Makes me wonder if the winner knows in advance, or if such stars assume they'll win. Either way, an hour's passed. My tux keeps my posture straight, as it hasn't lost the starch it came with. Ben's eyes are shut while the back of his head rests on the seat. Only thing missing is the cartoon bubble with a Z or a log getting sawed inside.

After a video montage honoring all the other bluesmen, –women and affiliated people who died this year—Ben won't open his eyes for that, though he's nowhere near asleep—the master of ceremonies, a white Memphian who edits the local free weekly, returns to the podium and says, "And now, ladies and gentleman, to present the award for Best Traditional Artist, Mr. Robert Junior Lockwood."

Hold on. I look at the program for the twentieth time, sure I saw Sam Philips listed as the presenter for our category. His name's still there, and would anyone other than Robert Jr. be in his place, I'd surely be disappointed. Philips is a bit of a wild man, you never know what he's likely to say. When I look up, though, I see none other than Robert Jr., who says in his unmistakable voice that Mr. Philips is a little under the weather and he's subbing for him tonight. Robert Jr. subbing for Sam Philips. It's too much. Ben taps my foot, and I shake his shoulder, a little rougher than needed. I don't care so much about the impression he wants to display for those seated around us, I want to certify that reading the nominees is Robert Johnson's stepson, Muddy Waters's peer, and goddamn, the man who accompanied Sonny Boy on King Biscuit Time and some of his finest sides for Checker. My face muscles tighten as my smile broadens past its typical spread. I'm fighting to stay still and wind up sitting on my hands like a disobedient child. Meantime, I'm praying Robert Jr. has his guitar somewhere or won't mind borrowing somebody's. More than any other bluesman, he's the one I want to play with. Only I don't know how to ask him. That is, I don't know how to phrase it in a way that won't make me gush or goof it up. That won't make me sound too much like Peter Owens instead of Silent Sam Stamps.

Beside me, Ben breathes leisurely and patiently, patting his hands together with the rest of the crowd. Onstage, Robert Jr.'s bald head gleams from the overhead lights, as he leans forward, reading glasses on, and tugs open the envelope. "And the winner is," he says, pausing like a pro to maximize the tension, "Brother Ben and Sam Stamps."

I hear the applause, a sound as familiar as my own breathing. Tonight, though, it sounds different. People stand and wave encouraging fists. The Professor whispers in Blind Deacon's ear. The old man looks relieved he won't have to walk to the stage. The mic barely catches it, but I hear Robert Jr. say, "This is their first one, huh?" And two rows down, Henry Taggart, his khenti-cloth scarf wagging, may be clapping loudest of all. Ben taps my elbow and I rise. Ben feebly crooks his arm in mine, but he's leading us out of our row and down the aisle.

We move forward, the slowest of all the winners. I'm pretty sure the applause grows louder, as we pause at each of the steps that lead up to the stage, and then struggle like contestants in a three legged race to the podium. Another hand on my arm surprises me: It's Robert Jr.'s, now sliding down to shake my hand. "You done well, son," he says. Then he's gone. My eyes can't follow to where he's gone. I'm sure I've had a dream like this, with a sudden appearance and equally sudden vanishing of someone I've wanted to speak with all my life. Now I face the crowd and feel, from behind, the MC placing around my neck a medallion on a silken ribbon. He follows up with Ben, whose stooped posture gives the MC an easier time. Applause subsides, though not completely, and the nominees and guests slowly return to their seats. While I swallow and lick my mustache and lips, Ben grips both sides of the podium, then reaches into his jacket pocket. I'll be damned if he doesn't retrieve reading glasses—the kind you pluck from a rack at Rexall—and a long, folded piece of paper. "Y'all gon have to give me a minute," he says. "I never been no best of readers. I usual just speak what's in my heart."

I don't know where he's going with this, have no idea what he wants from the audience. Or me. I am, however, staring at solid pieces of evidence that all his talk about us losing was just that: talk. And this unexpected detour to the home of the blues was as planned as every other stop. What's written on that page he's unfolding? Though the blood throbbing in my ears is half-angry, half-elated, along with everyone else in the Orpheum, I quiet myself to listen.

"I know y'all know," Ben says, still not reading the page he smoothes with his fingers and flattens with his palms, "that they's never just one man who make the music happen. And I didn't want forget nobody who he'p me along the way. So I axed Mr. Mabry, my manager, to put all this down." And then he starts reading, his voice so monotone it sounds like an entirely different person's, his studied problems with pronunciation painful to hear. Still, he lists heads of record labels—all nine of them—and several producers and festival promoters, some of who are here tonight. He even thanks Mankiewicz and Stern for, in his cagey words, "showin' me the way." Then he steps back and dabs at his dry eyes. He says, "This memoryin' bring back a whole lot of feelin' I ain't felt in a long while. I'm sure you all know I got to thank the dearly departed Reggie Carter."

A somber and reflective murmur passes through the crowd, until Ben says, "Y'all remember Bucket? Am I right?" He's answered with cheers and whistles and people calling Bucket's name. Ben continues:

"And can't forget Razor Sharp. Folks think we parted on unfrien'ly terms, but that ain't no truer than Santy Claus and the old Tooth Fairy. He still my good, good frien'. Always will be. And I can't let no evenin' like this pass without my sayin' thank you to Mr. Wilton Mabry. Without that man, I doan know where Brother Ben be today."

Absolute silence doesn't fall. I can hear a little applause, like the first sounds from a bag of popcorn in the microwave, but few here want to reward Wilton Mabry. The writers hate how he treats Ben, the promoters and producers despise his hard cash tactics, and the artists wish their manager was more like him. Now, though, Ben removes his glasses, pockets his list of names, then grabs the podium with trembling hands. "I 'spect ya'll know they's one name I ain't mentioned." He pauses, allows some noisy seconds to pass. "Course, y'all good people, y'all *blues* people, knew they's another man with me when I come walkin' down the aisle. Couldn't a got here without him, and I mean that two ways." He steps out from behind the podium, shuffles a few steps with one hand kneading his hip. Above the resulting laughter, he raises his voice and says. "He standin' here right next to me! Best harp player I know. Go by the name Sam Stamps."

And now the microphone's mine. In my belly, I feel the same flutter I had last night, out on Beale, certain what I planned on doing wasn't in Ben's script, wanting to show him his hold on my strings isn't as tight as he believes. Oh, I could say a lot of things right now. I can even hear it in my head, louder than any applause the audience can raise: "My name's Peter Owens, I'm from suburban Detroit and there's nothing I'd like better than to play with Robert Jr." Sounds like I just stood up at an AA meeting. Ben winks. "Go on, Sam," he shouts. I take my turn at the podium, step back to still the feedback and lick my lips. "Thank y'all," I say. Then I nod. Twice. As if to communicate any more would require a power I don't own.

● ● ●

Backstage, I clutch my medallion and look for Robert Jr. Unlike the Academy Awards, no press conference awaits us. A few reporters ask questions, but Ben feigns deafness and moves us toward the hands that need shaking. Congratulations are whispered by other winners and the performers and organizers of the show. On their way out to play a number, Clay Sampson's band gives us the thumbs-up, Clay even pausing to slap me hard on the back. An hour or two more in the spotlight would make this Memphis visit complete, assure that I'll return, whether Ben comes with me or not. Hell, I might move here, the way things have been in my first days. Ben then grabs me by the arm with a grip that conveys I need to listen closely. "You ready?" he says.

I let go my medallion. It thumps gently against my chest. "Ready for what?"

"To go back to the hotel."

I jerk out of his grasp. "Why?"

"This just isn't for us," he says. As if about to cross a busy street, he looks both ways, then at me. "Too many opportunities for missteps."

Missteps? On whose part? He can only be meaning me, and I resent the charge. "You think I'll mess things up," I say in my own voice. "Shit, Ben, you knew all along we were going to win and never even told me."

"Keep your voice down," he says, smiling for some people passing by and wrapping one of his arms around me. I lower my shoulders to avoid his grasp but think I see Robert Jr. standing by the entrance to the stage. Turns out to be Rufus Thomas. His daughter, Carla, stands by his side. Ben brings me closer, says, "Ask yourself. What would you have done if I told you? I could barely keep your damn feet on the ground when you found out about the polls back in February."

I grab my harp, wishing for once I played a chromatic. They're heavier than a diatonic and might do the damage I'd like to inflict on the other Best Traditional Artist of 2000. But ok. He's right. I may very well have been insufferable knowing we had such a reward as this awaiting us. At least now he can give me one thing more, so I ask, "Just let me stay, Ben. Let me jam with Robert Jr."

"Maybe next year," he says, almost before I finish my sentence. He laughs, lets go my shoulders. "Folks aren't gonna want to hear Mabry get praised again, so Blind Deacon and the Professor will win for sure."

"I really wanted to play with the man," I say, more for myself than Ben.

Still, he hears me—never mind he's been playing deaf all tour—and says, "I'm not up to jamming. I don't even have my guitar."

What happened to the man who joins in all those sessions in dressing rooms with bearded nobodies and their sterile renditions? For the first time we could play with peers and he says no. "You'll play 'Crossroads' with the next patchouli-smelling cat in Tuscaloosa," I say.

"This is different," he says, then coughs into his fist. Nothing showy—we're by ourselves—he just needs to clear his throat. "A different audience entirely and I can't stay on top of things the way I like."

Five years with the man, doing everything he asks, and this is what I get. Won't grant my one request. Makes me wonder just what it was he first saw in me. Am I at his side because I was the best man for the job or the kind of young brother he could keep under his thumb? I wondered this after the audition and when I learned the real story of Brother Ben. Now I close my eyes, punch a fist in my palm. "You bring me here at the last damn minute," I say. "Tell me it's a little treat, knowing all the time we had this won, and now . . ."

He cuts me off, pretends to wipe his mouth but holds his finger up to his lips. Then he whispers, "Keep it down. Sam."

"Sam is far away," I say, dialing down my volume but not shifting into Sam speech. My shoulders are up around my ears, so I let them fall, try to relax a little. "Just let me stay tonight for the jam," I say. "I want to play this one time."

Ben takes off his hat, positions himself so his lips graze my ear. "I let you play last night. Remember?"

"That's different," I stammer. I try to pull back but his hand clamps around the back of my neck.

"Because you played for a bunch of Beale Street drunks?" Ben says. "What if you messed up our little enterprise, playing in some armpit? For free? What did you know about those guys? Anything?"

All along I suspected he knew. Hearing him accuse me of something like sabotage angers me, though, even if he might be right. When his grip on my neck relaxes, I find my strength, my neck snapping backward, causing me to scramble to stay balanced. Ben tips his hat and says, "Ma'am" to Marcia Ball, who walks past, offering us both congratulations. I lift my hat and see Henry Taggart waving and heading our way as well, which leaves me only a little time to speak. "That's what it's all about," I say. "Money. What if I made us some new fans last night? You done that lately?"

Ben shakes his head. "You don't get it, Pete," he whispers. "This isn't about finances alone. It's about control. Did you have it last night? Did you?" I can't look him in the face or think of the right answer. Yet the words "I quit" keep rolling over my teeth, as solid as Life Savers. Only I can't say them now, powerful though they might be. Ben looks up. "Mist' Taggart," he says.

"You two staying around to jam?" Taggart says, shaking out his hair, then making sure his SPLC pin is visible on his lapel.

Ben yawns, the sound and motion of his face and shoulders so real, I momentarily forget my anger. But I snatch it back at once. To Taggart, Ben says, "I be carryin' some weary bones."

"Too bad," Taggart says, scuffing his heel against the floor. "Get my driver to take you back. He won't mind."

"So kind of you, suh," Ben says, shaking Taggart's hand.

"My pleasure. I just can't think of anyone more deserving of this award than you, Brother Ben." I stare at the press of their hands, Taggart so pale I can see the blue of his veins. In contrast, Ben's fingers appear darker than their pecan coloring. Taggart lets go, looks at me. "What are you doing, Sam?"

I wonder if he needs a harp player, if he's willing to cede a little control now and then. But no. I can't quit Ben just yet. Though I can get out of here, so I say, "Walkin'." I don't want any reminders of how close I was to playing Sonny Boy's music with a man who helped make it. I push my way out the exit, my medallion bobbing against my chest, and walk past the Orpheum, wondering just what in the hell Ben means by control but knowing I didn't have it last night, though I may have believed I did. I even stop on a street corner to play a few bars of "Your Funeral and My Trial," as if Ben might hear and know just how angry I am. How angry he's made me.

Beneath the night sky, I get turned around trying to find Turner's J.O.B, then remember Michael Hunt said he'd be playing with his covers act out at the Airport Marriot tonight. When I wind up on Third and Beale, I gaze at the lights of several other places where I might play my harp, show off my medallion like it might impress anyone outside of the Orpheum. Under the streetlights, the medallion looks duller and cheaper. Almost expect the shine of the metal to flake off like foil. Best thing to do is get to the hotel. After some heavy steps in that direction, I see Ben getting out of the limo and wonder if he arrived fast or did thought slow me down once again. Instantly, I speed up to join him. Then I stop, holding on to anger and the uncertainty if I'll ever really know exactly what he thinks and why he wants from me what he does. That's when he looks in my direction—at least I think he does—but he doesn't wait. He enters the doors of the Holiday Inn like he doesn't plan on staying long. I don't believe he's headed upstairs to pack his bags, but I speed up in case he is.

# 9.

**UNLESS THEY'VE BEEN TRAVELING ALONG–AND NO**
one's confused Brother Ben and me with the Grateful Dead—the blues faithful who show up in Tuscaloosa, Auburn, Athens and Atlanta have no idea they're viewing the best shows of the tour. Onstage, without looking at one another or saying a word, we segue from song to song. The time between numbers has shortened, our tempo has quickened, and Ben's playing demonstrates a liveliness and spirit belying the fact he's played these songs thousands of times. We're so synchronized I could leave

## Sad to Be Alone

the stage during the middle of a song, take a piss, flush, wash my hands and dry them, then return to close out a number. Once we finish, though, we're back in the dressing room only to collect our cases, as Ben's suspended the impromptu jams. And when we depart, in step like Buck and Bubbles, you might think

we shared far more than a similar taste in polyester slacks and faux-silk shirts.

Offstage, though, we're not talking. Sunday morning in Memphis, I expected a lecture that would have made my mother's ultimatums seem like suggestions. Now, in this, our first silent period, I wish he'd hollered. Twice now I've pulled up to a Ramada, watched Ben go to the reception desk and return with two different keys. No wink, not even the barest hint of a grin. From there, we set our departure time for the show—holding up fingers and grunting or nodding like primitive tribesmen—then enter our separate rooms. In my drawers, on my double bed, I eat junk food without Ben's lectures to upset my digestion. Watch SportsCenter to check on the Red Wings and see if the Pistons have a shot in this year's playoff race. Play some Sonny Boy or Little Walter to exercise my diaphragm until I'm ready for a nap. When Ben knocks on my door, I change into my stage clothes. Lately, I've been fond of a suit that shimmers blue and black like those boat-tailed grackles who squawk and shit all over Jackson Square. But on the way to the venue, Ben and I don't joke or talk mess. Quitting's no longer on my mind, but now and then, I worry he might fire me. Could be the only logical move. We've played these same songs together so long, might be best for both of us to end this show. Yet I'd hate to separate when we sound so good together. Only thing for certain is that I still don't know the man's mind, and he's taking his time to tell me or isn't going to tell me at all.

• • •

In Jacksonville, our single Florida gig, Ben's met in the Holiday Inn lobby by some veterans of previous tours, none of whom notice he and Silent Sam don't have anything to say to one another. I slink to my non-smoking room on the third floor and change into my track suit. I need to talk, though. Not to these hangers-on, who only want my "sho's" and "Thank you's" and "suh's" anyway. My mother and Grover are out, as I don't know the Ghanaian exchange and know already her advice: quit. No chance with Ben either, even if he weren't tangled up with another half-dozen people who want to ask what Sleepy John Estes's neck felt like.

Which leaves me with Heywood, though my first three tries at his home number don't get answered. I check my watch and remember we've entered Eastern Standard Time. In Pine Bluff, Heywood's an hour behind. Hungry, I head downstairs, ignoring the other ten pounds I've put on, easy. Passing the lobby, I hear Ben coughing and wonder if it's sincere. Without a glance his way, I keep going. My trip to the vending machine yields two packs of cheese and crackers. I want coffee but settle for a rusty can of Mr. Pibb. A pay phone reminds me to try Heywood again, then a silver-haired fellow with a tan darker than Ben steps in my path to the stairs. A short guy, he smells of gin and grips my wrist. "Y'all were just great last night," he says. Wearing a possible toup, a red windbreaker with Western Alabama stitched on the breast, and black pants, he doesn't look like somebody who went to the Brother Ben show. Still, I mumble "'Preciate you," as only Silent Sam can.

"Good luck tomorrow," he says. He lets me go and flashes a thumbs up before wobbling off. Stitched on the back of his jacket is a basketball dropping through a hoop. Did that dude think I was a ballplayer? My friends at Troy did, because of the melanin, but I felt far more useful tending goal. Had the blues not come around, I might have played in high school, tried to become the next Grant Fuhr. Now I climb the stairs to my room. On my fourth call, Heywood answers. "Pete," he says. "I heard y'all won a Beale Street! But I'm hurt, bro. Why didn't you invite me?"

"I didn't know we were even going until the last minute," I say, which is still true: *I* didn't know.

"Still can't believe Ben went, let alone y'all won."

"Man even mentioned you and Bucket."

"Getting generous in his old age?"

"Maybe," I say. "Right now he's in the lobby entertaining about six cats."

"'Y'all must be blues people,'" Heywood says in Ben's voice. "Why aren't you meeting and greeting, too?"

"Reason I'm calling you," I say. "One of them, that is." I summarize the strangest tour of my career, hitting hardest on Detroit, Memphis, Robert Jr. and Michael Hunt. And it feels good to hear my own voice, uninterrupted, purging my mind of all that's sat there like garbage in a can. I bring him to the point I'm at now: alone in my room, having said nothing to Ben today except "Pothole," when he pulled into the parking lot. When I finish, my lungs let go as though I've been drawing long on a note. But Heywood doesn't speak. For about ten seconds, neither of us says a word. I've had all the silence I need. I say, "Heywood?"

He laughs, and I can't tell if he's mimicking Ben's stage laugh or mocking me. "Any more?" he says.

"Nope. That's where I'm at. Waiting until six pm to head on over for a seven-thirty show."

"You want advice?" he says, echoing Ben but also sounding like the schoolteacher he is. "Or did you just need to vent?" I feel like a troublemaker who doesn't know if Mr. Sharp's going to tell me a story or break a paddle on my tailbone.

"Either way I'm here for you, Pete. I am here for you."

"What would you do in my place?" I say.

"Apologize. I mean, what were you doing up in that club? Not only did you play without the man, you also didn't get paid. He would have been happier if you'd played on the sidewalk. Least that way you could bring home some quarters and split the take."

"Think that's what he's all about? Money?" I tossed that at Ben in Memphis and thought about it several times since. We aren't making any new music, aren't even talking about it, just adding the totals of gas, auto upkeep, meals and lodging, then subtracting them from our performance fees.

"Would that be wrong?" Heywood says. "Man's entitled to protect his money and his way of making it. He should be mad at you, Pete. Messing up his shit."

Now I wish I'd called my mother. "Still, I'm getting tired of this role," I say.

"What role?"

"Silent Sam," I say.

Heywood clears his throat, and I can hear the difference in our playing. We both play diatonics, but Heywood's so chesty, he always boomed each breath through the comb, where I'm more inclined to cupping my hands and letting them do a lot of the work. Another difference I realize is this: He never made the top ten list, and he was born south of the Mason-Dixon. But I'll save that jab for later. "You know what," he says. "I *miss* being Razor sometimes." He pauses, then, before I can reply, he says, "Sometimes."

"For real?"

Heywood laughs again. "Act like you're the only one playing a role. How'd you like to try the one I've got tomorrow, an obsequious teacher at a rundown school who can't piss off the superintendent on his annual tour of campus?"

I'll admit, that sounds rough but doesn't distract me from what he said earlier. "What could you possibly miss about being Razor?"

"You don't ever get tired of being Peter?"

I sip some Mr. Pibb and close my eyes, sit on the edge of my bed. From kindergarten to commencement, being Peter Owens did require a lot of effort. I far preferred the one who sat up in his bedroom with his harp and Sonny Boy on the stereo to the black friend who quote-unquote wasn't like those *others*. "Ok, sure," I say.

"Then just think how lucky you are to have Sam. A brother who doesn't have to be checking every step and mincing every word. A brother who can dump hot sauce on a plate of fried chicken and not feel ashamed. Anytime you want, you can step right into his shoes and do whatever you feel. Then you can straighten up and go back to being Pete. Who'll know the difference?"

"There's more to it than that, though."

"Like what?"

I drink some more Mr. Pibb, as if for courage. "Like that role and Ben kept me from playing with Robert Jr."

"Ever think about the dudes who'd like to be in Sam's place?"

And fuck if he hasn't snared me with that one. He must be a good teacher, one certain to let his students—who are ninety percent black and poor—learn to tackle problems on their own, yet not so enamored of them that they run wild in his classroom. Different from my mother, who insisted always there was one way only: be like her. Plus, he's got me thinking. On stage I never find myself wishing I were Peter. And those last few weeks before the tour's about to start? I can't wait to be Sam again. Can't let Heywood know this. He might just tell Ben. No telling where I'd be then.

Lounging on my bed, I hear Heywood talking and ask him to repeat himself. "Sounds like you're thinking you're the one who knows what's right," he says. "Unless you're absolutely certain, that's a dangerous place to be."

I swallow hard, then say-sing, "So sad to be lonesome, too much unconvinion to be alone," a line from Sonny Boy's "Sad to Be Alone."

Heywood says, "You sound good, Pete."

Ignoring the compliment, I say, "What should I do?"

"How long you two been on this tour?"

Forever, I'm thinking, but it's not even three months. I tell Heywood and he says, "So you went a little nutty. All those well-meaning white folks can get to a brother. You showed your ass a little. Now you're sorry. Just tell the man. He'll understand."

There's a pause, and I look at the clock on my nightstand like a sleeper waking before the alarm. In an hour or so, Ben will knock on the door, signaling me without a word it's time to get dressed and on the road. My shoulders flinch in anticipation of that knock, then Heywood says, "You don't think you're ready to take over, do you?"

"Naw," I say, a little too quickly. "I've still got a lot to learn," I say, in case this does get reported directly to Ben. "Why do you ask?"

"Just checking, Pete. Just checking."

• • •

Nearly fifty minutes later, Ben's at the door. I let him in and we nod, then I grab my harp case, two empty pint bottles and Ben's flask, slip my grackle jacket on and slide past the mirror above the dresser before my reflection greets me. To avoid saying it in Sam's voice, I don't apologize in the lobby, where, along with my curious admirer from earlier, a host of others in red jackets surround twelve cats in warmup suits and sneaks, most of them black and none shorter than six-two. After certifying the older man's mistake—imagine my doughy ass on any basketball team—I want to share with Ben the joke, but he's headed out the door. I catch up and get inside the Brougham, then clear my throat and say, "I'm sorry." Ben turns the key in the ignition. The massive engine rumbles and Ben consults directions to the venue, a just-completed fine arts complex on the North Florida University campus, then looks both ways. I apologize again but this time he glares, only his eyes stay on mine briefly as he cranes his neck to gauge oncoming traffic. In both directions, it's streaming pretty thick and fast and a left turn is apparently what we need to make. Still, I apologize a third time, loud as I can go without shouting.

Ben nods. "Heard you the first time," he says. "Question is, what are you sorry about?"

I'm sure before long I'll be forgiven, but Heywood simplified matters too much. I should have also consulted Ben's "Tell Me True," which he ends with, "Your sorry don't mean nothin', until you make it true." I'll have to humble myself, follow orders and not fly off on my own. "I messed up," I say, "Back in Memphis. Shouldn't have shown my ass like I did."

"I'm trying to look out for you, Pete. I don't know if I can go much longer . . . . Fuck," Ben says, a word I've heard from him before, but still surprising from his generally decorous mouth. I follow his eyes to the four-lane road, where traffic shows no signs of letting up and no driver recognizes the Last True Delta Bluesman and lets him enter the flow. His long fingers flex on the leather-covered steering wheel as breath issues harshly from his nose. I look east, then at my watch. As ever, we're more than early. If it takes thirty minutes, we'll still have an hour before showtime. Traffic should slacken. My concern is whether I've neared the end of my apology or have a long road of humility to travel. What did he mean he's looking out for me? And doesn't know if he can go much longer doing what? "You said," I stammer.

"Hold on," Ben says, and yanks the steering wheel hard to the right. The Brougham angles past some just-braking SUVs, and Ben slips us into the center turn lane, then guns it and gets us heading west as a series of car horns sound to our rear and front. I'm so impressed by this maneuver, my hands come together in applause, and my mustache ripples from the smile forming below. Only we don't get much chance to celebrate. A pair of blue lights rolls in the rear view and like many a black man brazen enough to demonstrate the potency of his vehicle in public, we've wound up on the wrong end of the law.

"Shit," Ben says, looking forward. "What did your mother tell you about getting pulled over?"

"Don't get pulled over," I say. I took so long learning how to drive because my mother's lessons involved more precautions to keep out of the back seat of a cop car than the basics of ten and two and always check the blindspot. Every time I get behind the wheel, I recall her tips: stay out of residential areas, drive just below the speed limit but not too slowly and wave at officers—but not with excessive familiarity. If these methods failed, my mother instructed me to keep my hands in plain sight on the wheel, wait for a request before I retrieved my license and registration, and to yes-sir and no-sir as much as Baa-Baa Black Sheep. Which I'm prepared to do now. But Ben says, "We'll be fine. Follow my lead."

Some silent minutes pass until I hear the car door behind us shut. I stay the urge to turn around, grip my shiny blue-black knees tighter. I doubt my Best Traditional Artist medallion would impress our officer, and it's rattling in my harp case in the trunk, anyway. Then in my peripheral vision, I see this cat: almost a parody himself in his mirrored shades and Marine high and tight, one hand hovering near his holstered handgun. My heels drum the floormat, as I await another performance from Ben, one demonstrating the depthless variety of his repertoire. I suspect this hardass leaning toward the window has in mind some movie or TV-cop as his model. And I've got a part to play, as well. Just want it to begin so we can finish and get to where I perform best.

"License and registration, please," the cop says, his drawl too redneck for me to relax. Sweat slips down both sides of my trunk. I chew my mustache but halt, fearing that motion resembles the swallowing of contraband.

Ben says, "Yes, suh," but not in as bright a voice as the one I hear backstage or in hotel lobbies. He hands over the documents, one at a time, his movements shaky, as if beset by a sudden palsy.

The cop inspects them, clips them to his clipboard. "Mr. Mabry," he says. "You nearly caused an accident back there. *Accidents*, you might could say. One when you pulled out the hotel lot, another when you forced your way into the westbound passing lane. You aware of this?"

Ben's chin begins to tremble. He keeps his hands on the steering wheel as proof he won't reach for whatever weapon the cop's imagining or hoping for. I flatten my hands on my thighs, wondering whether next year we should buy a Honda.

The cop says, "You hear what I said?" His syllables deliberate, his volume higher, the preferred American method of speaking to foreigners and half-wits.

"I hoid, suh," Ben says, sniffling, the molasses in his voice thicker than ever. "And you gots to b'lieve me when I says how sorry I am. Lawd must been lookin' out fo' me and them folks back air."

The cop flinches, wipes a black-gloved hand along the bare side of his narrow head. Traffic still rushes past, raising dust from the road. The cop coughs, leans back to Ben. "I don't know about that, but you understand that that's why I stopped you. Reckless operation of a vehicle."

"Lawd but I hopes everyone all right," Ben says, his head tilting forward, his shut lids squeezing out tears.

"No one was hurt," the cop says. "It's just . . . " He stops, rubs a finger over his chin and turns to Ben's drivers license. "Just what brings you to Florida, Mr. Mabry?"

So here it is. Bad enough Ben was reckless—though I doubt the retirees slaloming through lanes in their Caddies earn more than a warning—we're dressed like pimps, operating a vehicle preferred by drug dealers, and an out of state one, to boot. Suddenly the timely arrival at the Fine Arts Center isn't a concern: Staying out of the Jacksonville city tank is. I read the cop's nametag and wonder if Officer Reese ever shed a tear for a song sung by Charlie Pride or O.B. McClinton. If it helps, I'll get out my harp and play "Okie From Muskogee."

Ben lifts his head, sniffles, and says, "My son and I here to look at some them whatchamacallits? What is they, junior?" He turns to me. Fuck if he doesn't wink. His son? We don't even look alike. "Them houses," he continues. "The connecteded kind."

"Retirement home?" Officer Reese says.

"No suh," Ben says. "Start with a c. Kuh-kuh-kuh."

My cue, I guess. I stammer, "Condominium," getting stuck on the c and losing track of how many m's are needed. I know Ben's scheming to make us seem harmless—not sharp or belligerent—and Officer Reese is now smiling at us, though he does click his ballpoint pen.

"That's it," Ben says. "Lookin at some them conda, conda, conda . . . . What you say, junior?"

"Condos," Officer Reese says. "That's what folks down here would say."

"That do make it easier," Ben says, rising up, gaining some inflection. Quickly, though, his shoulders slump. "But they some kinda expensive. Seem like I might be stayin' in Mississippi fo' my retarment."

"Y'all been looking just in Jax or elsewhere?" Officer Reese says and his chin juts forward, as if tugged by the line Ben's unspooled. I believed Ben wanted to expedite matters, get our ticket and make the show, but now I wonder if he hopes to skate past the fine, as well. So far, Officer Reese hasn't written anything, and his posture softens as Ben catalogues the expensive condo fees from Pensacola to Tallahassee and other points along I-10 that he, a simple Mississippi shipyard worker, encountered. He keeps swaddling himself in this stereotype until the infraction's nearly forgotten. And now he completes it: "And after I spent so much my pension on this here Cadillac, I can't be payin' no 800 hundred dollar a month." He then leans on the cough. His wheezing delivery gets Officer Reese's attention even further. Finally, he clears his throat and chuckles. "I wants to leave somethin' behind for my boy here, but oncet I saw this here car I said, 'Give me one nice car to ride in before some hearse take me to the boneyard.'"

Officer Reese's smile seems a permanent feature on his pink and unlined face. Just a kid he is. He clicks his ballpoint again, looks my way. "Your daddy's got a lot to say, don't he?"

"Y-y-y-yesss, suh," I stammer, pushing out my lower lip with my tongue and keeping my mouth open and wet.

"You both'll try and keep this Caddy in one lane from here on in?"

"Yessuh," Ben and I both say, his delivery crisp, mine dripping with spit.

"All right then," Reese says, pocketing his pen. He hands Ben back the license and registration. "Hope y'all enjoy the rest of your stay in the Sunshine State."

Ben waits until Reese is back in his car, then starts up the Brougham. The first breath of AC is welcome on the tight skin of my face. My armpits aren't as sweaty as I lift my hands from my knees at last. "Forget what I said earlier," Ben says.

I nod, flex my fingers, expel a breath so loud and long you'd think I'd been holding it since we left Memphis. Willing to forget, I'm still not sure what he was saying in the first place.

"All's forgiven," Ben says, then steers back into the street when a space opens.

"Lead the way, Pop," I say and lean back in my seat.

• • •

Our reputation for promptness still intact, but just barely, Ben and I arrive with five minutes to spare, leaving us no time for anything but park the car and meet the Fine Arts Center's nervous manager and his ugly wife. Then we hit the stage, where in our customary places—Ben on a folding chair, me standing to his right—we rock the house. The thousand or so concertgoers, most of whom saw us here last year in a drama theater, receive not only another in a series of hot shows, but the best, you ask me, of the tour so far. Tonight Ben sounds as though he really did smoke dynamite and drink T-N-T, as he scorches the strings with his slide and ups the volume of his voice past its typical Delta moan to a slightly citified holler. When we segue from "Big Legged Woman" to "Call Me Your Lovin' Man," I open my eyes and realize I haven't been examining the crowd tonight. Almost feels Ben and I aren't really playing for them but for each other. Perhaps it's adrenalin from escaping a ticket, but I hear traces of that rough and raw sound I heard first so long ago from Sonny Boy. And when it seems we can't push past the limits True Delta Blues imposes on us, Ben says, "Blow Sam," and allows me a solo of two choruses. I push those notes around like they looked at my woman and need a reminder not to try that shit again. When I finish, I turn to Ben and wave my harp. He says into the mic, "Call the fire department. That harp's smoking." Then, when he begins the final verse of "Back to Jackson"—"Doan wanna leave here angry, doan wanna find someone to blame"—I stick the harp back in my mouth but play with my arms stretched out and flapping, a trick I learned from Sonny Boy. With his nimble lips, he could hold the harp like a cigar and still play. Since I still have my teeth, I won't try that. Instead, I bring my hands back to my harp, match Ben's quick pace through the final notes, then wait, my heart racing, to hear his foot tapping out "Take My Chance."

• • •

More people linger near the dressing room after the show but Ben gets us out quickly by faking two narcoleptic spells. I take his arm while he hangs on and mumbles to the disappointed guitarists about giving all he can and having nothing left in the tank. When we get in the Brougham, he hands me the keys, laughing louder than I've heard him in some time but yawning too, a sign the can't-keep-my-eyes-open-a-minute-more routine is somewhat real, at least for tonight. I take my turn at the wheel then, keeping it slow—but not too slow—on the way back to the hotel.

It's ten o'clock when we return to our separate rooms, a little early for us without a post-show jam. I suspect Ben's getting ready to sleep—I thought I heard him snoring on the drive home—but my legs feel loose while my hands flutter and flex. If I hadn't called Heywood earlier, I'd be back on the phone with him. Problem is I can't quit imagining some other ways Ben and I might enliven our gigs, our career even. A sensible voice keeps insisting that tonight's show was one of a kind, not to be duplicated tomorrow night in Columbia or the next night in Greenville. We'll resume the solemn pace of the True Delta Blues and leave behind that racehorse tempo we had running tonight. We'll be the Brother Ben and Silent Sam who earned Best Traditional Artist for keeping the blues unchanged from the days of 78s spinning on victrolas. After some minutes of pacing in my room, exhausting the TV's possibilities and even paging through the Gideon, I think back upon our route home and recall a convenience store within walking distance—Ben's got the keys—and grab my hat, convinced a taste is will calm me down.

The walk's longer than I expected, and the air's thick and muggy. I arrive at the 7-11, breathing heavy and hoping my funk's not too strong. A pair of college-aged blondes looks at me as I hold open the door. I almost allow myself to think they're staring at me, instead of this suit that should be on the racks of a costume shop. Their giggling fades as I find the cooler and debate over a quart or a sixer. I haven't had another drink since Memphis. Six might wipe me out. The quart of Bud fits my hand and feels damp and cold rolling against my forehead. For a minute, I feel another pair of eyes on me and look up  in the rear corner of the store, where a curved mirror traps my tiny image. At the end of the snack aisle, a clerk turns around, headed for the checkout stand, but he lets me see he's watching my every step. He's a little bit darker than the white folks I've seen all day, even if I doubt he's a brother. His head's shaved to stubble but his head's a little blocky and his eyebrows thick and black. Hispanic most likely. Cuban if I had to guess.

When I reach the end of the aisle, I spot his hands reaching under the counter. Hope he's not grabbing the store shotgun. What he is doing becomes clear after he lifts his boombox and places it on a stool behind him. The music playing, though, can't be what I think I hear. I've fallen for this joke twice now, thinking somehow "Take My Chance" is playing on the radio. Again, though, it sounds unmistakable: That's Ben's guitar, that's my harp, yet the first instrumental bars keep getting recycled, and I hear us play that intro twice without hearing Ben sing, "Some folk say she's from Louisiana, some say she come from Paris, France." But this clerk can't be a blues fan, can he? Curtis Salgado plays a fierce guitar, and when he's not picking his solos faster than I can process the notes I could listen to Santana a good long time. On the counter, I place my bottle next to a display of a handsome black couple ecstatic over Newport cigarettes opposite an equally happy white couple lighting Winstons. As the intro plays again, I consider telling the clerk his CD's skipping while quieting my desire to claim responsibility for the harp playing. Only now I don't hear us. In our place, some bombastic brother raps, "Take . . . My . . . Chance, like Brother Ben did. N2K's here, to knock you out, kid."

"One-seventy-five," the clerk says, grabbing a paper sack for my quart and snapping it open, all the while grooving with the elastic rhythm of the hip hop number. I can't follow. Don't understand but every other word that's rapped and can't get over the fact we've been sampled. Thought that happened to James Brown, George Clinton, and other architects of fat, bass-heavy grooves, a category Ben and I have never been grouped in.

"One-seventy-five," the clerk says again, both hands around my bagged bottle of beer. He's even twisted the bag around the neck so I can drink easily in whatever lonely place he's imagined me heading.

I fish out five, place it next to his left hand. My change comes back quickly, though we're still the only ones in the 7-11. I reach for my bottle. The song on the boombox quiets, then fades, replaced by a hymn to big booties and skirts too short to cover them. The clerk nods his shaved head to this as well. I wonder if, sober as I am, I've been hallucinating. If I wasn't, things are still hazy, as I believed no one was allowed to lift a cymbal crash or synth riff without obtaining permission first. And Ben owns the rights to all his songs—that is, Wilton Mabry does.

The clerk coughs, a reminder to get going. I watch his eyes close as he mouths the words to the new song playing. In my own voice, I say, "That song. The one before this one. What's it called?"

" 'Out For Mines,'" he says crossly.

" 'Out for Mines,'" I say. "Who does it? What group?"

Sighing, he rolls his eyes. "N2K Posse," he says. "They the bomb."

His sudden homeboyism startles me. " N2K Posse?" I say.

"Niggas two thousand, yo," he says, then cups his hand around his mouth and hoarsely barks three times, which may mean something to him and others but serves as a signal for me to pick up my bottle and leave before things get stranger.

• • •

Back at the Holiday Inn, I stand outside Ben's room. This whole tour makes more sense now: Much, if not all, of the strangeness has been scripted by the master, in order to keep me occupied and unaware of the fact he's sold us out to some idiot rappers who probably don't know the difference between Bo Diddley and Bo Peep. My first knock doesn't summon him. None of his yawns and fatigue seemed part of an act earlier, but if anything's worth waking him it's to find out why he didn't think he could tell me. Wouldn't be the first time for that, now would it? And I'm getting weary of being the punch line of that joke. The next knock and the one after that don't bring him to me. I won't wear out my knuckles and don't want to wake the neighbors and wind up kicked out of the hotel. So I enter my room, call the front desk and ask for Ben, but the sleepy-sounding young woman who answers claims that guest has placed a block on all calls until his wake-up at six-fifteen. I look at my watch. Seven hours to wait. I take a sip of beer, but it's warmer than I'd like, and its thirty-two ounces is nowhere near what I need to quiet the noise in my head.

• • •

"Of course I gave them permission," Ben says. "But at a price, Pete. A good one, too."

Headed to South Carolina on I-95, he tells me this over the hiss of the AC and a Fletcher Henderson tape. Angry is how I've wanted to sound since I woke at seven, but each sentence out of my mouth has mewled and whined. I try again: "Why didn't you tell me the first time I heard it? I thought I was hearing things, and you knew it was us on the radio."

"They never told me when they were going to use it or when the record would come out." Ben says. Traffic around the downtown Jacksonville exits keeps us from moving too fast. Ben keeps scrutinizing the vehicles ahead and I can't detect any shiftiness or catches in his voice. Sounds like he's telling the truth, but when you lie as much as he has, you're bound to get pretty good at it.

I say, "I asked you twice about us on the radio. You denied it both times."

"I really didn't hear. Either time."

"And all this I-forgot-to-tell-you-Pete shit? You didn't make it up to keep me confused all tour?"

"Cross my heart."

"When you cross your heart to someone, you're not supposed to tell a lie," I talk-sing, again raiding the endless supply of Sonny Boy references.

"Pete," Ben says, flashing a white-toothed smile—he hasn't put the gold sleeves on yet. "You have been practicing, haven't you? Was some good in separate rooms, wasn't there?"

"That's not what I want to talk about." I look away. Don't want him to see his compliment has got me smiling. Composed, I say, "I need you to tell me there's no more surprises on this tour. I need to hear that everything between here and Maine is going to go as smoothly as it's ever gone."

Ben turns down the volume of the Henderson tape. "I can't make the world hold still," he says.

"That's not what I mean. You need to tell me right now, is there anything, anything, that you haven't told me of?"

He shakes his head. I'm about to say that's not good enough, that I need to hear him tell me. That's when he turns, his eyes clear. "Nothing else, Pete," he says. His right hand releases the wheel and he pinches his chin with his thumb and forefinger, just as the cars ahead of us start moving. The Brougham's engine roars briefly, but Ben slows us down when the odometer's needle nears the speed limit, as if he's wary from last night's near calamity. I sigh, thinking I've got what I need for now, maybe. Then Ben says, "But you never know." He laughs his stage huh-*huh* and smiles. "World's a funny place. A lot can happen, Pete. A whole helluva lot."

# 10.

## AT LEAST WE'RE SHARING A ROOM AGAIN. NOW I

can make certain Ben's not plotting some new trick. Still, even though I'm close enough to touch him—or punch, kick and strangle—Ben can always retreat to that place I've never fully entered: his clever and cunning mind.

I think I've figured out, at least in part, why he allowed "Take My Chance" to be sampled, aside from the hefty pricetag he dangled—a figure he hasn't yet shared. After our shows these past two weeks, from South Carolina to last night in Pittsburgh, we've heard told in emotion choked voices that we are definitely the preservers of the True Delta Blues, a music as rich as the soil from which it sprung, and that there's no one else like us in the wide world. Ordinarily, in such backstage scenes, I'd find my place on the periphery, waiting for either Ben's order to take him home or join in on the jam (lately, it's been "Take me home, Sam" a lot more than usual), but with N2K Posse's "Out 4 Mines"—spelled, as it is, with a 4 in place of the preposition—climbing the charts like a monkey, people need to share their outrage and commiserate with Ben and me. No one among the blues faithful suspects The Last True Delta Bluesman. They think of him as the most guileless creature to exist outside of fairy tales and believe N2K Posse outright swiped the opening bars of "Take My Chance" or the old villain, Wilton Mabry, has once again put profit over all else and sold out hapless Brother Ben. Either way, Ben's the victim and needs his legions to turn out and show they're on his side. Which has now twice, in College Park and Richmond, required a change from quieter, thousand seat venues, to larger auditoriums. Still

## Fattening Frogs for Snakes

no brothers and sisters in the mix, but on the mid-Atlantic leg of the tour I've seen some of the biggest crowds of my life and heard some declarations that make me wish I was the man people believed. One woman in Chapel Hill said, "What I can't understand is that these young men don't have more respect for Brother Ben, as a fellow musician and an African American at that." I don't know the young brothers in hip-hop, though I doubt any has a memory that creeps beyond 1978 or whenever rap broke big in the Bronx. Ben just coughed and wheezed and said, "I doan know, ma'am. Young folks today doan seem in'erested in no blues. Least these fellas knows my name."

This afternoon, in the City of Brotherly Love, we've got a whole day to lie around, as we play Temple's Center for the Performing Arts tomorrow. I'm looking forward to a day of cleaning my harps, cutting my hair leisurely, catching up on the Pistons' fate. A cheesesteak from Pat's is a must. But while I'm removing the dried spit and gunk from my Hohner, Ben takes his guitar out of his case. I put down my Q-tips and hydrogen peroxide, blow on my Marine Band. "What's up?"

Ben says, "Loose bridge," then plucks the heavy E with his thumb, creating a rattling and doleful sound.

"What's the cure?" I say. "Super Glue?"

"Irreparable," Ben says, flinging the guitar to his bed. It lands with a thump and an out-of-tune peal. "Care to look for a new one with me?"

I want to believe otherwise, but I'm still not convinced there's nothing but easy hours and simple days awaiting us—there haven't been more than two this whole tour—and I at least want my eyes open instead of shut. "All right," I say.

"Maybe you'll give me a cut when we get back?" Ben says.

"Will do."

In minutes, we're out of the room and the Holiday Inn Express. It's track suit weather at our bus stop but rainy. The Brougham's in the hotel's garage, as Ben figures we'd have a hard time parking the thing on Philly's narrow streets. Still, we catch the right bus like a pair of longtime SEPTA riders, though it's not to any majestic music store we're headed. He might stand by Dean Markley strings, but Ben feels no particular loyalty to Gibson or Fender, Martin or Guild. In fact, as Mabry, he's turned down endorsement deals to maintain his vaunted authenticity as Ben: With his no-name axes he appears frugal, if not cheap, and his playing sounds all the more impressive, coming from a guitar probably made out of Taiwanese balsa.

Rain's still falling when we exit the bus, waving to the smiling, high-yellow driver as if this is our everyday route. I wonder if it's sunny and eighty in New Orleans, while Ben locates his pawn shop—the smallest, dingiest and most nondescript of several nearby—a place called Pierce Loans. The bell above the door clangs once as we walk in on an older woman in a headscarf and overcoat haggling with the white-haired owner behind the counter. Between them rests a top-loading VCR. The woman points at it and says, "My son gave me this just a few years ago."

"A few?" the owner says. He leans back smiling, but his eyelids spring wide when he turns our way. Both hands disappear underneath the wooden counter, hovering over, I'm sure, the button that triggers the silent alarm. He's not even slick about it. "Help you gentlemen?" he says.

"Musical instruments," Ben says, in his everyday voice.

"In the back," the owner says, his snowy head rising to monitor us. I would have guessed Ben would go with a more Delta delivery, but judging from his present movement, he wants efficiency. A Mississippi accent might raise more questions than needed.

We pass jewelry and watch displays, squeeze past couches, stacked TV's and boomboxes, other VCR's, only to tangle ourselves among castoff trumpets, worn trombones and sad-looking violins. From up front, the woman says, "You can do fifty for this."

"Fifty?" the owner says. "Lady, the last time I got robbed at least they said 'Give me all your money, *please.*'"

I wipe away a laugh with my sleeve, snagging the material on some longer hairs of my mustache. Amusing as he is, I'm certain the owner's gathering details he'll need to give to the sketch artist for Ben and me. Dust fills my nose, as does a lingering odor of dried saddle soap. A sneeze doesn't help. I turn to locked accordions, a spiffy set of Ludwig drums, a bass with no strings. No harps, which doesn't mean somebody didn't try to sell any. No doubt the prime reason for these instruments being here is their ex-owners' poverty, though I'm sure some items were stolen or left behind with every intent of serving as collateral for a loan. I can't help but think about these phantoms. Who was a player just as good as Ben? Who quit when the rent was due? I've got no desire to buy anything, yet browsing here makes me feel like I'm taking something from someone more deserving.

"Like this?" Ben says. With his right hand, he holds a brown guitar by the neck. Doesn't have a pick guard, but that lack didn't stop the previous player from leaving a series of gouges beneath and above the sound hole. "Or this?" After picking up a blonder axe with his left hand, Ben moves them up and down.

"Both are pretty sorry," I say, then place a handkerchief over my nose and mouth.

"I don't know about that," Ben says, looking at the one in his left hand. Its body isn't as beat up, though it's hard to tell if the color is original or faded by the sun, and it's missing two middle strings. "That thing was left too many afternoons in the back seat of a car," I say.

"Neck might be a little warped," Ben says, holding it closer. I'm envisioning a spoiled suburbanite who couldn't play like Hendrix by New Year's Eve, then sold his Xmas present to buy dope. Meantime, the shop's owner and his customer still bicker over the VCR. Ben hangs the brown guitar where he found it. He strikes the strings of the other, shaping a sound the least musical among us would recognize as badly out of tune.

"Put it out of its misery," I say.

"Not yet," Ben says, leaning against an old Philco radio, tightening the pegs, then strumming an E chord that sounds empty and sharp. The owner and customer aren't talking as Ben tunes the four strings and in no time his nimble fingers race down to the bottom of the neck, filling the cramped space with bright, slippery notes that surprise me with their individual clarity yet fit together as neatly as stones in a setting. I have my harp, of course, but he's playing too fast. He plucks a last note, winks at me, and strides past, at his full height, carrying the guitar by its neck. I follow him to the counter, where Ben says, "How much?"

Out of his shirt pocket, the owner removes a pair of glasses and slips them on. "Seven-fifty," he says, reading the faded ink on the pricetag.

"You play beautifully," the woman says, tugging tighter her scarf. "Are you a musician?"

Ben looks at me, then shakes his head. "Sometimes, ma'am," he says. "Every now and then."

• • •

Back on the bus, Ben keeps the guitar pressed between his feet and his knees, and he stares out the window. I say, "Charlie Christian."

"Pardon?" Ben says, turning to face me, his eyes showing amusement, as if he knows exactly what I mean.

"Back there in the pawn shop," I say, sitting up in my seat. "That little run you played."

Ben looks away, but I catch the smile. "Eddie Lang," he says. "If you want the truth. A white dude, too, believe it or not."

Ignorant of jazz and much of its history, I nod. My tastes are ordinary, confined to the big names: Davis, Ellington, Armstrong. Can't stand Wynton Marsalis. Wouldn't cross Bourbon if he were playing for free on the other side. I begin to say something about Lonnie Johnson but think better of it. Then Ben says, "There's a Kinko's. Better check my email."

He spreads his knees, picks up the guitar and stands. When the bus stops we hustle off. We enter the Kinko's together, headed for a long table with MAC's on one side, PC's on the other. My address is etephcim@hotmail.com, which anyone who cared to unravel it would know to be Mich—as in Michigan—Pete spelled backward (Ben knew on the first guess.) Even at home, I only check it maybe once or twice a week. What fan mail I get arrives at Mabry Enterprises, Inc. in Jackson and typically features one or all of these questions: What kind of harp do you play? How long have you been playing? Is Brother Ben going to cut a record soon? But I don't reply. Ben does, as Mabry, in order to preserve the perception Sam's only slightly more literate than Ben. Today, I suspect there might be email from my mother. Few people in New Orleans know my address, and fewer know me well enough to care if I'm gone.

Now I find nothing but junk in my Inbox. Not even one from Heywood, which I was hoping for. So I write him at his school address, keeping it clean in case a colleague might be in the room when he reads it. Main thing I wonder is if he's heard of N2K Posse. I'm sure his students have. Maybe I'll arrange a visit to Pine Bluff—I've promised to come up before—so I can play for his students my tiny contribution to "Out 4 Mines." I also include news of Ben's seven-dollar guitar, then send along the message. You ask me, there'll soon be a blues released about e-mail. "Done looked in my Inbox," I muse, "ain't no messages for me." I log off, wait for my bill to print out. Ben's on his feet and headed toward the printer, which spits out my bill and his. "I'll get these," he says, then moves past me to the cashier. I walk outside, where the rain has stopped. Like an ordinary Philadelphian of color, I purchase a Kenya AA from the shop next door. When I exit, sipping my coffee, the Kinko's door opens. Ben clutches my wrist. He says, "Remember how I told you the world wasn't going to stop for just the two of us?"

● ● ●

Get this: N2K Posse, whose existence was unknown, I *thought*, to both of us a few weeks ago, has started a tour of their own. Two nights ago, they played Boston, followed by a date in Hartford—two sellouts. Their next stop's Manhattan, where we haven't played in years. Our Empire State gigs are in Binghamton, Ithaca, Syracuse and Albany—the college towns. Yet the Posse wants us, if we've the time, to swing by Madison Square, where we can meet the fellows in the group, pose for some photos, and stay for the rest of the show, if we like.

Ben claims he had no hand in arranging this. Printed out the email to prove the idea came straight from N2K's manager, Darnell Fuller. There's no protest I can raise, only suspicions. Maybe he hoped for such an invitation but didn't plan on it. Already the promotional gears in Ben's head are grinding and, to be true, probably have been since he licensed the sample. Whatever the case, this visit backstage, he's now claiming, is the most important stop on the tour—much more than the Philly and Binghamton gigs—and what everything else has been leading up to. "Imagine, Pete," he says, as we sit in our room. "If just ten percent of their crowd—five!—gets turned on to 'Take My Chance?'"

I don't say anything, but I have concerns. Whether you call it rap or hip hop, I know it's huge and has even crossed over the way blues did way back when. Yet I'm no willing listener. Some rap has real power and energy, and, yes, authenticity. No MC alive is as creative as Sonny Boy, but with that opinion I'm—as usual—in the minority. Still, for all its potency, rap's like a bulldozer. It only works in one direction: plowing right over you. Rare is the number that lightens your spirit. If it does, then people dismiss it as superficial. The other stuff often troubles me, especially when it's endlessly fascinated with keepin' it real, as if "real" can only be defined by money, bitches and guns. I'll never join the ranks of those like my mother who want rap's voices monitored or silenced. Lord knows they'd want to shut Ben and me down next, what with our celebrations of drinking and womanizing and picking up firearms with ill intent. But rap isn't for me. Blues got there first. Reached inside and never let go.

"Cheer up, Pete," Ben says, springing up and rubbing my head. "You act like I'm making you go to the dentist."

Don't need a mirror to know I look sullen, so I turn away. "You're still scanning the crowd every night," Ben says. "And what kind of audience might these little chumps bring to us?"

Now I close my eyes, as if to shut down the channel he's using to read every thought I cart around. He moves closer, touches my shoulder with his hand. He could keep me in this place if he wanted. He's that strong or I'm that weak. "Who knows?" Ben says. "Maybe an appearance with these boys will get us enough momentum to head back in the studio. After this tour's over."

That motherfucker. Long ago, when I learned of all his manipulations, I thought I'd never succumb to them. Yet, fully aware of his game, I let my eyes open, shining with a light that tells him I'm on his side.

• • •

Practice, practice, practice, goes the joke about getting to Carnegie Hall. Getting to Madison Square should require the same, yet here Ben and I are, on our way in a cab. Thanks to the invite of a group of black youth that, if I saw them on a side street in the Quarter, I'd likely shift my wallet to my front pocket, pick up my pace, and look for a cab, cop or crowd in a well-lit street.

It's not our first time in Manhattan. My first couple of tours, when we still played bars, we'd hit a place in the Village called The Dixie Mission, but Ben started getting tired of second hand smoke about the time the owners switched to an all country format. He's not been able since to find any venue willing to host us, which disturbed me at first—this was New York City, after all—but in truth we get more affection from the faithful upstate.

Now, stalled on Seventh Avenue, Ben's cell plays a few notes from " 'Round Midnight." "Mabry," he says. He recites a few uh-huhs, then says, "Ben and Sam are going out of their way to do this. We're on a tight budget and itinerary." This is the savvy businessman I wish my mother could see. Hear, that is, because unquestionably her eyes would narrow at what he's wearing. She'd let the sober black suit pass but the tomato red shirt with matching pocket square and socks would make her nostrils flare. "All right, then," Ben says. "Why don't you make that call right away."

"What's that?" I say, opening the pages of *Peep This*, the magazine that claims to be the "Voice of the Hip Hop Nation," and turn it to the profile of N2K Posse. Found it in a newsstand this afternoon, while Ben was taking the Brougham through a car wash.

"Fuller. The manager," Ben says, turning off his phone and slipping it in the inner pocket of his suit. "Just agreed to pay for our room."

"All right." Armed with info from *Peep This*, I've been waiting to needle Ben. I say, "Thought you might have been speaking with 2-SLO, Marv-E-Lus, Tastee and DJ Spin-sation-L."

His hard look might have withered me five years ago, but I've seen worse. "What are you talking about?" he says.

"N2K Posse," I say. "Your boys."

"My boys," Ben says, chuckling.

"Their manager's Af Am, right?"

"What makes you think that?"

"Darnell?" I say. "Doubt there's many white boys with that handle."

"Maybe he changed it from Edward or Chad," Ben says. "Show he's down."

"Right," I say, as the cab moves forward. This time, Ben didn't fool with any lessons on humility. Doorman at the Sheraton hailed one for us. A breeze now enters my slightly opened window and ruffles the collars of my tan suit and iridescent shirt. We left Philly so fast I didn't even get a cheesesteak, so I'm thinking of what I used to eat when we played The Dixie Mission. A few slices of pizza or a gyro or falafel might fill me up. Ben starts whistling, quietly at first, and I lean in when he's switched over to the words: "If I can make it there, I'll make it, dat-dat, anywhere." He needs a swipe with my porkpie, so I smack him across the shoulders. Doesn't stop him. "It's up to you," he continues. "New York, New York."

• • •

"Brother Ben and Sam Stamps," says a tall, fashionable brother outside the dressing rooms. Can only be Darnell Fuller. The color of drugstore cigars, with a *GQ* wardrobe, he has a perfectly smooth head and designer glasses. His subtle cologne practically defines him as a manager, and his Italian loafers are the best shoes I've seen since Mr. Habib's. Then again, sandals, workboots and ripped Chuck Taylor's appear regularly on the feet of the blues faithful.

"Mist' Fuller," Ben says, his left fingers curled and trembling while he reaches toward Fuller's manicured hand. When Fuller pauses and his smile fades, Ben explains about his "picking fingers," adding, "I doan even let Sam here touch 'em."

"Oh," Fuller says. He shakes my hand, his fingers dry as he tugs me forward. Then he hands over all access badges on cloth loops. I mime uncertainty until he says, "You wear it like a necklace." Ben dangles his badge, making it twirl as his pretends to be mesmerized by the dazzle and shine. "We need to get us some these, Sam," he says.

Impatient, Fuller watches us, his chin resting in the L shaped by his thumb and upraised forefinger, the thoughtful Malcolm X pose I saw affected a lot in my Black Studies class. An MLK fan, I chew my mustache and await the next order, which is to follow Fuller as he approaches two massive, dark, dark brothers with huge arms folded, square heads on wide necks, both as expressionless as bricks and just as dense. "Here we are, gentlemen," Fuller says, shaking his Rolex on his wrist, as we enter, Ben shuffling so slowly one of the security guards leans toward him, as if fearful of the old man's collapse. Knowing Ben, I'm sure he's taking his time to read the room. And as I look in over his shoulder, I see just what a spectacle it is. During my time touring, I've changed in rooms no bigger than my apartment's walk-in closet and as empty and drafty as unfinished houses, but this space provides an altogether new experience. Wide screen TV on one wall, lighted make up tables opposite. A huge rack of clothes in the back, standing next to four exercise machines. A carpet so plush my feet sink. Long sofas and chairs big and deep enough for two. Nothing here like the director's chairs we ordinarily slump in. My hand reaches toward the enormous food table, where five open pizza boxes lie, each pie as wide as a truck tire. Fuller tells us to help ourselves, yet Ben clears his throat, a suggestion to leave it alone. I stick my hands in my jacket pockets, rubbing my Marine Band as if it were a rabbit's foot, counting the bottles of Cristal massed by the waxy-looking display of fruit, cheese and vegetables.

"Those boys doan eat no chitlins, do they?" Ben says, letting the light catch his gold-sleeved teeth.

Fuller winces, shakes his head. About chitlins, I agree with the face he's making, but now, with Ben, feign amazement. "Thought they's southern boys," Ben says to me. "From No'th Ca'lina?"

"What I thought," I mumble.

Ben turns to Fuller. "Is they?"

"Well, yes, but . . ."

Holding up one hand, Ben slowly shakes his head, tucks his chin close to his open collar. "I know, I know. Times be changing."

I steer him toward a sofa and he falls into it as if his bones done give out. Just then, at the back of the room, four young men and three times as many young women stream into the dressing room. I'm sure they're the Posse, and as they get closer, I recall the faces from the profile in *Peep This*. There's 2-Slo in the Timberlands, baggy jeans and Oakland Raider jacket, his braids tight and shades drooping on his nose. He's followed by DJ Spin-Sation-L, who sports a Carolina Panther jersey, loose, shiny track pants and whiter than white sneakers. Jordans, I'm guessing. Light-skinned Tastee and squatty Marv-E-Lush both wear tank tops and baggy jeans belted around mid-thigh. Tastee's hair looks as though James Brown's hairdresser relaxed it, while Marv and the DJ have wobbly afros that carry a strong fragrance of pot. Much gold abounds. On fingers, around necks, in ears. 2's entire lower jaw seems encased in it. The girls—that's how young they look—are like clones: same hair weaves with cascading curls, tight dresses exposing augmented chests, skinny legs and high heels. They scrap to get closest to the rapper of their choice. Still seated behind me, Ben coughs, a few harsh notes to warm up for the room-clearer he probably plans on for later. Suddenly, Fuller steps between me and Marv, a brother so young his forehead glistens with grease and a recently popped zit pulses red on his nose. "Fellows," Fuller says. "This is Brother Ben and Sam Stamps."

"My grandmomma had y'all's records," Marv says and daps my fist with his, then stoops to hug Ben around the neck. After Marv gets up and grabs a bottle of Cristal off the table, an orderly procession follows, with each member of N2K offering me a handshake and Ben a hug along with some scripted line of gratitude. All the while, Darnell Fuller nods at each client, directing them to their own bottles as if in reward for spending time with we representatives of the last century of black aesthetics. All four bust open their bottles and start guzzling the champagne straight. 2-Slo wipes his mouth with his silver jacket sleeve and says, "Y'all want some Crissy?"

I shoot out my cuffs and shake my head. Ben sits up a little in his seat, reaches in his pocket. "Brought mah own, youngblood." He raises his flask, uncaps it, then tilts back his head for a swallow of caffeine free Diet Dr. Pepper. We didn't even flavor it with bourbon this time. Still, N2K all raise their bottles, DJ Spin-Sation-L saying, "Awright, Bro' Ben." Ben passes me the flask but I refuse it, waving my hands and stammering, "I ain't foolin' with that homemade."

The door to the dressing room opens, and one of the security guards escorts in a wiry Anglo with a backwards baseball cap and two cameras hanging from his neck. "Mr. Fuller?" the guard says. "Man here to see you."

"Excuse me, gentlemen," Fuller says, walking swiftly past Ben and me toward the photographer. Tastee plops down across from Ben on one of the sofas, picks up the remote and turns on the TV. In the *Peep This* profile, the writer, one Mustafa Hamwi, claimed the four were "two hundred percent hard, yo" and "roughneck as they wanna be." Such overblown praise makes me think these boys are no more survivors of Black America's meanest streets than I am. Didn't Tupac go to prep school? Didn't MC Run graduate from St. John's? Yet the tattoos seem too ghetto to be counterfeit. When Tastee's joined on the sofa by Marv for a game of *John Madden Football* on their PlayStation, pit bulls and gothic letters and broken chains sprawl across their arms and chests. Marv even has a sizeable cross on the back of his neck. I rub my hands over my sleeves, grateful this shit comes off.

"All right now," Darnell Fuller says, his voice as accentless as mine. Wonder if he too hails from the Midwest. "Jake here"—he points at the photographer, who shows us a clenched fist—"is going to get some shots. Why don't we set up around Brother Ben?"

"Gotcha nigga," Marv-E-Lush shouts, standing and pumping the buttons of his joystick. Beside him, Tastee rises, bumping his shoulder into Marv's but not preventing, on the screen, Marv's Carolina Panther from crossing the goal line and doing his touchdown dance.

"Fellas," Fuller says. "We don't have time to play."

When all four grumble and moan, I realize exactly how young they are, how much like children they appear despite their tattoos, dope and champagne. Moved about like manikins in a front window, they stand in a circle, behind Brother Ben, adopting poses and mugging like the kids in the Quarter who tap dance with bottle caps on their soles. Jake, the photographer, asks if there's a guitar, as it would be a nice prop across Ben's lap, but Ben didn't bring his and the closest thing to a musical instrument among N2K's equipment is a drum machine. Fuller asks if I've got my harp—he says harmonica—and Ben chuckles. "Doan go nowhere without it," he says, but Jake, snapping already from different angles, says no one could see it in a group shot.

I'm right behind Ben, my hands to my side, not smiling, as that's the look I conjure for photographs taken of Ben and me. As always, he'll smile while I'll wind up looking as scared or fierce as I did on the back of *Blues At Your Request*. There's plenty of photos of bluesmen, some gimmicky, others, usually candids, that show a genuine side of the subject. Who can forget Mr. Johnson's? Not the smiling dandy in the publicity photo for Vocalion, the other one, clearly posed—with his guitar and dangling cigarette—in a photo booth. Scholars say he looks like a "mean customer" or "someone you wouldn't want to meet in a dark alley," which, to be true, are phrases you hear about someone as harmless as me or as menacing as Mike Tyson. In that photo, especially in Bob's wide, vulnerable eyes, I've always seen somebody who wanted to believe, as I did, that he wasn't the only one out there. Maybe that's me projecting onto Bob my own vulnerabilities. In Sonny Boy's many photos, he never showed anything deeper than the surface: seemed always to be cutting up or playing harp. And tonight, I follow his cue. I tilt my hat, slump my shoulders, and look straight ahead, let the camera do its work.

• • •

"You two staying around for the show?" Fuller says, putting his hand on Ben's shoulder, while in the center of the room, N2K gather in a circle, their lady friends standing apart by a few feet. "We'd really like to see what you think about the music."

"Sho nuff?" Ben says, yawning and wiping at his eyes. He's not faked a sleeping spell yet, and has held off on the cough. "Seem to me young folks doan care what us ole timers think."

"No, no," Fuller says, holding up a fist and shaking his watch. "They really admire your work." He looks up from Ben and nods at me. I return the nod, look back toward the silent huddle of rappers and girlfriends, which suddenly becomes a moving body, the rappers raising their hands and jumping up and down in unison until they all shout "Jesus!" Can't tell if they're cursing or praising his name. Either way, they break their huddle, the girls tug at their too-short dresses and curl their fingers in their mostly artificial hair. N2K's members place their hands on each other's shoulders, and march in place out the door with their security guards at the front and the girls bringing up the rear.

Ben turns, his head cocked to the side so his hatbrim shadows his face "That ain't what you tole Mist' Mabry," he says. "He said you tole him those youngsters never heard no blues except for maybe Mist' King. And that's 'cause he do so many commercials."

"Mabry told you that?" Fuller says, and for the first time, the confident Buppie, who no doubt has many more acts in his stable and a portfolio that rivals Ben's, looks as though he might not be the head nigga in charge. "He must have been mistaken," Fuller says, taking off his glasses and wiping them. He looks at me, then Ben, smiles and opens his mouth. Then he says, "Better check on the fellows before they hit the stage."

Fuller's out the door, leaving Ben and me as the only ones in the dressing room. Still, Ben waits another five seconds before turning to me. He stretches, lifts himself out of his slouch. "Up to you, Pete. Wanna leave?"

I shrug. "Something about that cat," I say.

"That he's so full of bullshit and still smells like CK 1?"

I keep my smile longer than normal. "Sure," I say. "But there's something else."

Ben takes off his hat, twirls it on one finger like a vaudeville star. "Well, I don't need to actually hear these boys to know they can't carry a tune."

"Still, maybe they're helping us out. You said so."

"Maybe."

Yesterday, back in Philly, I expected Ben to show me graphs and pie-charts measuring the financial impact of allowing N2K to sample "Take My Chance." Now I sit down next to him, though neither of us needs to whisper. "You're not sure?" I say.

Ben yawns and I look up to see if someone else has entered the room. Door's still shut. Ben says, "We'll get some folks. But you need . . ." He pauses, yawns again, sets his hat on his head, askew. "I'm just tired, Pete. Been telling you that all tour."

I snort through my nose, straighten his hat and tug his red pocket square. "Been telling me that since the first day I was on the job."

It takes him a minute, but he closes his eyes as if reflecting, then leans back in his seat, laughing louder and longer than I've heard him all tour. Almost feel the need to quiet him, in case someone surprises us. But I don't. Wind up laughing myself. It's the first time on this tour when you could say I'm on top. "Got me there, Pete," he says. "Goddamn, you got me."

• • •

When Fuller returns and requests we at least hear a few numbers from N2K—along with the promise they'll perform "Out 4 Mines" early—Ben nods and we tip backstage. I keep both hands on Ben, especially as we maneuver past all the cords and boxes and switches. After Fuller gets Ben a padded chair, he helps me seat the Last True Delta Bluesman, then stands to Ben's left, slightly in front of us, and says, over the din, "What do you think?"

Impressed as I am by this view of the Garden, I know it'll be my last time here. I suspect, too, it might be N2K's single appearance here. You ask me, these brothers aren't that good. I've never been to a rap concert, yet I've a feeling this performance is nothing out of the ordinary. All but DJ Spin-Sation-L are shirtless and Marv, Tastee and 2-Slo jump around and pace the stage, shouting party-people chants: "Throw your hands in the air and wave 'em like you just don't care." Their delivery and exuberance suggests these boys believe they made this shit up, while I recall the same chants from Q-Dog parties in East Lansing, and am hoping the roof ain't on fire tonight. Plus, the act tires out the fellows. By the third song, spit clogs their throats and they strain to keep up the rapid patter their fans adore. Only DJ Spin-Sation-L consistently astonishes me. His hands blur over the turntables as he recycles the drum intro from "My Sharona," and Peter Tosh and Marley saying, "Get up, stand up." Others are whimsical: a bit of a Rice-A-Roni commercial, a phone sex operator moaning ecstasy while two dogs bark and a kitchen faucet drips. All this sonic genius while his MC's drop easy rhymes about their potency or hard times and mean streets and what they'll do to a bitch who gets out of line. The mostly black and brown audience—some white kids are out there, too—applauds everything these jokers do, their cheers loudest, though, when Marv hollers, "Give y'all selves a hand."

Seated beside me, Ben intermittently slumps and feigns narcoleptic spells. For now he's blinking and smiling, tapping his foot, though from what I can tell, Tastee's only telling the fans of the hard work they four have put into their newest record. Fuller's been on his cell the whole time, but now he turns to us and says, "Here it is." And sure enough, I hear Ben's slide and my quiet harp. But only for a moment, as the crowd recognizes the hit and obscures the music with their exhortations. I look to Ben. His eyes are shut. I jostle his shoulder and his lips part but he doesn't open his eyes. He can't really be asleep, not with this noise. Fuller leans over and says, "Great, isn't it?"

I nod, kneeling to look at Ben's eyes. "Ben," I whisper. "You all right?" I grab his knees and shake them, certain that despite his pains to maintain his health, some part of his body has betrayed him. "Ben," I plead.

"You thought I was asleep, but I wasn't," he says, like John Lee Hooker himself. Leaning forward to whisper in my ear, he says, "After you stung me so good back there, I had to keep you on your toes."

I stand, fooled after so many years but smiling. The rising applause reminds me of "Out 4 Mines," but clearly it's over. Fuller's clapping, too. He says, "Great, isn't it?"

Ben stands, clamps his right hand on his hip. "Hate to be leavin' so early," he says. "But they's a mattress callin' my name."

He doesn't wait for my aid. Instead, he extends his other hand for balance and shuffles back toward the dressing room, leaving me to convey our gratitude to Fuller. He watches Ben, then glances over my head at the stage. More mediocre rhymes and big beats echo. "Think he liked it?" Fuller says.

"Hard to tell," I say, leaning backward and shrugging. "Hard to tell," I say again, because that's all I've got.

Fuller pockets his phone. "The way Mabry talked, I was sure you two'd be happy to hear them play."

Beneath my iridescent shirt and foolish coat, my shoulders stiffen, and I wipe my hand across my mouth and mustache, wishing I could let Fuller in on the joke. "He kind of hard to read sometime," I say, a little surprised at the length of my sentence and its accuracy. I try to see if Ben's still visible in the shadowy corridor, but he isn't. I turn to Fuller, who shakes his Rolex like he's holding dice. He says, "But you liked it?"

Something's different in his manner or maybe his delivery. But now he's got his well-manicured fingers on my sleeve, as if to keep me here longer than I'd like. "Come on, cuz," he says. "You can tell me."

There: this isn't the voice I've heard from him all night. I've always suspected, especially after starting with Ben, that most brothers had at least one voice for work and another for home. But the smooth voice Fuller had in the dressing room and up until seconds before sounded much like mine: without an accent, precise, the kind my mother taught me to shape for those who'd be deciding if I could have a credit card or a college education, the kind Ben fought to form for himself after he figured he needed Wilton Mabry to keep any more financial calamities from befalling him and Bucket. Now Fuller says, "I know you be listenin' to some hip hop now and then."

Which voice is genuine? The manager's or the homeboy in the Dolce and Gabbana before me? A few minutes ago, I wouldn't have been surprised to learn he was from Ohio or Indiana or even Michigan.

Now I lower my hat to shade my eyes, shake my head. "Nawsuh," I drawl, my tongue slippery on the floor of my mouth. "Tell the truth, I never been nowise interested in none that rap."

The music cranks up behind us—I think I hear the theme from "Bewitched"—and I find myself wondering what Dane Connor's up to. Fuller still hasn't let me go. "Serious," he says. "You don't listen to no hip hop?"

It's well past time to join Ben wherever he is, so I pull my sleeve from Fuller's grip, but he steps in my way. All tour there've been these moments, where I want to get away but people want me, for whatever reason, to stay put, thus forcing me to remain Silent Sam. I shake my head again. "It ain't got what I want," I say.

"What's that?"

I straighten up, noting that, in voice, Fuller's left the streets and headed back to the suburbs. "Blues is true," I say, still in Sam's voice. "Real, what I mean. And them fellows back air"—I jerk my thumb toward the stage. "They doin' what everybody else be doin'."

"Hold on," Fuller says, his hand landing on my shoulder before I can duck. "N2K's doing the same thing as everybody else? That's what you're saying?"

What happened to the homeboy? I nod, purse my lips, as if to hold on to whatever else I've got to say. Fuller slides to his left, allowing me to pass, but as I get on the other side of him, he says, "And you all are just so, so, what? One of a kind?"

Damn but I wish Ben were here. This isn't what I'm used to, trading lines with someone who isn't ready to praise me endlessly for the train whistle sound I can create so easily, with just breath, tongue and flapping hands. Fuller doesn't let me reply. He says, "We could have picked any of your songs for 'Out 4 Mines.' Wouldn't have made a difference. Matter of fact, we didn't even have to use your stuff. It all sounds the same, blues does."

The last sentence stops me. I've heard it before, so has Ben, so has any fan or musician who played more than one number for a novice. And when I turn, I already know what I'm going to say. The words slip out as if greased: "Then you doan know blues."

In two hurried strides, Fuller catches up with me. He actually pushes up the sleeves of his jacket and shirt. If he takes off his glasses and watch, I'm going to bust him in the chin, though for now I keep my hands at my sides, unclenched. Still, I await his next move, tensing my flabby body and leaning backward. No one's taken a swing at me since my sophomore year when a drunk mistook me for another brother. He missed. Fuller says, "I know one thing. I know you're playing in front of white folks every night."

I'd rather he punched me.

He spreads his arms, palms up, the pose like Ali's after he just dropped another chump to the canvas. He says, "Brothers and sisters been tired for years with that old, broken-down woke up this morning bullshit of yours. Tired." I'm now aware of people watching, none of them Ben, but sound crew, maintenance men, the pair of massive security guards. Perhaps this audience causes my voice to rise, or I just want to be absolutely sure Fuller hears me. "Least we *playing* something. Besides other people records." Before Fuller can say another word, I've got my harp in hand and blow the intro to "Fattening Frogs up For Snakes." I keep my eyes wide open now, watching Fuller as each note flies past him. And because I'm sure he doesn't know the tune, I put down my harp and sing the first verse:

It took me a long time, to find out my mistake

Took me a long time, long time, to find out my mistake

It sure did, man

But I'll bet you my bottom dollar, I'm not fattenin' no more frogs for snakes.

Don't need to sing or speak another word. Pocket my harp, turn around, and there's Ben before me. I blink. My contacts shift and settle. "Sam," he says, "You done been practicin'!"

I look over my shoulder to see if Fuller's still there. He is, mouth open but with nothing to say. Ben takes me by the arm and pulls me toward the exit and out to the sidewalk. On Seventh Avenue, at ten pm, it's not easy to hear someone standing even as close as Ben is to me, so near we could embrace.

"Couldn't have drawn it up better myself," he says. "You just wrote your way into the book, Pete."

Traffic noise increases, battering my brain with squealing brakes, honking horns and mammoth trucks grinding gears. "What?" I say. "What book?"

"The Blues Who's Who or whatever's the next encyclopedia," he shouts. "You just wrote your first few sentences with that scene back there."

"Naw," I say. "You're kidding."

He shakes his head and winks. "Blues is true. Wish I'd come up with that one."

How'd he hear? I didn't see him until after I said that.

"Exactly the kind of hook every writer loves," he says. "Trust me."

A request I've heard before. And likely will hear again. But what is there to do now other than nod and follow him to the Brougham? This is Brother Ben we're talking about. He surely knows the way.

# 11.

**IN ELEVENTH GRADE ENGLISH, I LEARNED NEW** England was home to Emerson and Thoreau, Hawthorne and Melville, Harriet Beecher Stowe and Emily Dickinson, and more than any other region of the U.S., it produced the ideas that inspired a colony into nationhood. I was still trying to learn how to play harp then but never would have imagined I'd annually look forward to my arrival here. Ben and I always play New England when the tour's near its end, meaning soon I'll be back to a life as an almost nondescript, middle

## Eyesight to the Blind

class black man in New Orleans. Plus, this is the region of the country, where, quite honestly, Ben and I can do no wrong. From the University of Hartford to Keene State College, and every college town in between, from Lowell to Manchester to the Berkshires and Portsmouth, we're revered by many. They want our performances so badly, and we never disappoint. Ben says the people who attend these shows are most likely those who once traveled to the Delta to integrate its polling places or haunt jooks and general stores to discover Hurt, McDowell, and James. And for them, we are the last living link to that time when it seemed change, as Mr. Cooke sang, was indeed gonna come.

But because so many fans are around during so many hours of the day, we have to stay in character longer. To jog, Ben wakes around five. We spend little time out of our stage clothes and rarely speak in any voices other than those of Brother Ben and Silent Sam. The jams last longer than anywhere else though the proportion of talented musicians backstage increases. Past couple of years, the guitar players were joined by a few harpists, some of them pretty good, including a *junior* at UNH, a white boy who played a chromatic and pushed me outside the notes and chords I'm most comfortable with.

But this has been no ordinary tour, and I've given up trying to guess what might happen next. Ben keeps claiming he's emptied his trick bag. All we need to do is perform a few more weeks. More sooner than later, we'll be back in our homes, waiting for the next tour or another video crew from Prague or Okinawa to interview us in Jackson about the True Delta Blues. Ben hasn't said anything else about cutting a new record, and I'm not going to remind him, lest this might be another trap. Quite frankly, after the sampling of "Take My Chance," I'm pretty sure the only recording we'd make would be for a commercial. Maybe even under Kent Bollinger's direction. For the United Negro College Fund, perhaps. Or a fried chicken franchise.

• • •

In Hartford, I call my mother. When no one answers, I leave a message, keeping my voice steady, telling her and Grover nothing more than the tour's nearing its close. I call Heywood, too, only he's not home either, leaving me no confessors other than Ben, who's sleeping until it's time to leave for the gig. An hour to go before then, the batteries on my Discman are dead, and I don't want to fall asleep myself. So, wearing a t-shirt, my blue-black suit, and Ben's black boots—they pinch a little—I stroll to the elevator, wondering what to do. A drawback of touring is that cities can become indistinguishable. And even though I've been to Hartford five times, I've never stayed longer than one night. I don't know where the good newsstand is or the record store, or where to get the best cup of coffee. Once, I thought I'd explore all these new places. Now, the cities are names on a checklist, and I'm eager to get one crossed off and head to the next one to do the same.

I smooth my mustache with my thumb and forefinger, look away from the fuzzy reflection cast upon the elevator doors and think about buying a newspaper or playing video games in the Ramada's lounge. In the lobby are the potted plants, semi-comfortable furniture and scurrying hotel employees I see in every hotel, only today they're joined by a pair of middle aged white cats seated on a sofa. Instinct tells me to step back into an elevator, but I'm not the one they want. They might like to see Silent Sam, but it's Brother Ben they're after, judging by the pints of Old Crow each man clutches. Pretending not to notice either—though they both weight at least two-fifty, and I'm glad to see people heavier than me—I look into the lounge, find it's closed until six. I run my thumb over the ridges of the quarters in my pocket. A *Courant* machine's in the corner beyond the reception desk, yet such a purchase doesn't seem a move Silent Sam would make. Peter would. He's concerned about the Pistons and the Red Wings, the Tigers, too, now that it's May. But why would Sam Stamps bother himself with reading when it's well known that it makes his eyes tired? That's what Ben told an interviewer for *Stormy Monday.*

A lot of reflection for a simple trip through a hotel lobby, you ask me. Still, while eyes warm the back of my neck, I pretend to look out the lobby door, as if measuring the time by the position of the sun. Then I step toward the center of the room, about the time the pair leaves the sofa and advances. "Silent Sam?" one says. The heavier of the two, he sports a Ben and Jerry's t-shirt, jeans and duct-taped Chucks. A coppery goattee's trying to take some weight off his face but failing. His hand reaches for mine. "Gary," he says, jowls wobbling. "It's a real honor."

Nodding, I look at the other fellow, who's equally pale and balding and wearing a jean jacket so faded it looks borrowed from Parchman Prison. He's not as brave as his buddy, won't even come out from behind him or shake my hand. Then again, once Gary lets me go, I'm not exactly reaching out. Too busy offering my escape line: "Ben, he upstairs in the bed."

"Oh," Gary says, looking over his shoulder at his buddy. "He's asleep?"

I can't resist. "Soon as his head hit the pillow."

Both nod. The quieter cat is a few inches shorter. Slipping down his nose are wire-rimmed glasses, with thick lenses that make his eyes swimmy. He leans forward, then steps back. "Y'all bring those fo' Ben?" I say, pointing to their pints.

"Yeah," Gary says, looking at the flat bottle as if he forgot it was there. He hands it over to me and his partner does the same. I watch both men, expecting a song request, questions about the after show jam or whether Ben and I still make pallets on the floors of our rooms. "Y'all need somethin' mo'?"

"Is it true?" the shorter cat says, stepping behind Gary.

Gary nods like a dashboard dog. "Yeah, Sam," he says. "Is it true?"

Though he never copped to this as a reason he stopped touring, Heywood told me that keeping up with the entire mythology of Brother Ben worked him harder than he wanted. To the question now before me—"Is it true?"—I might as well say yes. But I'd like a little more information than they've given. "What true?" I say, struggling to fit two pints in one pocket.

"About that rap group's manager," Gary says. "Major heard on the radio you just punched him. I read on the net that you knocked him out."

"And you told him to stop thieving, too," the partner—Major, I guess—says.

I blink a few times, clink the bottles together in my hands. I can see the moment as each man describes it. Been a lot of people on this tour who needed a beating, and Fuller's near the top of that list. I doubt I could inflict harm on anyone, though Sam's said to have scrapped all his days. Just look at the scar above my eye and that crooked middle finger. Never mind the scar's an old hockey injury and the middle finger got hurt after a tumble from a top bunk. Yet this new chapter—Sam the ass-kicker—has me stammering for real. Almost think about breaking the seal on one of these pints, but Old Crow tasted like turpentine the one and only time I took a sip, which is why we flavor our flasks with the far more palatable Jim Beam. Tugging his goatee, Gary says, "He deserved it, whatever you did."

"Totally deserved it," Major says, watching his shoes.

I stop chewing my mustache and roll my shoulders like a boxer before the match. If I punched the air near Gary and Major, I'd frighten the shit out of them while confirming the reality of the lie they both want so much to believe. I slip one pint in my pants' pocket, clench my fist and say, "And he won't be messin' with Brother Ben and me no mo'." Though I just *show* them the fist they heard so much about, Gary and Major back away. As if it were real, I feel the rush of contact with Fuller's jaw, then bring my fist up to my mouth and wipe a knuckle against my mustache.

"All right," Gary says, putting out a shiny pink palm. I slap him five but go gentle. Still, he cringes as if expecting the weight of a masonry block. Major wants his five, and I oblige. Then I look at both men and say, "Best be gettin' back to the room."

"Sure, sure," Gary says. "You'll tell Brother Ben it was us who gave him the Old Crow, right?"

"Just keep following that crow," Major sings.

I nod, the man of few words that I am. Then I shake my legendary fist and turn to the elevator.

• • •

Ben says he's got nothing to do with this rumor of Fuller and me throwing down, but lately it seems my best method is to disbelieve everything he says. Meantime, the rumor follows me from Hartford to Providence, where it builds during the early Massachusetts gigs. I try my escape lines in hotel lobbies and dressing rooms, yet more and more the blues faithful want to talk to me. Silent Sam, that is. The basic outline of the rumor stays the same: still my punch either knocking Fuller out or dazing him. It hasn't developed to where I clock the N2K Posse and their road crew, then take on LL Cool J and Master P for fun (though in Lowell six people spoke of Fuller sighted wearing a neck brace). There's no talk of me playing harp or singing "Fattening Frogs For Snakes," yet everyone claims to've heard of threats Sam hurled, and they all involve further ass-whuppings unless Fuller promises to stop stealing from Ben and me.

It's all a little cliché and makes me wonder why so many intelligent people need to cast bluesmen as bad niggers—even scholars, like Graham. Sure, there are some actual killers among the blues pantheon: Pat Hare, Leadbelly, Robert Pete Williams, Bukka White. But there are victims too, Little Walter and the first Sonny Boy, among them. Which is why I prefer to take my cues from Sonny Boy II: He lived to a ripe old age.

Still, I always believed you picked up a guitar or harp so you wouldn't have to fight anyone. You learned to play so well people would run to your defense. Now Ben tells me to be flattered over the whole development, and I am, to some extent. I just wish that the badass persona—do I need a new nickname? Swinging Sam Stamps?—was not so quickly accompanied with the part where Sam doesn't understand the aesthetics and legality of sampling. Nor does he understand that Mr. Mabry has been paid to use those opening bars of "Take My Chance." Good, old Simple Sam. Now I want to find some way to let it slip that Sam may not be as easy a read as everyone believes. Yet I don't know how, other than to be Peter, whom nobody can know. Early on, Ben told me he'd do most of the talking. I was to watch and learn from him how to read people and utilize the veneer of his limited intellect. In the end, I don't know I've learned these skills. Wouldn't surprise me to hear from Ben himself I haven't learned much at all.

• • •

Boston's our last gig in the Bay State and we're playing the Musical Theater on the B.U. campus, one of the largest venues we've seen all tour, outside of Madison Square, and home to over a hundred empty seats during last year's gig. For a return date, Ben charmed the Musical Theater's manager as Mabry *and* Ben over the phone. Now, en route from the hotel, he calls the ticket booth on his cell and in his Wilton Mabry voice asks if any tickets are available. "No, huh," he says for me to hear. "Sold out last week?"

Good news, I'd say, and evidence of the power of publicity. Either N2K Posse's single or the rumor of Fuller and me is bringing out the blues faithful in droves. Tonight, when we reach the parking lot, the crowd doesn't appear made up of those who listen to the urban radio stations that play N2K. They so strongly resemble last night's crowd, I think I see some of the same faces from Framingham. Then again, I hope I've not succumbed to as erroneous and small minded a view about whites as that held by those who claim all blacks look alike. But unless my sunglasses are fogged, I believe Major and Gary from Hartford stand up ahead and wave madly, both men dressed as they were when I first saw them a week ago. I tilt my hat over my eyes, then look out the rear window while Ben eases us forward. More enthusiastic bands of folk slow down, but no one stays in the path of the Brougham. They know better than to get in Ben's way when he's behind the wheel. Just ask those people in Phoenix who swear Ben drove over the feet of two promoters.

We make it to the performers' entrance with no one riding the hood of the Brougham or snapping off the aerial for a souvenir. A burly fellow in a yellow windbreaker stands next to a sawhorse. Ben toots his horn and the guard raises the board, signaling Ben to drive into the reserved lot. The Jump and Jive had six security guards and N2K Posse didn't move anywhere without their two behemoths nearby. So we're not that popular. Not that Ben might get biggity. Just me.

As soon as we're out of the car, we're met by this cat with spiky, black hair slicked straight back. He looks Italian, his skin not much lighter than Ben's. Wide as a wrestler, he's far more eager to see us than I'd expect. "Brother Ben?" he says as if he doesn't quite believe he's seeing The Last True Delta Bluesman, dressed in an undertaker's black suit. He reaches so quickly for Ben's hand, he almost gets the picking fingers, but Ben slips him his left. "This is fricking awesome," the rent-a-cop says. "I'm Rico. Jeez, I can't believe it's Brother fricking Ben."

His cop cadence has me about to raise my arms in surrender though I've done nothing wrong. Still, I wonder how long Rico's been this big a fan of Brother Ben. Typically we don't see too many ethnic whites among our pasty throngs. The surnames of the New England blues faithful are straight off the Mayflower. They're members of families who've endowed buildings and scholarships at the campuses we play. Swiftly, Rico turns to me. "Need any help, Sam?"

I've already got my harp case in my hands. Shrugging, I shake my head. Meantime, Ben's shuffled back to the trunk, wearily fits his key into the lock. Rico's shoulders shift beneath his jacket, as if he'd like to help Ben out, but he brings himself up straight as a stick, saying, "I was gonna help you with your guitar, Brother Ben, but I don't want it busted over my head."

"Never let another man touch yo' guitar, son," Ben says, grinning, his gold sleeves particularly lustrous tonight. "That's what Mr. Son House tole me when I was just a youngster."

"Wow," Rico says, closing his eyes and nodding. He steps out of the way as Ben picks up his battered case. Then the old swindler grunts and has to try twice before getting the trunk to latch shut. Ben says, "You gon see the show?"

"Yeah," Rico says. "My first ever." He follows as we walk toward the performers' entrance door. I smell his cologne, frank and abrasive, certainly something off the shelf at Shaw's, then let him and Ben enter together. Rico says, "You guys gonna play 'Big Legged Woman' tonight?' That's my favorite."

I truly believe it is. No one could fake such enthusiasm, except for Ben, who stops inside the hallway leading to the dressing room. "You likes them big-legged women or the song?" Ben teases.

Rico nods. "Both, I guess."

"Me too," Ben says. Then he tilts back his head, rubs his grizzled chin thoughtfully. He says, "Hey, Sam," and awaits my reply. I nod.

"Think we kin fit in 'Big Legged Woman' fo"—he pauses, turns to Rico. "What you name, son?"

"Rico."

"Rico," Ben says. "Think we can play 'Big Legged Woman' fo' Rico?"

I shoot out the cuffs of my blue-black jacket. "Guess so," I say.

Rico says, "Thanks, Sam. Thanks, Ben."

" 'Preciate you, suh," I say, and lift my hand to shake his. Only he's not looking in my direction. He turns to see my open hand and ducks, raising his bent arms in defense. "Hey, Sam," he says, "watch it."

"Then doan get him angry none," Ben says.

• • •

No matter how well we played, no matter how loud the cheering tonight, after we finish "Old Black River," Ben and I pack up and exit the dressing room, disappointing a group of about fifteen people lugging guitar cases and pints of Old Crow. Ben tells them about our gig tomorrow in Keene tomorrow night, and makes sure to yawn and slouch so I have to slip my arm under his for support. Even I manufacture a few yawns as we walk away to the Brougham. When Ben asks if I'm tired on the drive back to the Days Inn,

I almost tell him we don't have an audience anymore but turn instead and see he's looking serious for once. Truth is, I'm a little wired, as I often am after shows near the end of the tour. Instead of tiring of playing the same songs in the same order, I get enervated, as if there's no promise of playing them again next year. Plus, that racehorse tempo was with us again tonight and hasn't left since we whipped it forth in Florida. No audience has minded, even though I wonder if it's True Delta Blues we're playing anymore. Now, behind the wheel, I tell Ben I'm feeling ok, and he says, "You want to get a drink?"

He's asked me this before. During our first two tours, though neither of us ever got drunk. Since, I can't say I've ever seen him finish a bottle, can or glassful, which is why I say, "You want to what?"

"Get a drink. You and me, Pete."

He can't want to go to a bar. We don't know in which bars we might be most anonymous. I've got enough trouble staying on this one street, Soldiers Field, and not getting lost on the way back to the motel. That's when he spots a convenience store and tells me to pull in. Hands me a twenty, grinning. "Don't get wild," he says.

I'm in and out in little time, toting a bagged twelve of Michelob. I don't know his preference for beer precisely—we never praise it in songs, only wine, bourbon and homemade—but I figured if he had a preferred brand it'd be Michelob, a beverage for a man of color in his sixties, one with a little more money than he ever dreamed. A little classy, but not showy, American made, and not likely to be sold in single bottles that fit neatly into brown paper sacks. Back in the Brougham, I drive cautiously—still mindful of our Florida escapade—and we wait until we've entered our hotel room before we unbag our bottles and sink them in a bathtub full of ice. We get out of our stage clothes next, and soon are both in bathrobes, seated on our separate beds. Ben clinks his bottle against mine. "This is all right, isn't it?" he says.

I take a sip—cold, tasty, just what I needed—but I don't know what Ben's talking about. "What's all right?"

He leans against his headboard, removes the gold sleeves from his teeth and puts them in a small plastic case on the nightstand. "All of it," he says. He blows over the top of his bottle, but it's too full to produce much of a whistle. "Ask a lot of folks, I think they wouldn't mind a few hours of total adulation, followed by a relaxed time with your main man and a few Michelobs."

"I know that voice," I say. "You're about to spring something on me." In his direction, I toss my bent beer cap. When it lands, Ben plucks the cap off his green bedspread and flings it back at me. I don't duck in time and the cap catches me on my bare chest. "That's gratitude," he says, then sips from his beer. "Tell some young motherfucker he's your main man and first thing out of his mouth is suspicion."

"Can you blame me?" I rub the spot on my chest, where it still stings, more from surprise than pain.

"Ok," he says. "Ok." His shoulders slump as he reaches his hands for his feet. "But I'm serious, Pete. We are lucky, you know."

I get off the bed and find a seat at the table to provide a better view of Ben. His mood's hard for me to gauge. I've never heard him talk this way before. Guardedly, I sip from my beer and say, "Bet those no-talent N2K's are drunk on Cristal and smoking blunts."

"And rubbing up against some fine young things."

"So we aren't the luckiest," I say, slipping off my socks and tucking them inside the boots. My left toes still feel the press of the narrow toes, a sign I shouldn't wear my calfskins tomorrow.

Ben puts his bottle on the nightstand between our beds. "In two years, those fellows are going to be killing each other trying to get back where they are now. I can tell."

"You know?"

Ben closes his eyes, leans his head against the headboard. "Trust me." Then, before I can respond: "Wouldn't have let them use our stuff if I thought they were going to be around a while. Couldn't risk the tune being identified more as theirs instead of the rightful owners'. Pete, they're going down as we speak."

I laugh into my bottle. " ' My health is fadin on me, oh yes I'm goin' down slow'" I say, trying out my Wolf impression, though St. Louis Jimmy wrote the song.

"And I also predict you're gonna apologize when it turns out I'm right." Ben grabs his bottle and drains it, then he strides toward the bathroom in his tank top and drawers, not shuffling or slowing down at all or meeting the description of most men in their late sixties. My stomach feels especially flabby now, as do my legs. From the bathroom, I hear the slosh and scrape as he digs in the ice for more beer. When he returns, he's carrying two bottles. "Seriously, though," he says, opening a bottle. "You mark my words." He extends to me the bottle with a loosened cap, but I snatch the unopened one from his other hand. "You know what Sonny Boy told Robert about drinking from a bottle with a broken seal," I say.

"All this time," Ben says, "and you still don't trust me." He sighs, slumps his shoulders and paces toward the nightstand, where he sets down the bottle and hops on the bed, landing on his stomach like a ten-year-old at a sleepover. "Guess you learned *something*," he says, winking.

• • •

Four beers later and things have gotten as merry as a Louis Jordan record. Ben's telling tales about him and Bucket in the early years, before Mankiewicz and Stern arrived in Clarksdale. I've never heard one of these—they for sure aren't in any books—and I doubt no one other than Heywood has either. "Bucket was the ambitious one," he says, arms folded behind his head. "Anybody who came to Clarksdale who had a record out, and I mean anybody, blues players, singing preachers, rockabilly guys like Charlie Feathers. Bucket'd be hanging out by the dressing room, blowing harp, trying to get noticed. That summer I was still thinking about college. Fisk or Alcorn."

"Heywood told me about that." I'm in the bathroom, eliminating a good portion of the beer, but feeling fine, not wobbly or fuzzy-headed.

"Serious. I was older, but had good marks back in school."

That doesn't surprise me. "But you did play street corners with Bucket, right?" When I finish pissing I wash my hands and take out my contacts. I put on my glasses and walk out with two bottles, damp and dripping with melted ice.

"Thanks," Ben says, when I hand him one. "Me? I didn't pluck a string unless there was up-front money involved."

"Always about those dollars," I say.

"And those days of working for free, Pete. They were hebben jes like ole marster said?"

He's got me there, which is no big news. I think for a blues couplet about money so we can change the subject and land on Sonny Boy's non sequitur, "Her daddy must have been a millionaire, I can tell by the way she walks." My harp's in my pocket, otherwise I'd play the solo from "Eyesight to the Blind."

Ben says, "Why don't we do this more often?" He sets down his empty and opens another. "Tie one on?"

"You tell me?"

"Here's one reason," Ben says. He chugs from his bottle. "If I got drunk I might tell people to kiss my ass, then play mixolydian scales all night like I was Ornette damn Coleman or something."

"Tell me more about you and Bucket," I say, leaning on my elbow, outside the bedcovers.

"You know that story," he says.

"Only what Heywood told me."

"And?" Ben says, gesturing with his bottle. So I relay the tale I learned from my predecessor, about young Wilton's moves back and forth between St. Louis and Clarksdale, the convenient and coincidental arrival of the two northerners and the plans and schemes—on both sides—that followed. Like a showoff kid, I include the bit about his courtship of Martha, then sit up to sip my beer. Ben belches, a wet rumble with volume, tremolo and bass. Grinning, he eyes me, and I recognize he's still got one gold sleeve in, the one he wears on his upper right front tooth. He tilts back the bottle again. "One thing Heywood left out," he says. "But he never knew the whole story. Neither did Bucket." Another swallow, then he places the bottle next to an empty on the nightstand, but he won't now complete the tale. Instead, he gets under the covers and pulls them up to his neck. If the subject were anything else, I'd let him go to sleep, wouldn't let him smile to himself before he told me, knowing how easy I am to manipulate. But I've got to ask: "What's the whole story?"

"Every story like ours has got to have some serendipity in it, you know?" he says. "Can't ever just be the plain old truth. Always got to be that, you know, thunderclap of chance, to let everyone believe there is some divine plan in keeping the blues alive."

"Why're you stalling?" I take off my glasses, set them next to the nightstand's alarm clock.

"I'm just saying, Pete. Just saying. But I mean, it's always John Hammond comes looking for Robert, who's dead, but he finds Big Bill Broonzy, that sort of thing. And it's always black men getting discovered, you know. Like we didn't exist as individuals until somebody with a tape recorder spotted us playing a guitar."

"Like Christopher Columbus," I say. "Discovering what was already here."

"Hey, now, don't knock Chris. You know I like hustlers, and he was one of the slickest. Anyway," he pauses, and I can hear him mumbling, then he sits up to drop the last gold sleeve in the container. "Those two didn't stumble across me and Bucket. I saw them walking around Sunflower Avenue, lost. Back then you could spot a Yankee in a hot second, especially on a summer day. First time in my life I saw Nantucket red trousers."

"Go on."

"I went and got Bucket, but I didn't tell him why we'd be playing so close to the bus station. Usually, people getting off ignored us and the folks headed someplace else were holding on tight to every dime."

"Sure."

"But I grabbed Bucket and we played until the Ivy Leaguers staggered back to the bus station. Man, I made them *believe* they'd discovered us."

I want to see his face, but my glasses are on the nightstand and he's switched off his light. I can't tell if this story is the plain old truth or not. It's not often he reveals so directly his magic. If I don't catch it with my own eyes, he's said before, then I need to learn to pay better attention. Now Ben sits up, almost as if I've willed him to, and rests his weight on both elbows. I can see his form, not specific features, though I squint and reach for my glasses. "After those dudes left us to start making calls back home, Bucket said, 'Wilton, I think you hexed them mens.' And then we were off."

"He always called you Wilton, didn't he?" Somehow, this single purported quote from Bucket makes the entire story sound plausible. My glasses still on the nightstand, I roll over on my back, look up at the blurry ceiling. "It's like with Sonny Boy," I say. "Everybody called him Rice."

"My wife, too. She never called me anything but Wilton. Something to think about, Pete."

We're quiet for a minute, as I consider asking him about his wife and wonder whether it's time I started calling him Wilton, too. Then Ben says, "Hey, Pete."

"What?"

"This one's my last."

"Say that again?"

"You heard me. This one's my last."

I bump my head against the headboard but ignore the pain to turn over. Ben's holding an empty bottle of beer. "You can have all the rest if you want them," he says.

"Damn," I say, rubbing the back of my head. "Thought you meant something else for a minute."

Ben laughs, not a stage laugh, just a single, sharp note.

"Ben," I say. "Wilton?"

He doesn't answer. I suppose I could get up and shake him—he's not asleep once his head hits the pillow—but I fear the answer he might give. So I turn out the light, then sit here in the dark room, waiting for my eyes to adjust.

# 12.

## "LAST QUESTION, BROTHER BEN. SAM," SAYS MARTY

the DJ. "You've both done very well for yourselves. You've certainly improved your lots in life. So tell me: What keeps you singing the blues?"

Goddamn. If Sonja Hutch's or Dane Connor's questions weren't the most often asked to bluesmen and -women, this one is. Worse than the frequency is how smug people get when they ask, as if they're the first to think it, as if they've caught us in an inconsistency or a lie. Still, today, the afternoon of the last concert date, in the studios of WPTL, the public radio station of Downeast Maine, Mr. Marty Sloan will not let this interview end without our answer. He wants us to call him Party Marty, but it's clear he doesn't know who he's messing with. And from his previous banal questions and the brief conversation we had before the taping, I can tell he only knows Ben by name and reputation. He wears a Bonnie Raitt t-shirt and his frame of reference goes no wider than Slowhand to Robert Cray.

**One Way Out**

I've got an answer for Marty: You mustn't try to oversimplify blues. It's a complex animal, both a feeling anybody—black, brown, white or in between—can experience, and a musical form that, for much of its history, has been mostly perfected by black musicians. But this isn't the place for such discourse, especially not out of the mouth of Silent Sam Stamps. Besides, I've got Brother Ben next to me, and he's already started his reply: "You know, the music I started playin' when I was a youngster, didn't nobody call it blues. Momma said it was devil's music. Daddy called it good-timey. Ain't no way to make no livin', he said. No one in my family liked it, seem to me. But one night I snuck out to play with Bucketmouth Carter at a fish fry. And when them other people heard me on my git-tar, boy, I didn't care what it was called, I wanted to be playin' it."

"That's great, Brother Ben, but what I wanted to know," Marty begins, but Ben interrupts: "You know, blues ain't like no other kind of music. I mean, you can lissen to jazz, rocker roll and country. And you can hear them same chords and some the same words what you hear in blues, but to play blues"—and here he pauses, grows solemn. Nobody does solemn like Brother Ben. Makes me wish we weren't just in a radio studio, taping, but broadcast over every New England TV set and those beyond. People have to see the Last True Delta Bluesman's pecan-colored face, the tremor in his eyelids, the tremble in his lips and chin. He even generates some wrinkles where previously his face was smooth. In my swivel seat, I turn to look closer. Tears leak from his eyes, and I wonder if he's got a tack in his shoe. He starts to speak again, but his voice catches—twice—while I chew my mustache, trying not to spoil this nostalgic masquerade with laughter. I look to Marty. His chin's on his hand, mouth agape, and he's blinking as if Ben's too bright to take in all at once.

Ben wipes his tears with a crumpled bandana, continues: "If you ain't been in them words you singin', folks gon know, and they ain't gon believe your blues is same as theirs. 'Cause that's what you got to play. Blues that ever'body knows. And I tell you. I been in them blues. I remember ever' time we didn't have nothin' to eat, ever' time I rode the back of a bus, ever' woman who left me, ever' job I lost. Yeah, I been there. And Sam has too. Know what happen to me and Sam just 'bout a month ago, Mr. Marty?"

Marty's slow to take in that he's been addressed. His chin rises from his fist and he blinks, then says in his radio-smooth voice, "What happened?"

"We's in Florida. Doin nothin' but drivin' to the show. And this policeman pulled us over. I doan have to state what color he was. He didn't know me and I didn't try to tell him. So yeah I made me a little money. But I done traveled that road I sing about. So you right, Mr. Marty. We drivin' a nicer vehicle, but Sam and me drivin' down that same road today. Right, Sam?" He turns to me. "Tell Mr. Marty like you told that fellow back in New York."

It can only be Fuller he's talking about, though I recall telling him a lot of things. I lick my lips, cough, and say, "Blues is true," hoping no question mark sneaks into my enunciation.

"That's right," Ben says. "Blues is true, like Sam say." He stands, picks up his hat, motions for me to do the same. "And we thank you, Mr. Marty, for lettin' us tell you what we can about them blues."

I want to applaud but get out of my swivel chair, bump my shiny knee against the console, then follow Ben as he exits the studio. He's been particularly energetic today, starting with the four miles he ran in the morning in Portsmouth, New Hampshire, and the pushups and situps that followed in our Ramada room. Feel like I've been two steps behind all day. Once we get outside to the Brougham, I say, "I couldn't have done that." Since our night in Boston, I've been trying to call him Wilton, but I'm struggling with that task. Wind up saying no name at all, most of the time.

Ben waves his hand. "You did your share," he says, starting up the car. From L.A. to Maine, after three oil changes, one tire rotation, and seven automatic washes, the Brougham still roars like a jet engine when he starts it, and rides smoothly over downtown Portland's cobbled streets. He scans the light traffic and steers us in the direction of the Fairfield Inn near the Jetport.

"The double throat catch," I say. "That was sharp."

"A gimmick. Anyone can do that."

"Still," I say. "Everything out of your mouth sounded like gold."

He waves his hand again, steering the Brougham to the on-ramp, and we're on I-295. A drizzly day, traffic's heavy going north, up toward the bargains in Freeport. I've been to Maine now five times and never been inside L.L. Bean, whose sweaters and Blucher Moccasins I've worn since my mother got her first catalogue.

Ben says, "You talked to your folks?"

"Not since we saw them."

"Here." He raises his thighs to steady the steering wheel, then fishes his cell out of his jacket—a green you typically find in sluggish bodies of water—and hands it to me. "Go on," he says. "I need to use up some of that time."

I punch in the numbers, get the machine but don't leave a message. Relief and sadness alternate through me like waves, as I don't know if I'm glad they're cutting me off or fearful that no living body in the world wants me home. I reach the phone back to Ben. "Don't worry," he says. "She'll come around."

"She will?"

"Trust me. I know these kind of things." With his free hand he punches me in the shoulder, like Bill and Theo in a touching *Cosby* episode.

After exiting 295, we find the hotel, our usual place to stay, near the Jetport, where I can fly home while Ben drives the Caddy to Biloxi. A couple of times, I've shared the drive back with him, and he's an entirely different person then, stopping at tourist traps and wasting money on roadside attractions, as ordinary an American as this country has allowed its darker citizens. Now the front tires splash through a puddle on the way into the parking lot, and we pull under an overhang to park. I know there are many parts of this great land where a coffee-colored Cadillac wouldn't fetch much attention, but here among the snowbirds and Mainers it does, as does the presence of two genuine bluesmen in their stylish vines, walking up to the reception desk. We barely shake the rain off our hats and stomp it off our shoes before the latest group of admirers shamble forward, bearded, be-denimed, all of them. Memories of Sonja and April return as I measure these patchouli-smelling men. Not one night since has a woman, any woman, been waiting for us. Ben whispers, "I'll take care of this." Then he pats my hand with the phone. I pocket it. "Call her," he says, and slips me the key to our room. For once, I do as I'm told, no questions asked.

• • •

But even with all his powers, Ben can't force my mother to pick up the phone. Anyway, had she said "Hello," I think I might've hung up, unable to say a word to her that she'd like. So I turn to Heywood, who should be tired of me by now, yet he answers on the fourth ring. "My man," he says.

"How'd you know it was me?"

"It's always you in the middle of an afternoon, especially when you forget you're in Eastern Time Zone."

"My bad. At least it's Saturday."

"True, true. You in New Hampshire now? Vermont?"

"Maine. Last gig."

"No shit. You gonna get your ass up to Pine Bluff like you're always promising?"

"We'll see," I say, knowing good and well I should, only wondering how I'd fit in among Heywood and his students, if I should try them out as Peter Owens or Silent Sam. I say, "You need to get the man himself in to your classroom. Show those hard-heads just what the blues is."

"That's a hard sell, Pete. These kids, boy. I don't think he's ready for them."

"Weren't you the one telling me black folks were coming back to the blues?"

"I told you to be patient," Heywood says, his laughter bringing out some from me. "Didn't say it was gonna happen today. I'm talking about the future."

I take out my harp. This Marine Band's so old I can barely make out the numbers stamped over the holes. "The future," I say. "I can't see it."

"What are you worried about, Pete? You won't be around?"

Must confess I don't like his tone, which is too close to Ben's when he's about to say, "Want some advice?" But Heywood doesn't say that. Instead, he says, "You know that the man and I still talk some, don't you?"

"Had my suspicions." Shoot, I sometimes believe Ben speaks through Heywood, and their act is as corny as Willie Tyler and Lester. At the same time, I recall the Michelobs and stories Ben and I shared, and how Heywood might not know all he believes about Ben. I might be the one who knows Ben best. A scary thought, you ask me.

"He knows what you're thinking," Heywood says. "Even when you don't tell him."

I've had my suspicions about that, too, but as I consider this, another thought finds its way to me. "Did you know about 'Take My Chance?'" I say. "That he'd allowed those rappers to sample it?" I place my harp on the nightstand, then toss my hat on the floor and drag my palm over my stubbly head. I hope he tells me no, because I don't want to start mistrusting everything he says, too. But Heywood sighs, and I think his throat catches, before he says, "He told me about some negotiations. But I didn't know until I heard the song myself."

I chew a corner of my mustache. It'll come off tomorrow, for sure, just like all these clothes. Covering the phone with my hand, I laugh through my nose, but suddenly, I feel wary, as if my words will travel from Heywood to Ben. And I don't want to piss Ben off. Already seen what that's like. Still, Heywood's holding out on me is a stone letdown. Who am I going to confide in now? Grover? The nut on Tchopitoulas Street who directs traffic in his drawers and combat boots? I'm reaching for my harp when Heywood says, "What is it that you want, Pete?"

Oh man, is that a loaded question. But what the hell. If my answers get to Ben, so be it. He won't find out before tonight's show. I won't arrive to see somebody else in my place. Probably should tell the man myself someday. "I want to know it's worth it," I say. "That the act doesn't ruin how much the music means to me. But I look out in the crowd every night and never see just what I'm looking for."

I hear nothing from Heywood: no laugh, no breath, no rasp of his stubble against the receiver. I clutch my harp and say, "When's that future gonna be here, Heywood? When will some brothers and sisters be in the crowd to hear what we do?"

"You heard, Pete."

"What?"

"All the way up in Michigan," Heywood says. "You heard."

"But that's," I begin, though I don't close it out. Heywood laughs—or at least I think he does—and then he says, "Think about it, Pete. But I'll leave you alone. You got a show to do."

• • •

It's early to be getting ready—two hours before our typical takeoff—but Heywood's got me thinking, and Ben's not back from his lobby shenanigans with the bottleneck players of southern Maine. I lay out stage clothes on the bed: blue-black suit, burgundy shirt with the sphinx head, dark socks and the pointy boots my tender feet have finally adapted to. Must admit, this outfit will make me look like somebody you wouldn't want to trifle with. Hell, unless I smiled, you couldn't *see* me in a dark alley.

In the bathroom, I shear my head and neck with clippers, then figure what the hell and lather up with lime-scented Barbasol. The clear swaths of scalp don't frighten me, as I'm looking forward to an entirely clean dome, that I will promptly cover up with a bluesman's hat. As soon as I finish shaving, I shower to remove the prickly stubble off my neck and shoulders, then emerge into a steamy bathroom. I wipe the mirror with my towel. In the mirror my face looks puzzled, and I grab my chin and turn it side to side, expecting Ben to come in and say something like, "Admiring the view," or some dig about my vanity. Still can't quite figure what's wrong with my reflection, other than the fact I haven't spent this much time looking at it all tour. I wipe the mirror clean again, then turn my chin one way. I see Peter with a mustache. I cover up the mustache with my finger and see a clean-shaven Sam. If I ever speak again to my mother, I'll claim her warning about making funny faces wasn't true: mine didn't freeze that way.

When I cinch my towel around my flabby waist, I hear a door shutting. Time for dinner's nearing, Ben should be here, so I step out of the bathroom. "Ben," I say. No answer. A look into the room reveals his empty bed and mine, where my clothes lie like a cat in thrift-shop threads who fell asleep. I sit next to the suit, cross my bare legs. Need to get some drawers on. One look at the room service menu will tell me what to order Ben. Though up here in New England, chefs create interesting vegetarian dishes. Might have some actual choices here instead of those sad platters of cauliflower, broccoli and baby carrots Ben's gummed through. What could he be doing down there? Certainly he's answered all their questions about open tunings and chopping cotton, chord progressions and mistreated women.

I don't know whether to call room service or get dressed and go downstairs to haul that old fraud back up here with me. I pick up my harp, start playing scales, then slide into "Juke" and "Good Moanin Blues"—I sure love both Walters—and find myself blowing Sonny Boy's "One Way Out." First time I heard the damn song was the Allman Brothers' version, never knowing there was this harp player—never knowing you called a harmonica a harp—who did it first and did it better. I still like the Allmans. They're not just good white players, they're good blues players. Best music Slowhand ever made was that when he had Duane pushing him. You ask me, that's the key, no matter what kind of blues you're playing: You need somebody to keep you moving forward, not letting you coast or slide backwards. Makes me wonder, though, if Ben's doing that for me. If I'm doing it for him.

I've had enough time alone, so I dress, tug the boots on and trot to the elevator—the slick soles aren't made for stairs. In the lobby, I find Ben still surrounded by the faithful, and I wonder if he's having a good time, then think of how he was putting on the same performance yesterday in Portsmouth and the day before in Manchester. While I move to break it up, though, one of the pale figures in denim turns to me and fuck if it's not Major from Hartford, who showed up also in Boston. And while I look for his buddy Gary, Major leans in my direction. At the same time, Ben nods, a gesture acknowledging he knows it's time for dinner and will be upstairs in a few. Then he says, "But you know ole Tommy. He mighta drank that Sterno but he didn't die as young as you'd think, no suh." A Tommy Johnson anecdote, that's good. Better to claim you played house parties and rode the rails with an enigma like Tommy rather than Wolf or Mud. Who'd be around who could contradict you?

I'm backing away toward the elevator when Major takes his first solid step toward me. He was shy back in Hartford, though now he seems determined to talk to me. I see it in the breath he takes and the way he closes his eyes for a second, then almost bounds to cut me off. "Silent Sam," he says, sounding strangled.

I look him over from his no-name running shoes to his thinning hair. Bessie Smith's head is on his black t-shirt, with the legend, EMPRESS OF THE BLUES, in silver underneath her chin. His glasses slip down his nose and are spotted with rain. I don't think it wise to call him by name, but try to show a little recognition in my eyes, though I need him far enough away so he won't see my contacts.

"Major," he says, looking at the floor. "I met you with my friend? In Hartford?"

"Sho," I say, my right hand limp but extended in his direction. His grip is damp and hasty. He drops my hand before I can his. Then he reaches into his back pocket and pulls out the inevitable pint of Old Crow. Something about his demeanor's so pathetic, I almost want to tell him of the bourbon's inevitable fate. Yet I accept the bottle, say thanks, and promise it'll get to the man himself. Seems like my time here's done, so I turn toward the elevator, as Major says, "What about you, Sam? What's your drink?" Again, he won't look at me. I feel a sympathy I'm not used to in such situations. Most of the time, I want these clowns to clear out, to quit reveling in Ben's act, give us some space and a couple hours out of character. With Major, every time I lean forward, he steps back. I could wear a Spartans' sweatshirt, talk like Paul Robeson, and he'd never suspect I might not be the man he believes I am. And now, for whatever reason, he's got to know what that man drinks. I show him the Old Crow. "Not this."

Major smiles but wipes it away quickly. His eyebrows furrow and his glasses slip further down his nose. "What do you like?"

Blinking, I take a step back, considering what beverage should be my favorite. Whatever I claim will show up in the hands of the faithful when the next tour commences. Also need to be sure I don't say anything incongruous. Mud drank only champagne, had a rider in his contract demanding certain vintages, but that ain't right for a boy not long out of Natchez. Wind up telling the truth, which Ben says we can always work around. "I'm a beer drinking man," I say. "But it doan matter what brand." Only after I speak do I realize I've fallen into the occupational hazard of twelve-bar speech.

"Cool," Major says. Behind us, Ben pulls himself into his slump, while the five other men line up to shake Ben's claw-like hand. The ones waiting for their brief contact with the legend whisper to each other. All appear ready to spread the gospel about Brother Ben.

"But why don't you like Old Crow, like Brother Ben?"

I turn toward Major, but he steps back. Again, I go with the truth, but have something else to add. "I think it nasty," I say. "Plus, it named after a thievin', dirty, black bird."

Ben's got two more hands to shake. I walk backwards to punch the elevator button for up. Still an arm's distance away, his glasses fogged over with steam, Major follows me, but his voice smoothes out when he says, "No. Crows have a bad reputation, but they're really smart. And cooperative. You can train one." His voice is rising and his eyebrows are too. "They know how to use tools." His mouth stays open after he's finished speaking, a man not used to saying so much at one time. He takes off his glasses and rubs them with the tail of his shirt.

"For real?" I say.

"Ornithology," Major says, his weak eyes blinking. "It's another of my hobbies."

I stammer, "Orna, Orna, Orna."

Major says, "The study of birds. Ornithology." Backing away, he nearly bumps into Ben, who announces, "The voice willin', but the flesh weak." He shakes his head, shuffles forward and says, "Who this, Sam?"

"Mr. Major," I say, but he's already too far away to hear and running toward the door.

In a voice unfit for the stage, Ben says, "What were you two talking about?"

I press the elevator button. The doors open. Walking inside, I say, "Beer. And ornithology."

Ben winces, as if I've drawn a note too sharply. "The Parker tune?"

I shake my head. "No, the study of birds. Real crows," I say, handing over the pint.

"That's four," he says, clanking them together in his pockets. "Just from this afternoon."

On our floor, we step out, but Ben stops me before we get to the room. Reaching for the floppy collar and yanking on it, he says, "The sphinx is mine."

Not like I'm going to fight over the damn shirt. I swear, it's made of a material that can stop bullets. I unbutton it in the hallway and say, "What about the boots?"

"Keep 'em," he says. "They actually look better on you."

• • •

Outside the hotel, an hour and a half before the show, it's still drizzling, and the parking lot's empty. "You drive," Ben says. An odd turn of events. Considering the energy he's had all day, I believe he's joking. Never have I driven him to the venue. Heywood used to, but Ben's always limited me to interstate driving, and I've never complained. When he lets himself into the passenger's seat and puts the key into the ignition, though, I take my place behind the wheel. My eyes slide over his frame as he stretches and yawns in a way that doesn't seem at all affected. Soon after I start the Brougham he returns to form, though, lecturing about my cheeseburger platter and fries. "Want some advice?" He doesn't wait for my reply. "You need to get your cholesterol checked."

Tonight's show was scheduled for a one thousand seat theater, but two weeks ago, it got moved to Veteran's Memorial, which holds thirty-five hundred. I doubt we'll fill this, the largest venue of the tour, but maybe such a visible sign of our renewed popularity will get Ben back in the studio. Who knows if next time on the road we might be in joints like this one from the start? Now, as I drive cautiously on 295, passing Saabs and Audis with bikes on the roof, I remind myself to stay focused. Most important thing to do is get us to the gig, on time, unhurt. Wouldn't want to disappoint the colossal number awaiting us.

Idly, I observe, "Last show of the tour."

"Mm-hmm," he says, leaning forward to punch in a tape. The music that springs out of the speakers is clearly jazz, a flurry of notes so thick I can't identify but half of them. No chance I could keep up with my harp. "Who's that?" I say.

"Parker. 'Ornithology.'" Ben's eyes are closed but the nimble fingers on his left hand keep busy on a fretboard of air.

"All right," I say, catching the groove that does lie beneath the whirlwind.

After we exit 295, it's only a few traffic lights and a left hand turn before we come up on Vet's Memorial. Ben's name alone is spelled out in letters two feet high on the marquee. Wouldn't bet against the notion the man himself requested to keep my name off the marquee. Always wanting me humble. I'm not sure "Ornithology" has ended, but as an employee in a rain slicker waves at us, Ben ejects the tape, secrets it in the glove box. The employee directs us into the echoing garage beneath the auditorium. Seagulls shriek as we exit the Brougham and grab all our gear. Air's thick and I smell salt and seaweed, which makes me want a taste of lobster or fried clams before we go. Ben can't abide seafood—closes up his throat.

An elevator ride takes us two floors up, where we're greeted in the hallway by the auditorium's manager, a lanky cat named Morris St. Onge, with khakis and an alligator shirt. His blonde wife wears his blue blazer over her shoulders and says what an honor it is to meet us. More people hover nearby, but Ben says, "Need us some time alone befo' the show," then bows and scrapes and shows all the gold in his mouth. The dressing room's not quite as large or as well-furnished as the one at Madison Square, but the carpet shows the tracks of a fresh cleaning, and someone's put freshly cut flowers in two vases by the makeup tables. I open my harp case, retrieve two empty pints of Old Crow. One I upend on the counter between the flowers. The other has a tiny line of brown at the bottom, and I look at Ben before uncapping the pint and swallowing. Just as nasty as ever. I toss away the cap in the trashcan, upend the bottle next to it on the floor, then go to the restroom to wash the taste out of my mouth

When I get back, Ben's seated in a director's chair, strumming clear and ringing chords. Though we don't need to rehearse, I grab a harp, my oldest, and listen for a place where I can jump in. While I'm moistening my lips and the comb, he shifts from rhythm to lead and the tune he's playing is the same from the cassette earlier, only he quiets the strings with the meat of his right hand.

"Nice," I say, duly impressed. There are jazz harmonica players, like Toots Thielman, and the stuff Sugar Blue does is in its own category, but I'll stick to twelve bars.

Ben nods, stares at his fingers on the strings, then stops. "First song I learned to play," he says, "was 'Froggie-Went-a-Courtin'.'"

"Think I know that one," I say, remembering *Ten Simple Tunes for the Harmonica!* There I was wanting to play "One Way Out" and "Juke," but first had to stumble through "Greensleeves" and "This Land is Your Land."

"Could you still play it?" Ben says, eyes still on his fingers. Now he shapes new chords but doesn't strum.

"Give me a couple bars."

Ben pulls his fingers off the fretboard, leans the axe against a beige love seat. "Last show," he says, closing his eyes.

"For now," I say. The clock on the wall tells me we've got forty minutes until showtime. I flex my fingers and roll my head on my neck to get loose. Probably should listen to the man more about diet: He's old enough to be my father and seems as spry as I am tight and knotted-up. Now he stands, walks to the mirror, where he brushes lint off his shoulders and shoots out his cuffs. I pocket my harp and follow him, hearing my mother complaining about trashy Negroes and waiting to get from Ben the judgment on whether in my suit and rust colored shirt, my black fedora angled with the brim flattened out in the front, I look the part of the bluesman tonight. Don't really need him or the mirror to confirm this fact. The shirt's a little tight around my shoulders, though. Must have dried it too many times on high. Ben turns around, clamps his hand on my shoulder. Before he speaks, though, he yawns, shutting his eyes and shaking his head. What happened to all his energy from before, I wonder. He says, "The voice is willing, but the flesh is weak, Pete."

"You don't need to remind me," I say. "Heard that same line about ten times since Indiana, heard it tonight in the lobby."

He smiles, but there's not a trace of treachery. Doesn't even show his teeth. Just a simple smile, the kind old friends show each other all the time. "What if I were to tell you this was the last show?" he says.

"It is the last show," I say, spreading my collars to my shoulders.

He takes his hand off me, tilts his head. His smile fades, then flashes back. "I mean the last show."

I can't check the laughter that bubbles up my throat. "Last show ever?" I say. "Naw, Ben. Don't even try to play me."

He places his hand across his heart. "I'm tired, Pete. Been telling you all tour."

"You're saying this is it?" I say. "Brother Ben's last show? Ever?" The words don't sound right. I laugh again, without much heart in it. He nods, and I wait for a wink. None comes. For a good minute or so, we stare at each other until he says, "That's right, Pete."

"You mean it," I say, unable to pitch my voice like a question.

"Yes," he says, and walks back to his director's chair.

I'm about to ask him what I've wanted to ask a long time, yet with this opportunity, I don't want to get anything wrong. I walk closer, put my hand on his and clear my throat. "What are you tired of?" I say.

Could be a number of things, I suspect. The grind of touring. The loneliness of a musician's life. The fact he's sixty-six and pretending to be seventy-seven and has been performing, in more ways than one, for nearly all of his life. With all that weighing on me, man, I'd be tired, too. Only what I want to hear him say is that at last he agrees with me: That he's tired of having to be the kind of black man we pretend, tired of the people who demand he be this man, tired of being Brother Ben. Slowly, he forms an undeniably genuine smile. "Just tired," he says. "It's time to get some real rest."

I squeeze his hand with mine, as if to keep him in one place. "You're not tired of having to be Brother Ben?"

"Never was him," he says, still smiling.

I let go his hand, lean back in my chair. "You're not Brother Ben?"

"He was just a figment of some folks' imagination," he says. "To play some good music, I wear his threads now and then. Like you are now."

I stand. The light here is too bright to obscure the truth my eyes discover: I'm not wearing the blue-black suit. Instead, I'm in Ben's black suit, the one he wore backstage at Madison Square. My hand finds my harp in the pocket, and I wonder just how this all went down, recalling that noise when I was in the bathroom but how I saw little to make me suspicious.

"Good fit," Ben says, standing and tugging at my lapels. "Question is, what are you going to do?"

"What you mean?" I say, my mouth slightly behind my brain. Without even trying, I sound like Sam.

"This little enterprise. You going to let it die? Or keep it up and running?"

I close my eyes. Don't—or can't—say a word.

"Did you think I'd last forever?"

Eyes still closed, I bring my harp to my lips but just breathe, don't try to shape a single note. "Think about it," Ben says. "You've got time."

When I open my eyes, Morris St. Onge is knocking on the door and opening it. "Packed house," he says. "Thought you might like to know."

"We thanks you," Ben says, his Delta enunciations back as if they never left.

"Do you have a minute, Brother Ben?" St. Onge says. The lights overhead reflect on his glasses so I can't see his eyes behind the lenses. "Some people from Nova Scotia who really want to say a few words."

"Up air in Canada?" Ben says. "I give them a listenin' ear, sho."

"Great," St. Onge says, holding open the door, his eyes still obscured by the light.

"Sam, he need another couple minutes to hisself," Ben says.

"Sure," St. Onge says, shutting the door after Ben exits.

I look at the suit again, shake my head at how black it is. A greasy, oily black, from cuffs to lapels. How did he get it on the bed? Doesn't help that my shirt's still tight. I stretch my arms out, then flap them up and down a few times. Feels better but still a little confining. And just what did he mean he never was Brother Ben? I don't know why or how, but the next vision to cross my eyes is that of a smooth brother in garish rags like mine—the cat I don't want to see in the mirror. And fuck if he isn't winking.

• • •

Maybe because it's our last night or we're so in synch, maybe it's because I feel so doggoned strange—the weirdest night on the oddest tour ever. Whatever the case, after we hit the stage, and Ben counts off "Last Drink of Liquor," we tear that place up. Each note I play emerges sharp and defiant, light as granny's biscuits, hard as a slap in the mouth. I doubt the audience hears any distinction between this performance and our last one here—though maybe Major, out there in the shadows, knows something's afoot. Still, they cheer each tune as though they know this is the finale, the end of Brother Ben's journey down that long road of the blues. When "Last Drink of Liquor" bleeds into "Troubled," we don't let up. Seated in his padded folding chair, tapping out the beat with his shoe, Ben's playing is rock-steady, tight. Nothing showy, and maybe even quieter, with more spaces for my harp to fill. As I change harps for "Mind Me Woman," it occurs to me Ben's announcement backstage might have been another ploy. To assure a sizzling set, he tricked me into thinking this was our last show together. After Vegas and Memphis and Manhattan with N2K, I shouldn't be shocked to learn later tonight a new story that undoes all that I'd been lead to believe. Yet I don't slow down one bit.

Every night we play I hear it occasionally: that rough and raw and real sound I heard for the first time in my bedroom. Usually in a few notes or, at best, a song or two. Tonight, though, that's all I hear. Every harp player I stole from is in my ears. Big Walter Horton's mellow phrasing, Junior Wells's showmanship, James Cotton's rhythm, a whole lot of Little Walter's bends and Sonny Boy's trills and draws. Plus there's my own sound, my own blues blowing for all to hear. It's a different kind of blues, I have to say. It's coming from all those lonely nights in Troy, later in East Lansing, when I listened at night to black men from another generation—another world, it seemed—and played along, yearning to connect but never dreaming I'd actually get a chance to play next to one. I only hoped I could take a harp and make it talk to me in a voice I understood.

• • •

As the applause ebbs for "Take My Chance," I wait for Ben to stomp us into "Old Black River." I open my eyes for what seems like the first time and my contacts shift, blurring my vision of the crowd. I blink and the lenses settle back in place, as the blues faithful grows silent, knowing this is the finale. Ben's most famous lyrics, "I been a fool to travel, Lord, I been a fool to roam,/But that Ol' Black River, always lead me back home," will be shouted by everyone in the auditorium, almost louder than the volume Ben's mic can produce. I fan myself with my hat now, wipe the sweat from my mustache, and turn to see Ben, with a manufactured tremor in his knees, standing up. He grips the mic, says, "Blues faithful, y'all been so good to Sam and me, you make it easy for us to be good to you. And I know y'all know they's just one mo' song tonight, a song about the river that run right next to our home state." Ever a pro, he pauses, allows the crowd to scream the title and build their emotion until it washes up on us like a wave. Ben stands there, his smile toothy and filled with gold. He says, "And I doan want to keep you waitin', 'cause I knows how much y'all loves that song." Another pause. Another roar. I study the pointy tips of my boots. They're pinching again and my shirt feels tight around my shoulders still. "But I got somethin' to say I suspect didn't none of y'all expect to hear tonight. This here perfo'mance, this here's my last. That's right. Y'all seein' the last of Brother Ben."

Shock and disappointment echo in the auditorium. By chewing my mustache, I manage to remain stoic and ever so Silent Sam. The pause in playing has multiplied my thoughts: If Ben's interests are purely financial, then why would he stop now? I wince at the possibility of having to admit I was wrong about him. Did Heywood know? What will my mother think? Plus, I still can't figure out how Ben switched suits on me. Then, as a full and utter silence replaces the noise, I fear Ben has miscalculated. Blues legends don't *retire*. If they don't die young under mysterious circumstances, they play until they drop dead on stage in Japan, like Johnny Guitar Watson, or some college town far from home, like Luther Allison in Madison. Or they give the show of their life, as Wolf did, then go quietly. Sonny Boy was playing right up until the moment he died. Wouldn't surprise me to learn he gripped a Marine Band of his own when they finally put him to rest.

The crowd's continued muteness spawns these thoughts and more, and I edge backward, not expecting boos, as in Vegas, or the spray of empty bottles and cans. Still, I want to get closer to the exit. Then Ben says, "But I got good news, blues people. Been tellin' folks all tour 'bout how my voice be willin' but my flesh, my flesh weak." To accentuate this, he reaches a trembling hand toward his chair back and slumps. "Y'all lookin' at a tired man." And here he coughs, not bothering to move the mic, but forcing all to endure his phony racking. Then he says, "But they's a strong, a strong man wit' me. Think y'all know him. Go by the name Silent Sam?"

The silence ceases. Men and women lunge toward each other, slap high fives and grapple in awkward embraces. My face burns from Ben's maneuver, though I don't know if it's from shame or anger. The ploy wasn't his retirement. The ploy was his suggestion I might decide what to do with this traveling costume ball. I want to snatch the mic from the Last True Delta Bluesman's palsied hand. This would be a fine place and time for the truth, starting with the unveiling of Wilton Mabry and ending with the introduction of Peter Owens. Yet I don't reach for the mic. I stand there, stiff as a post, my armpits greasy with sweat.

"Blues is true," Ben says, stealing my line. "And they ain't never gon die."

The audience quiets a little, like children who know they're going to get lectured, but with recess afterward. "And you gon be surprised. Count on that. Done kept Sam out the light too long. Now is his time to shine. If y'all think y'all know who he is, you in fo' a surprise. This a whole different man. You know, folk call me the Last True Delta Bluesman? Well, when you open up yo' ears and hear Sam do his thing, you gon be hearing the First New Delta Bluesman. Ain't no one play them new Delta blues like this man here." He turns to me slowly, the soles of his shoes scuffing the wooden stage as me mimics infirmity. "What you say, Sam? You gon keep Brother Ben's blues alive? You gon stay true to the blues?"

In the exhortation that follows, Ben whispers, "Sounds like you'll need a manager to handle your affairs. Happen to know of a good one." I look at the pointed toes of my ridiculous boots, eye the sphinx on Ben's sweaty shirt. If I look any higher up, I'll see his face, and he'll wink at me, the signal how easy, how natural, it would be to maintain this charade. Over five years he's been telling me they want us to be Brother Ben and Silent Sam. We might as well benefit, he's always said. Now he tilts the microphone my way. As it nears, my eyes close, and I swallow.

Before our first show: That's when I asked Ben if the story about him and the judge was true. A month earlier, I'd learned Wilton Mabry and Ben were the same person. I should have known the story was no truer than the rumors already floating around about Heywood and me scrapping like Godzilla and King Kong. But I was so nervous then, fearing anyone who looked at me for more than a second would detect the real truth: I was no more ready to play the blues than the spoiled suburbanite I actually was. No one did, though, then and thereafter. Each year I began to believe that, as Ben promised, this trick would work. Even if I hadn't lived the blues as my heroes had, I could play them. It wasn't 1932 or 1954, or '68 or '82. What counted most was what I could do with my harp, and about that, there was no doubt. That night, after Ben smiled and squinted at me, he said, "Shit no, the story isn't true. But why settle for the plain old truth when you got a story and a guitar that sound so good together?"

Tonight, at Veteran's Memorial in Portland, Maine, the biggest city in the Pine State, I blink and swallow. My contacts shift again, and the lights are brighter than I believed. The people are too far away for me to see faces, though I'm sure Major's sweaty and beaming in his Bessie Smith shirt. I wouldn't mind seeing Officer Rico, Bollinger, Audrey and April, Michael Hunt, Dane Connor, Darnell Fuller, or any of the characters we've met this time around. I wish Sonja Hutch and Heywood were here. Grover. My mother, for sure. Sonny Boy and my father, were that possible. I wish that one person I'm always on the lookout for was here, too, that single sister or brother who believes, as I did—as I do—that this is the music that matters most for us. But I can't see him or her. Never have been able to. What I have for certain is Ben. And I'm here too, watching as he displays further weaknesses for the crowd. Then his long fingers find a firm grip on my shoulder as he nudges the microphone closer. I'd be a fool to say this whole tour makes sense now. It's difficult not to believe Ben's conjured every step, and I'm just another of the many unable to avoid doing exactly what he wants. Or maybe he's engineered everything so he can pass it on to me. My inheritance. Why should I turn it down? At this crossroads, it's not the devil I'm making a deal with.

My heart races a few beats, then, just as quickly, it slows, resumes a steady pace. I turn my shoulder, whispering, "There's gonna be some changes, right?"

"Sure."

"Natural fibers, sometimes?"

Ben laughs through his nose. "Whatever you want, Pete." He pauses. "Well, almost whatever you want. Now, what are you gonna tell the faithful?"

He turns to the crowd, says, "You gonna keep Brother Ben's blues alive?"

I don't know. I want my first words on stage to be good ones, but nothing's coming right now. We turn to face the crowd. I tilt back my hat, shake out my cuffs, then flap my arms and raise my harp to my lips. This is, after all, the way I've been communicating most clearly for the longest time. On the low end, I draw in that train whistle any hobo would recognize, then start chugging. I send the freight down the track slowly at first, slide my lips toward the middle of the comb, then flutter my hands like wings while I draw another sharp whistle. I learned this trick way back, a long, long time ago, before Ben even, but that doesn't keep me from making everyone inside this building think they're close enough to the tracks to feel the breeze and the heat. Yeah, man, this is my train, and I'll bring it back here next year. Tomorrow I might be Peter Owens, and the day after that, too. But for now I'm playing Silent Sam, and I've got the train going really good, you ask me, picking up speed and gaining ground. I send the train hurtling faster, then stop it with those air brakes a harp shapes so well. Ben picks the slide intro of "Old Black River." We look at one another and wink. And when I grab the mic and drawl, "Ben, you know I is," it sounds like I've been saying that all my life.

# ACKNOWLEDGMENTS

This book has been a survivor, and during its various forms and incarnations, there were a number of people along the way that kept it (and me) going. I like to think the blues artists who sustained me through the composition are already well represented, but Sonny Boy Williamson II (aka Aleck Ford, aka Rice Miller, aka Little Boy Blue) still seems like my co-author, so I'll thank him for every word and musical note he brought into the world.

As for those who helped the book along at its many stages, the thank-yous are many: To CD Mitchell and the staff at what was then called *River City*, who first saw something in the short story this once was; to the Arkansas Arts Council, who funded a few early novel drafts; to Nat Sobel and Emily Russo, who made it better than it had been; to Cary Holladay and Jack Butler, who both believed in it longer than I did; to Dan Wickett, who remembered it when I'd nearly forgotten it; to Ben Tanzer, who wanted to see it; to Leah Tallon and Jacob Knabb, who made it better again; to Victor Giron, Lauren Allison, Alban Fischer, and all on the Curbside roster who gave it a home like I'd never imagined.

Finally, to my wife Carmen Edington and our son Finn, who daily make it possible for me to deal with my own blues.

**TOM WILLIAMS** is the author of *The Mimic's Own Voice* (Main Street Rag Publishing Co). He has also published numerous stories, reviews, and essays, most recently in *RE:AL, The Collagist, Booth,* and *Slab.* An associate editor of American Book Review, he is the Chair of English at Morehead State University.

## ZERO FADE A novel by Chris L. Terry

*"Kevin Phifer, 13, a black seventh-grader in 1990s Richmond, Va., and hero of this sparkling debut, belongs in the front ranks of fiction's hormone-addled, angst-ridden adolescents, from Holden Caulfield to the teenage Harry Potter."* **—Kirkus Reviews** *(starred review)*

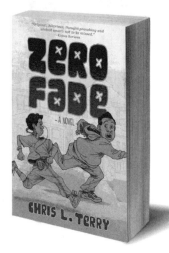

Thirteen-year-old Kevin Phifer has a lot to worry about. His father figure, Uncle Paul, is coming out as gay; he can't leave the house without Tyrell throwing a lit Black 'n' Mild at him; Demetric at school has the best last-year-fly-gear and the attention of orange-haired Aisha; his mother Sheila and his nerdy best friend David have both found romance; his big sister Laura won't talk to him now that she's in high school; and to top it off, he's grounded.

## MEATY Essays by Samantha Irby

*"Blunt, sharp and occasionally heartbreaking, Samantha Irby's* Meaty *marks the arrival of a truly original voice. You don't need difficult circumstances to become a great writer, but you need a great writer to capture life's weird turns with such honesty and wit."*

**—John August,** *acclaimed screenwriter and filmmaker*

Samantha Irby explodes onto the page in her debut collection of brand-new essays about being a complete dummy trying to laugh her way through her ridiculous life of failed relationships, taco feasts, bouts with Crohn's Disease, and more, all told with the same scathing wit and poignant candor long-time readers have come to expect from her notoriously hilarious blog, www.bitchesgottaeat.com.

*Don't Start Me Talkin'* is a comedic road novel about Brother Ben, the only remainin
True Delta Bluesman, playing his final North American tour. Set in contemporary societ
Brother Ben's protege Peter narrates an episodic 'last ride,' laying bare America'
complicated relationship with African American identity, music, & culture & like his her
Sonny Boy Williamson once sang, Peter promises "I'll tell everything I know."

"Tom Williams' *Don't Start Me Talkin'* reminds me of why I
started reading in the first place—to be enchanted, to be carried
away from my world and dropped into a world more vivid and
incandescent. . . . Williams handles this ironic tale of the Blues,
race, pretense, and life on the road with intelligence, grace, and
abiding tenderness."

　　　　　　**—John Dufresne,** author of *No Regrets, Coyote*

"A master storyteller, Tom Williams enters the living history
Delta Blues and emerges with his own thrilling tall tale, al
with American music, American legend, American heart."

　　　　**—Matt Bell,** author of *In the House upon the Dirt betw
　　　　　　　　　　　　　　　　　*the Lake and the W*

"Tom Williams writes like Paul Auster might if he were f
nier or like Stanley Elkin might have if he'd ever been a
to stop laughing. Darkly charming." **—Steve Yarbrou**
　　　　　　　　　　　author of *The Realm of Last Cha*

ISBN 978-0-988480

9 780988 480